ALSO BY TINA FOLSOM

Prequel Novella: Mortal Wish
Samson's Lovely Mortal (Scanguards Vampires, Book 1)
Amaury's Hellion (Scanguards Vampires, Book 2)
Gabriel's Mate (Scanguards Vampires, Book 3)
Yvette's Haven (Scanguards Vampires, Book 4)
Zane's Redemption (Scanguards Vampires, Book 5)
Quinn's Undying Rose (Scanguards Vampires, Book 6)
Oliver's Hunger (Scanguards Vampires, Book 7)
Thomas's Choice (Scanguards Vampires, Book 8)
Silent Bite (Scanguards Vampires, Book 8 1/2)
Cain's Identity (Scanguards Vampires, Book 9)
Luther's Return (Scanguards Vampires – Book 10)
Blake's Pursuit (Scanguards vampires – Book 11)
Fateful Reunion (Scanguards Vampires – Book 11 1/2)
Blake's Pursuit (Scanguards Vampires – Book 12)

Lover Uncloaked (Stealth Guardians – Book 1)
Master Unchained (Stealth Guardians – Book 2)
Warrior Unraveled (Stealth Guardians – Book 3)

A Touch of Greek (Out of Olympus – Book 1)
A Scent of Greek (Out of Olympus – Book 2)
A Taste of Greek (Out of Olympus – Book 3)
A Hush of Greek (Out of Olympus – Book 4)

Lawful Escort
Lawful Lover
Lawful Wife
One Foolish Night
One Long Embrace
One Sizzling Touch

Venice Vampyr

JOHN'S YEARNING

SCANGUARDS VAMPIRES #12

TINA FOLSOM

John's Yearning is a work of fiction. Names, characters, places, and incidents are the products of the author's imagination and are used fictitiously. Any resemblance to actual events, locales, or persons, living or dead, is entirely coincidental.

Cover design: Leah Kaye Suttle
Cover photo: Period Images
Author Photo: © Marti Corn Photography

Printed in the United States of America

1

Shortly after sunset, John Grant pulled into the underground garage of Scanguards' headquarters in the Mission District of San Francisco and parked in his assigned spot. Sunset, as well as sunrise, was one of the busiest times at the large building: shift change. The human employees left for the evening, as the vampires arrived to take over. By the time John reached the second floor, where his office was located, the place was buzzing with frenetic activity. Just like every night. He was glad for it, because it helped him take his mind off other things. Things he'd rather keep buried in the dark vaults of his memory bank.

As he walked along the corridor leading to his office, he acknowledged several of his colleagues with a nod, exchanging wordless greetings. He'd almost reached the door to his office, when a voice called out to him.

"John, wait up."

John turned around and watched Gabriel Giles, his superior and second-in-command at Scanguards, walk toward him. After many years of working with Gabriel, he'd gotten used to the other vampire's gruesome appearance: a large puckered scar reached from his left ear to his chin, disfiguring an otherwise handsome face to the point where he could strike fear into any opponent with only a grim look. Yet, despite his appearance, there was nothing evil about Gabriel. In fact, he was a fair man, a balanced individual thanks to his loving mate, Maya, and their three hybrid children, two of which were bodyguards-in-training at Scanguards. Gabriel had everything John had tried so hard, but failed, to achieve.

"Evening, Gabriel," John said, not letting the fact that he envied the powerful vampire color his voice. It wasn't Gabriel's fault that he had everything John desired.

"Glad I caught you." Gabriel motioned to the thick manila folder in his hand. "SFPD sent this over for us to have a look at." He shoved the folder into John's hand.

"Detective Donnelly?" John raised an eyebrow and accepted the file. "Another crime involving a vampire?"

Because of their arrangement with the City of San Francisco, and their connections to the mayor and the chief of police in particular, their liaison at the police department referred all suspected vampire-related crimes directly to Scanguards. Only a few officers at the SFPD knew about the existence of vampires, and by outsourcing any cases involving vampires to Scanguards, they made sure word didn't get out. If it did, there would be panic, which both the mayor and police chief wanted to avoid. Besides, Scanguards was better equipped to handle any rogue vampires not adhering to the law. They dealt with them swiftly and efficiently. Scanguards hunted them down, then brought them before the vampire council to be prosecuted. The verdict would be execution for the worst offenders, or a lengthy stay in the vampire prison in the Sierras for those who could be reformed.

"Donnelly isn't sure. But he's got no leads at all, so he wants us to take a crack at it."

"Sure. What's it about?"

"Child abductions."

Something churned in John's gut. "How many?"

"Over a dozen in the last six weeks. All girls. Young, too."

Though he wasn't keen on hearing the answer, John asked, "How young?"

"All between nine and twelve."

Disgust spread in his body, reaching every cell. He exchanged a knowing look with Gabriel. "You think vampires could be responsible, maybe using the kids as blood whores?"

Gabriel shrugged. Simultaneously, his scar twitched, a sure sign that the topic affected him on a deeper level. "I hope not."

"Wouldn't be the first time."

Gabriel nodded solemnly. "Look into it, will you? But if it becomes clear there's no paranormal involvement, turn the case back over to Donnelly. As much as this disgusts me, and I'd love to help out SFPD and find those girls, we don't have the manpower. Our regular assignments, the patrolling, and now our new arrangement with the Stealth Guardians…" He rubbed his nape, where his long dark-brown hair was tied into a ponytail. "Frankly, I'm not sure how we'll manage what's already on our plate."

John nodded. "Time for the next generation to pull their weight." The next generation were hybrids, the sons and daughters of vampires, who by nature were half vampire, half human, and thus combined the advantages of both species within them, making them stronger and more versatile, and ultimately less vulnerable than pure-blooded vampires.

Gabriel let out a breath. "We're getting the hybrids ready as quickly as we can. Some of them are already scheduled for their final practical examinations. But let's not forget that they're still in training."

"I think you underestimate them. Ryder is a very responsible young man," he said, referring to Gabriel's oldest son. "As are Amaury's twins." Amaury, one of the three highest-ranking directors at Scanguards, had two boys by his blood-bonded human mate Nina.

Unfortunately, John couldn't extend the praise he had for Gabriel's and Amaury's sons to Grayson, the oldest son of Scanguards' founder and CEO, Samson. The twenty-one-year-old was a hothead. His body had reached maturity on his last birthday, and would stay the same for the rest of his life, but so far his mind hadn't done the same. Grayson was impulsive, arrogant, and unpredictable. Not to mention constantly in competition with his older sister, Isabelle, and anybody else who he believed was getting ahead of him.

Gabriel chuckled softly. "And they all think they're invincible. Which they're not. Ryder is only twenty, as are Amaury's sons. They haven't even set into their final bodies yet. They're still vulnerable."

John sighed. "I understand. But they'll heal just as fast as a full-blooded vampire." Which was the truth. But they developed scars. If Ryder got injured and received a disfiguring scar—like Gabriel had when he was human—it would become permanent once he set in his final form. But apart from that, being a hybrid was better than being a full-blooded vampire. "Don't forget that they have advantages over us. They don't have our limitations."

His boss grimaced. "Don't I know it? But just because the rays of the sun won't fry them, doesn't mean they're safe on their own. Who's gonna watch over them by day?" He pointed to John and then himself. "We can't do it."

"Maybe it's time to take the training wheels off and let them prove to us that they're ready. I don't remember having anybody watch over me when I was a young vampire. Did you?"

For a moment, Gabriel fell silent. "Different times back then."

"Not any less dangerous."

"Different dangers though." Then Gabriel suddenly straightened and pointed to the folder. "Let Samson and me know tomorrow night whether we need to take this on."

John gave a quick nod. "Sure. I'll keep you posted." He turned and opened the door to his office, closing it behind him a moment later. He slipped out of his jacket and hung it over the back of his chair.

The file folder was thick, and according to the table of contents taped to the inside flap, contained over a dozen police reports, including photos of the missing children and anything else the police deemed relevant. John glanced at the clock on the wall. This would take a while.

He took out the first police report about a girl who'd been missing for just over six weeks, and began reading. He'd finished the second police report and was just beginning the third, when his desk phone rang. He looked at the display and picked it up.

"John Grant."

"It's Louise from reception. I've got a visitor for you. Her name's Savannah Rice."

"Don't know her. What does she want?"

"She was referred by Detective Donnelly from SFPD."

"Hmm." If Donnelly had sent her, it had to be important. "Fine.

Have her escorted up to my office."

"Will do." The receptionist disconnected the call.

John closed the folder and checked his office for any suspicious signs. But everything was clean. The bin was empty, the small fridge beneath his desk where he kept an emergency supply of human blood was locked. Scanguards provided bottled human blood for free, trying to minimize their employees' need to hunt for blood among the human population of San Francisco. Of course they couldn't prevent anybody from taking blood directly from a human's vein if they wished to do so, but the fact that they provided easy access to the nourishment they all needed—and more often than not, craved—made resisting the urge to bite a human easier.

John had fed upon rising, and felt perfectly satisfied with the blood he'd consumed. It would sustain him until the next sunset.

Another look around his comfortable office confirmed that nothing was out of place. Good. Since the person who wanted to see him had been referred by Donnelly, chances were that she was probably human, though he couldn't be sure. There was always the possibility that a vampire had contacted Donnelly, aware that he had a direct line to Scanguards.

A knock at the door announced John's visitor.

"Enter."

The door opened and the aroma of a human wafted into his office, though the sight of her was blocked by the bulky vampire guard who'd escorted her.

"John, a Savannah Rice to see you." He stepped aside and let the woman enter, then pulled the door shut behind her.

John should have heard the guard's footfalls as he walked away, but the blood rushing through his veins drowned out any sound. Any sound but the heartbeat of the human woman who stood in his office, hesitating.

Damn you, Donnelly, damn you for sending her to me!

She was a stranger, a woman he'd never seen before, yet when he looked at her, his heart leapt with recognition, with hope, with lust. She was everything he'd wanted to forget for four long years. Nicolette, the woman he'd loved and lost. He saw her in this woman, though he knew it wasn't possible. He saw the similarities, but he also saw the differences.

Like Nicolette, Savannah Rice was a beautiful woman, sensual and graceful. She was tall, but not skinny. She had curves in all the places that mattered, all the places a man wanted to feel warm, yielding flesh beneath his fingers. She didn't show much skin—few women in San Francisco did, the nights being too cold even in the summer. But what he saw heated his blood. Smooth and rich, and a little darker than milk chocolate, her skin stretched over her elegant fingers, her strong cheekbones, her flawless neck. A neck where a vein pulsed in concert with her heartbeat. He imagined his white skin against hers, his hands clasping her shoulders, as he latched onto that vein to drink from her, to drink from his blood-bonded mate.

But she wasn't Nicolette. He was lucid enough to realize that. Her face looked nothing like Nicolette's. Her eyes weren't the dark brown Nicolette's had been, but a vibrant blue that hinted at a white parent or grandparent. Her black hair was long and wavy, so different from Nicolette, who'd kept her hair shorter and much curlier, the way nature had intended. There was a mysteriousness that surrounded this woman, this stranger, something that seemed to be hidden behind the blue color of her eyes.

When she inhaled, his eyes were drawn to her top, a V-neck sweater that fit her like a glove. It hugged her most precious curves, two round globes more perfect than he could have ever imagined. And one other thing was evident too. He'd glimpsed it immediately when she'd entered his office: she wore no bra. Firm breasts without any help. Without support. He felt his fangs itch at the thought of how it would feel to sink them into her flesh and feel her moan beneath him. With difficulty, he pushed back the need that was suddenly trying to control him. The need to have this woman. To take her. To ride her. To bite her.

But he knew it was wrong. She wasn't Nicolette. And just because she and his dead mate shared physical similarities, didn't mean that this woman could fill the hole Nicolette had left. Chase away the emptiness he'd lived with for the last four years. Just because his body responded to her the same way he'd responded to Nicolette, didn't mean his heart would too. It was best to forget about it.

"Mr. Grant?"

Her voice, a soft trickle akin to a mountain spring, jolted him into action. He jumped up from behind his desk and approached her, extending his hand.

"Mrs. Rice, how may I help you?"

She quickly shook his hand, then let go of it just as quickly. "It's Ms.—there is no Mr. Rice. I'm a single mother. Buffy has no father."

Somewhat confused, John searched his memory. Was he supposed to know who Buffy was? The only Buffy he'd ever heard of was a fictional vampire slayer from a 90s TV series. "Buffy?"

"Yes, my daughter. She disappeared three days ago. Didn't Detective Donnelly fill you in? He said—"

The phone on his desk rang again. He was glad for it, because it meant he could avert his eyes before she realized that he couldn't stop staring at her. Most likely drooling like a hapless idiot. "Excuse me." He looked at the display and recognized the number of the San Francisco Police Department. "This might be him." He reached for the phone and picked it up. "Mike?"

"Hey, John. Just thought I'd give you a quick call about your new case."

"That's still to be decided," John said, knowing Donnelly would understand what he meant.

"Yeah, sure. Anyway, there's been a development. The mother of the last girl that disappeared. She's not happy with us."

"Uh-huh."

"She thinks the police are all incompetent. You know the type. So I figured I'd send her over to you so you can assure her that we're doing everything in our power. Her name's—"

"I know what her name is," he interrupted.

There was a tiny pause. "She's in your office, isn't she?"

"Thanks for the heads up." He made sure Donnelly heard the sarcasm in his voice.

"As I said, she's not happy with us. Squeaky wheel, if you know what I mean. I can't get any work done with her showing up every five minutes, demanding an update."

Great! So she was one of those types: bossy, demanding, insistent. "Well, thanks for the referral. I'll be sure to reciprocate when I can."

Donnelly had the audacity to chuckle. "No need. Just keep me posted, and honestly, I hope you find this thing has a paranormal stink to it, because I've got nothing. No ransom notes in any of the cases. No eye witness accounts of the abductions. Nothing. Not a whiff of a lead."

"Keep you posted."

He didn't wait for Donnelly's reply and put the phone back on the receiver. For what it was worth, this was his case, at least for tonight. And he would let nothing get in the way of his professionalism. He'd been a bodyguard for longer than he cared to remember, first for the vampire king of Louisiana, and the last four years for Scanguards. He was trained to show no emotion, and that's exactly how he would handle this case. Though it wouldn't be easy having to deal with this human woman whose blood permeated his office with a scent that made his fangs itch and his cock harden in spite of his better judgement.

He inhaled her aroma, filling his lungs with it, before steeling himself and turning to face her again. When he met her eyes, he instantly knew that she'd been scrutinizing him the entire time he'd been on the phone. And for some inexplicable reason that fact made it hard for him to show indifference.

"Ms. Rice, please take a seat."

2

Savannah took the proffered seat. John Grant wasn't what she'd expected, though she wasn't really sure what she'd thought she'd find when Detective Donnelly had suggested she go to him to get help finding her daughter. For starters, she'd expected him to be older, much older. Hadn't Donnelly said John Grant was highly experienced when it came to missing persons? How could he have gained that kind of experience when he was clearly still in his thirties?

And then there was his looks: for a private investigator he was too good looking, too tall, too athletic. Would somebody with model-like good looks like his really choose a career where he'd come into contact with criminals and violence on a daily basis, when he could easily find employment in modeling, acting, or fashion? His long dark mane alone could advertise any hair product and make it a bestseller.

"How may I help you, Ms. Rice?"

His question pulled her from her reverie. She pushed her thoughts about his appearance aside, remembering the glowing praise Donnelly had sung about him and Scanguards. To make sure they were legit, she'd looked into the company and found only complimentary reviews. It appeared that even the mayor enlisted their services from time to time, and what was good enough for the City of San Francisco, she hoped was good enough for her.

She swallowed and folded her hands in her lap, forcing herself to remain calm. It was hard, because every time she had to recount what had happened, tears inevitably came and choked off her ability to speak. It helped no one, least of all Buffy. For her sake, she had to pull herself together.

I won't give up till I find you, baby, I promise.

"Ms. Rice?"

She snapped her gaze to his face.

"Detective Donnelly said your daughter disappeared three days ago.

Can you tell me what happened?"

She nodded. His voice was laden with concern now, and it helped put her at ease. He was willing to listen. "Mr. Grant, thank you for seeing me—"

"Call me John, please. Tell me about your daughter. Buffy's her name?"

She nodded. "She's only ten." And she was probably frightened to death wherever she was. "She disappeared after school."

"Tell me everything. Start on the day she disappeared."

"She attends Grattan Elementary in Cole Valley, has since kindergarten. I normally drop her off just after eight and then go to my office in SoMa and—"

"Normally?" he interrupted.

While it wasn't too far to drive from Buffy's school to her office in the largely commercial South of Market district, she'd had to go straight to her office that day. "Yes, but that morning I had an early business meeting, so I asked my neighbor to take her. Her son goes to the same school, so Buffy rode with them."

"And you trust your neighbor? I will need her name and address."

Savannah made a dismissive hand movement. "That's not when it happened. Buffy got to school alright. She was there all day. The teachers and the students all confirm it. It happened sometime later."

"Sometime later? Has the time of her disappearance not yet been established?"

"Yes and no." And that's where her frustration with the police had started. They were dismissing some of the witnesses' claims, just because those witnesses happened to be children. "She goes to the after-school program there, too. And while some of the students said they saw her there, others said they think she'd already left."

"Why's that?"

"They were doing an impromptu field trip."

"Where to?"

"Just a few blocks away to a lookout point called Tank Hill."

John nodded. "I know it. Is it unusual for such a field trip to take place without any planning?"

"It happens on occasion that due to teacher availability or bad weather, activities are shifted from one day to another. You see, it was completely fogged in the day before, so they couldn't take the walk on the day they were supposed to. When the fog cleared that afternoon, the teacher decided to take advantage of it."

"And you say that nobody is sure that your daughter went on the walk with her class?"

"The teacher said she was with them, she'd even ticked her off the register before and after the walk when they returned to the school. But several of the kids said they didn't see Buffy."

"Hmm." John steepled his fingers under his chin, closing his eyes for a moment.

The gesture drew her attention to his long dark lashes and the full eyebrows that curved over his eyelids. When he suddenly opened his eyes again, his gaze collided with hers, pinning her.

"What time does the after-school program end?"

"At six."

"And you were there at six to pick her up? Were you waiting or were you late?"

Savannah edged forward on her chair. "Neither. I had a meeting that ran over."

"So you asked your neighbor to take Buffy home again?"

Was he judging her, because she couldn't be there for her daughter when she needed her?

"No." Savannah realized how agitated she was becoming, but she couldn't stop her distress from seeping into her voice. "Her son doesn't go to the after-school program. I called my babysitter. She went to pick up Buffy. But when she got there, Buffy wasn't there."

"I'm assuming your babysitter—what's her name?"

"Elysa, Elysa Flannigan."

"I'm assuming Elysa is on the list of authorized persons to pick up Buffy?"

"Yes, the school only releases the kids to somebody on their list. And Elysa is on the list."

"Was she on time?"

"She said she was." And Savannah believed her. Elysa had been babysitting for her since Buffy was three and was very responsible. "She was on time. She's always on time."

"Even if you tell her last minute that you need her to come and pick up your daughter?"

With that, Savannah lost her temper and jumped up. "What are you implying? That I'm a bad mother? That I don't look out for my child?"

John rose and walked around the desk. "Please calm down, Ms. Rice."

"You're right, it's my fault! I didn't have enough time for her. I put work before her, when I should have been the one picking her up, when I should have kept her with me rather than put her into an after-school program so I could spend more time at work. It's my fault."

"It's not your fault, and I'm not suggesting that you're a bad mother. I'm just trying to establish what happened and how it happened. I'm not judging you. I'm sure raising a child on your own is hard enough."

His last words calmed her a little. She felt awful for her outburst. "You must understand Buffy is everything to me. I love her more than my own life." Tears welled up in her eyes now, and she no longer had the strength to hold them back. "The thought that she's out there somewhere, taken by somebody, alone and frightened, is killing me inside. I have to find her. No matter what it takes." She wiped the back of her hand over her wet cheek. "The police are too slow. The Amber alert yielded no results. And they have no idea what to do next. No suggestions, no plan." She looked straight at him now. "Do you have children?"

Something seemed to jolt him, but then it was gone again just as quickly. "No, I don't."

"If you had children, you would understand that I can't leave a single stone unturned. Whatever it costs, I need you to find Buffy. I need you to bring her home."

He stood there, clearly contemplating something, almost as if he didn't know how to say what he had to say. "I need to be honest with you. Detective Donnelly might have overestimated what Scanguards can do. I don't want you to, uh…"

"What are you saying? That you won't take the job? I assume your services aren't cheap, but I can pay whatever—"

He lifted his hand. "It's not about money. In fact, if the disappearance of your daughter is indeed connected to the other disappearances in the Bay Area, and we take the case, the city will pay us."

She shook her head. "I don't understand. Other disappearances? How many have there been?"

"A dozen girls around Buffy's age have disappeared in the last six weeks alone. The police—"

"Oh my God!" Savannah reached for the chair to steady herself, but before she could do so, John had gripped her elbow, helping her to keep her balance. She'd read of a few disappearances, but those things happened, and for a large metropolitan area one or two a month wasn't unusual, but a dozen? "The newspapers. Why—"

"Why did the papers not report on it extensively? Because the police and the parents of the children decided it was in everybody's interest to keep this under wraps so the police could investigate without a bunch of crazies flooding their tip line with made-up sightings and theories."

"Under wraps?" Anger churned up in her. "Had I known, I could have protected her. I would have hired somebody to watch over her twenty-four-seven!"

"I know you would have."

Surprised, she met his eyes. Their chocolate brown color was shimmering with understanding as if a flame was turning it into a golden brown.

"I received the file from the police tonight." He pointed to a thick manila folder on his desk. "I'm going to see if I can connect your daughter's disappearance to that of the other girls and find a common denominator. If there's something there that connects these cases, I will find it."

The confidence in his voice was infectious.

"Thank you!"

"Don't thank me yet. I can only tell you if we'll accept your case once I've checked out all the details. Did you come by car?"

A little confused about the abrupt change of subject, she shook her head. "I took a taxi. There's never any parking in the Mission."

"Good. We'll take my car. It's in the underground garage."

Her forehead furrowed further. "To do what?"

"You're going to show me all places connected to you and Buffy: your home, your work, Buffy's school, your neighbor's home, your babysitter's home. I need to make myself a picture of Buffy's life."

She glanced at the clock on the wall. It was well past eight o'clock and dark outside. "You mean now?"

"Security is a twenty-four hour business."

Savannah found herself wanting to hug this man. His willingness to go the extra mile and not waste any more time, but jump into action immediately, filled her heart with hope.

Hold out a little longer, Buffy, Mommy is coming.

3

John grabbed his jacket, held the door open for Savannah and motioned her to walk through it ahead of him. A gentlemanly move, yes, but it also meant that he could follow her with his eyes, eyes that instantly dropped to her ass. Maybe for once he should have foregone his Southern manners, because looking at that shapely ass, those firm, round cheeks, gave him all kinds of ideas wholly inappropriate for this situation. He prided himself on being a civilized vampire, a man who kept his needs and desires firmly leashed. But just looking at Savannah as she sashayed out of his office and into the hallway, made him want to snap that leash and toss all his good intentions out the proverbial window.

Savannah suddenly turned and looked at him. Startled, he froze. Shit, had she somehow sensed that he was checking out her ass?

"Where to?"

"Uh, this way," he said and motioned to the elevators. As he walked next to her, the silence between them felt awkward, so he asked, "Ms. Rice, I'm sure that even with Detective Donnelly's recommendation, you considered other companies to help you with the search for your daughter. Why choose Scanguards?"

"I spoke to several of the other companies in the field, but none of them struck me as even remotely qualified." She gave him a sideways look. "They all started the initial meeting by laying out their fee structure and per diems, expenses, and what not. I knew then that they couldn't care less whether they found Buffy or not, as long as they could bill me a bunch of hours."

"Hmm." He would have had the same concern had he been treated that way.

"But when your first move was to ask me to tell you about Buffy and what had happened, I knew Scanguards was different. Detective Donnelly's recommendation certainly helped, but I don't rely on other people's opinions. I form my own."

Maybe that attitude was what Donnelly had meant by *bossy* and *opinionated*, but John considered it good instincts. Very good instincts.

"I'll do my best not to disappoint you."

When they arrived at the elevators, John pressed the button, and Savannah turned to him. "I didn't have much confidence in the police to begin with. But after what you just told me about the other children, I know I can't rely on them to find Buffy. I hate to put more pressure on you, but Scanguards is my last hope."

Before he could respond, the elevator doors opened and Amaury, Scanguards' founder Samson's best friend and a high-ranking director of the company, stepped out. As always, he was casually dressed in cargo pants and a shirt that was open at the collar. His long dark hair, shorter than John's, touched his shoulders, shoulders that were as broad as a tank. He was linebacker material for sure, though John knew Amaury had never played American football in his youth, which he'd spent in sixteenth century France.

"Hey, John," Amaury greeted him and nodded to Savannah.

"Amaury, evening."

"Glad I'm running into you. There's been a small change in the schedule."

John raised an eyebrow. Would he have to hand Savannah over to somebody else? "Yeah?"

"Damian and Benjamin requested to do their hands-on-training exercises with you starting tomorrow night. Take 'em patrolling and find something for them to do." Amaury grimaced. "Sorry, but I had to approve it, or they would have talked my ear off."

John shrugged and reached for the elevator door, preventing it from shutting. "I don't mind. Like I said to Gabriel earlier, the boys need to start pulling their weight. We need the extra pairs of hands."

Amaury slapped him on the shoulder. "Glad you see it that way. Not everybody is keen on training the next generation." He made a motion to walk away, then stopped and grinned. "Oh, and I told them that your word is law. They run roughshod over me, 'cause I'm their father, but there's no reason for you to tolerate such behavior."

John had to chuckle involuntarily. "They're good boys. You could have done worse."

Amaury winked at him. "Yeah, I could have gotten Grayson as a son." With a nod and a "Ma'am" to Savannah, he left.

John looked at Savannah and motioned to the elevator. "Shall we?"

Inside the elevator, John pressed the button for parking level two and watched the doors slide closed.

"I couldn't help but overhear that you're patrolling. What kind of patrolling?" Savannah asked.

"We have a contract with the city. For security services." When she gave him a curious look, he added, "The city's police force is too small to handle all of the city's security needs. So they hired Scanguards to patrol certain areas at night. Make sure the city is safe." Safe from creatures of the night. From creatures like him.

"The city seems to have lots of confidence in Scanguards."

"We've been working with them for a long time." The former mayor of San Francisco, a hybrid and a friend of Samson, had negotiated the deal. When the new mayor had taken over, he, as well as the chief of police, had been let in on the secret that vampires existed. Fortunately, they'd agreed to honor the prior mayor's arrangement and sworn to keep the existence of vampires, witches, and other paranormal creatures secret. The deal worked well for both sides: the city was safe, and Scanguards received steady pay from the city's treasury.

The elevator doors opened. "Go ahead, my car is parked to the left." He followed Savannah out into the clean, well-lit garage.

"The SUV?" she asked, pointing to a blackout van, one of Scanguards' preferred modes of transport because it shielded the vampires riding in it—including the driver—from the sun.

John shook his head, clicked his key remote, and the lights of the car next to the SUV flashed briefly.

Savannah's gaze snapped to it. "The sports car?" There was a hint of surprise in her eyes, as if she hadn't expected him to drive a sports car or make enough money to afford such an expensive vehicle. Or maybe it was just appreciation for the fine German machine he owned. For whatever reason, he had a hard time reading her.

The black Mercedes AMG was a sleek two-seater and his pride and joy. It had also been made vampire-safe, its windows coated with a film UV-rays couldn't penetrate, while still letting in enough light so the car didn't look suspicious.

He opened the passenger door and waited for Savannah to slide into the leather seat, before closing the door behind her. Then he got in on the driver's side and engaged the engine. Moments later, he merged into traffic on busy Mission Street, before turning North toward Cole Valley.

"We'll start with the school," he announced.

"There won't be anybody there right now. It's night."

"Doesn't matter." In fact it was better if he could snoop around without any school staff asking him questions. Besides, a visit during the day was out of the question. "I'll be able to see what I need to see."

"You work nights a lot?" she asked.

"Mostly." Though not by choice.

"Don't you mind it?"

"You get used to it." After a couple of hundred years.

"Hmm." She looked out the side window and fell silent for a moment. "Yeah, I guess you can get used to a lot of things if you have to."

He could sense sadness in her voice, and knew it was time to guide the conversation in another direction. Just as well, because he still had plenty of questions pertaining to Buffy. "You said there was no Mr. Rice. So where is he, Buffy's father?"

She turned her head to him. "I don't know. Why do you ask?"

"Because we can't rule out the possibility that he might have kidnapped her. It happens all the time that non-custodial parents kidnap their own children in order to get back at their ex-spouse."

"I was probably not very clear earlier." She sighed. "There is no father. None that Buffy would know. I was never married."

"Your ex-boyfriend then?"

From the corner of his eye he noticed her shake her head. "I wanted a child, but I didn't want a man in the bargain. Buffy's biological father has no idea he has a child. He donated his sperm to a sperm bank, and for all I know, he has lots of children he doesn't know about. He was a very desirable donor."

That news surprised him and made him curious. "What do you mean by desirable?"

She shrugged. "You can choose from profiles at the sperm bank. You know, to pick the kind of attributes you hope the donor will pass down to your child. He had a PhD from MIT, an IQ that put him in the top brackets at Mensa. I know some people would judge me for how I chose him. But I wanted the best genes for my child."

Stunned at her words, John stared at her. "Those were the only criteria they gave you? Nothing else to identify him by?"

She shook her head slightly. "I knew he was Caucasian, had blue eyes and dark hair. But they don't give you much else. No pictures, if that's what you mean."

"Hmm, I see. So I assume he would never find out that his sperm had resulted in a child." Knowing how strict privacy laws were, John didn't expect an answer. "Just like you don't know his name, he doesn't know yours." A dead end then.

"No, sorry. Maybe I should have gotten more information on him back then, but I didn't."

He cocked an eyebrow. "What do you mean? How?"

"Their systems are hackable."

"Hackable? How do you know that?"

"I'm a programmer. I was tempted to find out more about Buffy's potential father back then. I got into their system. It was easy." She sighed. "But I didn't go through with it. In the end, I decided it was best not to know too much. So I never accessed his file. What I knew was enough. The sperm donor was healthy, young, and intelligent. That was all that mattered."

John nodded, contemplating her words. She'd made a wise decision not to pursue the matter any further, though one thing made him curious. "Do you still use your skills as a hacker?" After all, it could be entirely possible that by hacking into a system, she'd drawn somebody's attention on herself, who now wanted to hurt her by kidnapping Buffy.

She shook her head. "I actually work in cyber security now. That experience showed me how vulnerable certain organizations are. So I made it my business to help them patch those areas that are vulnerable to a cyber attack. One of my first independent jobs was to shore up security at the sperm bank."

"You run your own business? As a cyber security expert?" He glanced at her, running a long look over her feminine features.

"Why does that surprise you? Because I'm a woman?"

"I didn't mean to—"

She lifted her hand. "No need to apologize. I get that a lot."

"It's just that when I think of a cyber security consultant, I imagine somebody a bit geekier." And Savannah was anything but geeky. She was sensual, sexy, like sin itself. And he was back to thinking about her sexually again. How long had he managed to keep his mind off her delicious curves by acting professional and asking her about things that should have been completely innocent? Five minutes? Ten?

If he continued like this, one of two things would happen. He'd either find himself pressing Savannah against the nearest flat surface, burying his cock in her while he drank her blood, or he would return home at sunrise, needing either an ice-cold shower or a hand job, or possibly both.

The former, he couldn't allow under any circumstances, and the latter didn't sound in the least bit appealing.

4

John had suddenly fallen silent, and Savannah wondered whether she'd said something wrong. She hoped her confession about Buffy's father or her foray into hacking hadn't turned him against her, because she couldn't risk Scanguards not taking her case. She needed to find Buffy, needed to bring her home. It was all that counted. And she would play whatever role was necessary. Remaining silent during the rest of the drive to keep from saying anything else controversial, was a small price to pay to secure Scanguards' help.

When they pulled up next to Grattan Elementary, Savannah was glad to get out of the car. The school building took up more than half of one city block, with a single row of houses facing away from the schoolyard occupying the remainder of the block.

"Show me where the parents pick up their children."

She nearly shrieked at the sound of John's voice next to her. She hadn't heard him walk around the car to join her.

"I didn't mean to startle you," he said gently.

"It's nothing. My nerves are just frayed." She motioned to the street corner. "This way."

The sound of a beep came from behind her a moment later, indicating that John had locked the car doors. The fog had descended on the city again, and the cold, humid air seemed to seep through her sweater, making her realize that she'd left the house without a jacket. She shivered involuntarily.

"You're cold," he said matter-of-factly.

"It doesn't matter."

But he was already taking off his jacket, and a moment later, he'd laid it over her shoulders, the inside still warm from his body heat. She couldn't help but pull the garment tightly around her torso so the heat wouldn't escape.

"Thank you. Normally I don't get cold that easily. But I haven't slept much since…" She didn't complete the sentence. She knew she didn't have to. She pointed to a gate. "That's where the parents line up with their cars, and the kids get signed out by a teacher."

John nodded. "Wait here."

Savannah watched him walk to the gate, peer in, then take in his surroundings. He didn't just look at the school, but also at the opposite side of the street, the houses facing it, and the buildings up and down the next street. When he walked up the short incline and turned to look down onto the school's roof and the teachers' parking lot, which abutted the children's playground, she wondered what he was looking for.

Moments later he was back.

"What were you looking at?"

"If I were to abduct a child from this school, I would have to scope it out first, figure out where the teachers would be, who could see me depending on where I was, and where the best place to hide would be."

"But you can't possibly see enough at night. It's too dark."

"I'll come back tomorrow during the day," he promised, "but I wanted to get an idea tonight so that I know what I'm looking at when I go through the police report." He took her elbow. "Now let's drive to your babysitter's house."

In the car, she gave him Elysa's address and he entered it into the navigation system of his car. It wasn't far to her Laurel Heights flat, which she shared with two roommates. Outside, John stopped the car, but didn't turn off the engine.

"Do you want me to introduce you to her?" Savannah asked.

He shook his head. "I don't want her to know who I am. I'm not going to talk to her directly, not right now anyway. I don't want to spook her, if she's involved in Buffy's disappearance. I'll be watching her to see if there's anything of concern."

"What now?"

"I'll drive you home. Then I'll look into a few things."

She gave him her address in Lower Pacific Heights. It wasn't far, and there was very little traffic at this time of night. She was looking for something to say, to drown out the silence between them, when John suddenly said, "You mentioned you run your own business. Any employees?"

"I have two IT experts working for me, Rachel Ingram and Alexi Denault. Why?"

"Have they met Buffy?"

"Of course. Occasionally, I take Buffy to my office with me when school lets out early, or when I can't get a babysitter. They know her well."

"So both of them have been employed by you for a long time?"

"Alexi is relatively new. I hired him about eight months ago. But Rachel has been with me for almost three years. Why are you asking?"

"Most abduction cases involve people who know the victim," he said.

At the last word, she sucked in a breath. She didn't like to think of her daughter as a victim. It dehumanized her. Made her an object.

"I'm sorry," John said quickly, as if he understood. Did he?

She glanced at him and nodded. "So you think Alexi or Rachel could have something to do with Buffy's disappearance? I don't see it. Neither Rachel nor Alexi ever showed much interest in her. You know, they're not into kids. They were nice enough to her when she was in the office, but I could tell they weren't that keen on having her around, asking questions and making noise while they were trying to work. Buffy is a curious little girl. Some adults find that exhausting." But she never got sick of answering her daughter's many questions, satisfying her curious mind.

"We can't rule out the possibility. Email me their home addresses and the address of your office. I'll look into their backgrounds," John insisted.

A moment later he pulled up in front of her home, a condo in a two-unit Victorian building situated on a quiet side street.

"Do you live upstairs or downstairs?"

"Upstairs."

"And the neighbor who took Buffy to school that day?"

Savannah pointed to a single family home on the same block. "Two doors down. The little yellow house. Nancy lives there with her husband and their son."

John nodded. "I'd like to see Buffy's room."

"Of course." Savannah reached for the door handle and got out of the car.

When she walked around the car, she noticed John glancing down the street at her neighbor's house, then looking across the street, assessing the surroundings just like he'd done at Buffy's school. She couldn't help but wonder what the street looked like to his trained eye, whether he recognized any dangers past or present. Could he immediately ascertain the weak points in a place, the way she detected vulnerabilities in rows and columns of computer code?

At her front door, John joined her, though his gaze remained vigilant, scanning the deserted street. There was something reassuring about him standing there, waiting for her to unlock the door. Confidence exuded from him. This was his profession, to see things other people didn't see, to find what was hidden, to protect those who needed protection. Standing there at the threshold to her flat, Savannah felt it as if he'd recited his resume, as if he'd told her about every case he'd solved, every person he'd saved. The knowledge wrapped around her like the warmth of his jacket.

"No security system?" he asked when she opened the door and started walking up the narrow staircase.

"It's a pretty safe area. And I don't really have anything worth stealing." There were many larger mansions only a few blocks away. A burglar would find those more appealing.

He didn't answer, but followed her. In the long upstairs hallway, a feature of so many Victorian flats, she flipped the light switch. "Buffy's room overlooks the garden."

She walked to it. But at the door, she hesitated. John caught up with her and stopped next to her. "Something wrong?"

She looked at him. "It's been hard for me to go in here since she disappeared. Seeing her room all empty just brings reality home, you know?"

He put his hand on her shoulder for only a second and said, "If it's alright with you, I'll go in alone."

Savannah nodded and John opened the door and stepped inside. She remained standing just outside, but her gaze drifted to the interior of Buffy's room, her empty bed with the stars over it that lit up in the dark, the chest of drawers that contained her socks and underwear, her T-shirts and sweaters, its surface overflowing with projects for school, the multi-colored bean bag in the corner, where Buffy loved to sit and read, sinking so deep into it that she almost disappeared if she was wearing colorful clothing.

Savannah turned away. She couldn't look anymore, or she would start crying again. She couldn't allow herself to fall apart.

"I've got everything I need so far." John's voice was behind her, closer than she'd expected. "Is this picture of her current?"

She turned and looked at him holding a snapshot of Buffy sitting at the kitchen counter, eating cake. Savannah smiled. "I took it only a month ago."

"May I take it?"

She nodded.

"Thank you, Ms. Rice." He cleared his throat. "I'll contact you tomorrow evening to let you know what I've found."

"Thank you. I appreciate it."

He tipped his head slightly, almost as if he was performing an old-fashioned bow. "Have a good night."

He let himself out, and she locked the door behind him. When she walked into the living room and switched on the light there, she suddenly realized that she was still wearing his jacket. She rushed to the window, but John's car was already in motion and was gone a few seconds later.

5

John kicked the gas pedal down. He needed to drive. To clear his head. To drown out the memories that were assaulting him. But he realized within minutes that the drive through the nearly deserted streets of San Francisco did nothing to stem the swell of memories that rushed over the wall that he'd tried to erect inside himself. It was all Savannah's fault. Her fault that he was reminded of the tragedy that had befallen him. A tragedy that felt as if it had happened yesterday.

He stopped the car on the next block and pulled a bottle from a secret compartment underneath the passenger seat. Maybe a few gulps of blood would help calm him. He unscrewed the top and set the bottle to his lips, took a sip, then another. He felt the viscous fluid coat his throat and ease some of his pain. But he knew it wouldn't last long. It never did. He had to keep busy, keep moving, keep working. Keep outrunning the memories like he'd done for the last four years.

He stared at the clock on his dashboard. It was getting late. He turned the car around and headed back toward Laurel Heights, where Buffy's babysitter lived. He would start by checking her out to see if anything was amiss. While he didn't necessarily suspect her of kidnapping Buffy, she was the one person who probably knew the child's movements the best. She could have—inadvertently or not—given the kidnapper information that made it easy to snatch Buffy at the moment she was least protected.

When he approached the block where Elysa Flannigan's flat was located, he could already hear the noise of people partying. Earlier when he'd stopped by with Savannah, he'd seen lights in the flat and several people milling about, apparently preparing for the party. Now, loud music droned from open windows, laughter and loud voices mingling with it. John stopped the car on the opposite side of the street and looked to the building. Through the lit windows of Elysa's flat on the second floor, he spotted balloons among the dancing crowd. A birthday party. But not Elysa's. The name he could make out on the banner that hung across the front door—and which hadn't been there earlier, when he'd passed by with Savannah—read Tracy. One of her roommates.

A car approached, blinding him for a moment, before it came to a halt in front of the building. Two guys in their twenties got out, and the car drove off. They sauntered up the steps. John followed them with his eyes. He didn't hear a doorbell, instead the two visitors simply opened the door. John watched them disappear inside. Clearly, nobody was checking who was entering the flat. It would be easy to mingle undetected.

John exited the car and crossed the street. Just like the two young men before him, he turned the doorknob and let himself in. The music was louder inside and got even louder as he ascended the stairs and reached the narrow hallway. It was crowded here as people tried to get from the living area in the front of the flat to the kitchen, where presumably the liquor was being served, in the back of the place. Nobody took any notice of him. Nobody asked whose friend he was, or whether he had an invitation.

He wanted to shake his head. Humans. They had no idea about the many dangers that lurked in the night. But even if they knew vampires existed, they would probably still assume they were safe, believing the false lore that a vampire couldn't enter a house uninvited. Well, he was here, inside their private space, and nobody had invited him. Just as well that he wasn't here to do any harm. But he was here to snoop around, to get a feel for Elysa and the company she kept.

The crowd was young, most of them in their early to mid 20s with a few younger ones sprinkled in. Youngsters who were definitely below the legal drinking age, yet enjoying the freely flowing alcohol as readily as their older counterparts.

John made his way through the hallway, peering into the rooms along the way. Each room was occupied to varying degrees. Some guests lounged on beds and chairs, bean bags or simply on the floor, others leaned against walls and doors, or sat on window sills, unconcerned that a wrong step by a fellow partygoer might send them tumbling out the open window. Others danced to the music that was too loud and seemed to have no discernable melody, just a hard, deep beat that resonated like the amplified heartbeat of a creature in pain and made the old wooden building shake to its foundation.

At the entrance to the kitchen, John stopped. It was packed here too. Several men and women were doing shots. From the smell that drifted to him, he knew they'd mixed Vodka with cherry- and strawberry-flavored syrup and chilled the mixture. Several of the drinkers were already so wasted that with each new shot they downed, half of it spilled on their skin and clothes, leaving streaks of red that in the right light looked like blood.

"You must be one of Elysa's friends." The female voice came from next to him.

John glanced at her. She was a good foot shorter than him, affording him a perfect view down her cleavage, though he hadn't aimed for that. He lifted his gaze just a bit, taking in her petite frame, her heart-shaped face and the blond pixie haircut.

"Why do you say that?" John replied.

She leaned closer and gave him a definite come-hither look. "Because she always invites the hottest guys." She made a dismissive hand movement toward a group of men in the kitchen. "Real men. Not like these boys."

"Well, I guess that's Elysa." He craned his neck. "Where is she?"

The girl jerked her thumb over her shoulder. "In the living room I think. But I'm sure she's busy. Why not hang out with me for a bit?"

"Sure, why not?" After all, this girl would probably eagerly talk about Elysa and her roommates just so she could spend time with him. He knew the type: eager to please. "So how do you know Elysa?"

"I'm her roommate, Nikki. And what's your name, handsome?" She tried her bedroom eyes on him. Unfortunately, the move was wasted on him. She was exactly the opposite of his type.

"John." He smiled, pretending he was here to enjoy himself. "So, you live here." He looked around appreciatively. "Nice flat."

"I can show you my room." She batted her eyelashes at him.

"Sure, later," he placated her. "So, you're in the same type of job as Elysa?"

She grimaced. "Me? Looking after little brats? No way! I'm not a saint." She winked at him.

"Not like Elysa, huh?"

"She's no saint either. But then who am I telling that? You know her. She'll do anything to make a buck. Even look after children."

John chuckled. "That's Elysa! She told you about what happened, right? With the girl she was babysitting?"

"Oh, yeah, what a shocker."

"Must be tough on Elysa."

"Yeah, and the rent is due in a couple of weeks."

"Excuse me?"

"Yeah, you know, now that the little vampire slayer is missing, she's out of a job. Don't think she's got much saved up."

"Little vampire slayer?"

Nikki giggled. "Yeah, you know. Her name's Buffy. I mean, who names their kid Buffy? So whenever we talk about her, we call her vampire slayer."

"Oh, funny." Not.

"Yeah, right?" Then she shrugged. "But anyway, with the girl gone, Elysa is scrambling to find a job to tide her over. You know, until they find the girl."

While this didn't exactly reflect well on Elysa, it also suggested that the babysitter wasn't involved in the kidnapping. If she had indeed helped somebody abduct the child, she would most likely have gotten paid for it, and not be struggling to make ends meet.

"Though, between you and me"—Nikki leaned closer—"once a kid's been missing for a few days and there's no ransom note, chances are the child's dead already. I mean, I watch Forensic Files, I know what's going on."

"So there was no ransom note?" John knew that already, but he wondered how Nikki knew.

"No, not according to Elysa. She said that's why Buffy's mother is so devastated. She's loaded, you know. Elysa said she would gladly pay anything to have her daughter back. So if there'd been a ransom note, she would have paid it already."

"I see."

"But hey, let's not talk about sad stuff. We're partying tonight."

"Yeah, Tracy's birthday. I should congratulate her. Where is she?"

"In the living room, dancing. I'll come with you."

But he blocked her quickly and said, "Hey, could I ask you for a favor?"

"What's that?"

"Would you be a darling and get me a drink and then meet me in the living room?" He motioned to the kitchen, where one counter was littered with bottles, some full, some empty. "And then we can party, how about it?" He looked deep into her eyes, giving her the impression her charms were working on him. They weren't.

"Sure," she purred. "See you in a sec."

Very unlikely.

John turned and walked down the hallway, dodging tipsy guests, and made his way to the living area. He let his eyes roam and sniffed the air. Apart from the aroma of pot and alcohol, various perfumes and body odors, all he could smell was human blood. Nobody in the room exhibited the tell-tale aura of a supernatural being. And all his senses indicated that there was no vampire, apart from himself, among the partygoers. At least that meant that Elysa and her roommates didn't have any vampires among their acquaintances. Or they would surely have been invited tonight. And would have attended with certainty. After all, a party was like a smorgasbord for a vampire. So many different types of tasty blood. And by the end of the night, everybody would be drunk, and a vampire would barely have to use any mind control to bite a human without being detected.

For a moment he was tempted to stay. But his sense of duty was stronger than his desire to suck on the vein of a living human. He had leads to follow. And by the looks of it, Elysa Flannigan was a dead end. For now. He would run a background check on her later when he was back in his office.

John left the party before Nikki could find him and stepped out into the cool night air. He crossed the street, just as his cell phone chimed. He pulled it from his pocket and looked at it. A reminder flashed.

Shit! He'd almost forgotten about that. Maybe because he didn't want to go to the appointment his cell phone was reminding him of. Unfortunately, being a maker came with responsibilities.

6

The psychiatrist's office was in the basement of an old Edwardian home in the Nob Hill area of San Francisco, a fancy neighborhood nestled on a hill. Up there, peekaboo views revealed themselves, showcasing the beauty of the city, particularly at night. Corridors of light became visible whenever John turned a corner and glanced down the streets leading into the shopping district, the financial district, or the neighborhoods leading to the Bay.

But John didn't take the time to enjoy the views. He was already late. No legal parking spot was available, so he parked in front of the shrink's driveway, blocking it. The good doctor wouldn't mind.

He let himself in by the tradesmen's entrance, not bothering to knock. He knew the drill. Inside the basement with the low ceilings, harsh light greeted him. The white waiting room was empty. In fact, he wasn't sure why there was a waiting room at all. John had never seen anybody waiting here. Anybody other than the person who was joining him for these sessions.

With a click, the door eased shut behind him, and the receptionist finally lifted her head from her paperwork behind the equally white counter.

"Mr. Grant," she purred, adjusting her utterly skimpy pink top that stretched so tightly over her breasts that he wanted to take cover in case a button popped off and took out his eye.

Her platinum blonde hair was styled like Marilyn Monroe's, and her makeup also mimicked the movie star's face, her lips a deep red, her skin as pale as porcelain, her lashes black and long. The perfect pinup. He'd never bothered to memorize her name, in fact, he couldn't even remember if he'd ever asked for her name. So in his mind he always called her Marilyn.

Marilyn ran her gaze over him in a leisurely fashion, not concealing her interest in the least bit. He assumed she treated each male client—he refused to call himself a patient—in the same manner. A vampire woman, she was different from human females, less docile, more demanding, and clearly not shy when it came to letting a man know what she wanted. However, he wasn't biting. Literally or figuratively.

John pointed to one of the other doors. "Doc in?"

"They've both been waiting for you for ten minutes," she said, a light scold in her high-pitched voice.

"I bet." His protégée was always punctual. And the doc charged by the hour and made sure not a single minute of his time was wasted. They'd probably been bitching about him for the past ten minutes, discussing all the ways he wasn't performing his duties as a maker.

Without another word or a knock, he entered the doctor's office, letting the door slide shut behind him.

This was the fourth time he'd come here, and he didn't like it any more than the first time. He still hated the tasteless black coffin-couch that looked like it belonged in a cheesy horror movie rather than a physician's office. Just as he abhorred the fake gothic window murals— for the room didn't actually have windows—which looked like they'd been copied from the set of the Addams Family. The stone floor could just as easily have been found in a crypt, and the filing cabinets sported handles that looked like stakes. Perhaps so a patient fed up with the doctor's annoying questions could stab himself—or the doctor.

At least Dr. Drake, the only vampire shrink in San Francisco, dressed like a doctor: white lab coat, a white shirt, black pants, and black dress shoes. He was a tall, skinny vampire, and apparently many of John's colleagues had consulted him at one time or another. Many voluntarily. Not so John. He'd been mandated to attend these sessions. He and his protégée, Deirdre.

She was sitting in the chair opposite Drake's, drinking from a bottle with a straw. He recognized the label. She'd gotten herself a drink from the vending machine in Drake's waiting room. Well, at least that meant she wasn't as squeamish about drinking human blood as she'd been just after he'd turned her.

"John, so nice of you to finally join us," Drake said with a good dose of sarcasm.

"Some of us have jobs," John replied and slunk into the armchair next to Deirdre. "Hey, Deirdre."

She tossed him a quick look. "John."

The greeting was frosty with a side of ice storm. Great. Not that he'd expected anything different. After all, Deirdre was pissed at him. Actually, she was pissed at the whole world.

"Well, then let's get started." As usual, Drake's jovial words grated on John, but he swallowed his distaste.

"Yes, let's."

"Tell me what's been going on in your lives since I saw you both last," Drake demanded. "Deirdre, why don't you start?"

She set aside the half-empty bottle of blood and sat up straighter. She tossed her long light-brown hair over her shoulder, revealing more of her face. She was an attractive woman, but there were hard lines in her face, lines that attested to the battles she'd fought, the vast experience she'd gathered over several centuries, centuries she'd spent as a Stealth Guardian.

The immortal warriors were a race sworn to protect the humans from the demons of fear, a evil preternatural force that fed on the fear of humans and thrived during times of war and conflict. Over the centuries, the Stealth Guardians had developed invaluable skills to fight the demons, one being invisibility, the other teleportation. Yet, the fight against the demons was taking on new proportions, and thus they'd formed an alliance with Scanguards. Scanguards could draw on their skills when needed, and the Stealth Guardians used the vampires' sense of smell to identify demons, who unlike other preternatural creature didn't have a tell-tale aura by which they could be identified.

Deirdre had been a leader of her race, but she'd made decisions that had led to her race punishing her for treason. They had stripped her of all her supernatural powers during a prolonged incarceration in a lead cell, an act that had turned her human. Later, circumstances had led to her being turned into a vampire, turned by John.

"What is there to say?" she started. "I sleep during the day. I'm awake at night. I drink human blood. I don't see the sun. I feel like a caged animal."

"Hmm." The doctor cast his eyes at John. "Would you care to comment, John?"

Careful not to aggravate Deirdre's already explosive mood, he said, "At the beginning it's an adjustment. I know it wasn't your choice to be turned into a vampire, but had I not done it, you would have died." He shrugged. "I know it's hard to accept what you are, considering where you came from, what you were…" A creature more powerful than a vampire, with less vulnerabilities.

"It's not about that!" Deirdre blurted. "I've accepted what I am. What you made me." She glared at him. "But what now? What do I do now?"

John exchanged a look with the shrink.

"What do you mean by your question?" Drake asked.

Deirdre jumped up. "Do I speak Greek?" She marched to the fake window, then turned and leaned against the mural. "You don't get it, do you?" She huffed. "I was a warrior. I was useful. I was a leader of my race. I made life and death decisions."

"Well, things change," Drake said. "We all go through changes in life. We adapt. Just like you'll adapt to your new circumstances."

Deirdre grunted and glared at the shrink. But before she could let out the barrage of insults that clearly sat on her lips, John spoke. "You're looking for a purpose in life."

She spun her head in his direction, surprise flashing in her eyes. She didn't say anything, but he knew he'd hit on the cause of her dissatisfaction.

Drake cleared his throat. "That's all well and good, but as a new vampire, barely out of diapers"—he chuckled to himself at his tasteless joke—"you have to learn to walk before you can run. You're not yet fully in control of all your—"

"Shut up, doc," John hissed. "Can't you see that you're only making things worse?"

He looked at Deirdre who was shooting a poisonous look at the shrink.

John directed his gaze back at Drake. "What makes you think that Deirdre can't handle being a vampire? Just because her turning happened only a few months ago? That might be true for a human who's been suddenly thrust into our world. But Deirdre was already part of this world. She was a preternatural creature for many centuries. All that's changed for her is that she's a member of a different preternatural race now. Still immortal, still powerful. We've done it your way for the last three sessions, and nothing came of it. You said we needed to take it slowly, one step at a time. And I followed your advice. But I'm done with it. We're doing it my way now."

When his eyes locked with Deirdre's, he saw gratitude in them for the first time.

"You want to be useful to your new species; make your mark in this new life. I should have seen it earlier." With a sideways glance at the shrink, he added, "I shouldn't have listened to other people telling me it's too early to get you to think about what you want to do with your new life." But he'd never been a maker, never had responsibility for another vampire, one who needed guidance. "I can help you with that."

"John, with all due respect," Drake interrupted, "this is not how this works. The mind of a new vampire is a fragile thing. You can't just bulldoze your way over it and pretend there aren't any underlying issues of guilt and resentment between the two of you. Let's talk about that."

Leave it up to the shrink to kick up some shit. John grunted to himself.

"You feel guilty for having turned Deirdre, because she was in no condition to give her consent. Tell us about that guilt, John."

John glared at the doctor. "Well, look at you, stirring up shit again! Ever heard of letting sleeping lions lie?"

"It comes with the profession."

"Does it?"

One side of the doctor's mouth curled up. Sadistic bastard!

"I sense a lot of resentment between the two of you. You hate the fact that you're responsible for her, and you, Deirdre, hate it that he has power over you as your maker."

Deirdre narrowed her eyes and pushed away from the mural. "You know nothing about me or about John. And frankly, I find these mandated *couples* sessions useless. Who came up with this harebrained idea?"

Drake lifted his chin, giving an air of superiority. "The vampire council prescribes these sessions for new vampires and their makers these days. And if you must know, I suggested it to them after seeing all kinds of suppressed issues crop up years later. It's best to nip these things in the bud."

"Yeah, I know what I'd like to nip in the bud," Deirdre murmured under her breath.

John had to suppress a grin. He hadn't realized that his protégée had a sense of humor.

"Be that as it may," Drake said, undeterred, "you have no choice but to attend these sessions."

"Attend maybe," Deirdre hedged, then winked at John, "but nobody can make me say anything I don't want to say."

Before Drake could respond, John added, "She's got a point, doc. Last time I checked we weren't in Scanguards' interrogation room. I'm afraid you'll have to make do with what Deirdre and I are willing to share. True, we have to be here for what—five sessions, maybe ten? But stay the crap out of my head. And out of Deirdre's. Just because you were able to convince the vampire council to mandate these sessions, doesn't mean somebody else can't convince them that they're useless and make them drop them just as quickly."

"How dare you—"

John rose, cutting him off. "You're not the only one who knows people in high places. I'm sure you're aware that I worked for the vampire king of Louisiana for many years. And that we're friends. I believe he has great influence with the council. I'm sure the vampire council dropping mandatory counseling sessions will cut into your income, won't it?"

When Drake glared at him, John motioned to his protégée. "I think we're done here. Do you need a ride, Deirdre?"

She smiled at him, the first genuine smile he'd ever seen her display. "Actually, I do."

Together, they marched out of the doctor's office, past fake Marilyn, who stared at the clock on the wall, perplexed, but silent.

John turned his head to Deirdre as they walked toward the end of the driveway. "Where can I drop you?"

"I don't actually need a ride. I just said it to piss Drake off and walk out with you."

John chuckled. "So you didn't like him much, huh?"

She tossed him a get-real look. "The guy is a pompous ass with a mail-order degree from a third-grade university. I'm just surprised you stuck it out as long as you did."

He raised an eyebrow. "I felt it was my duty as your maker to—"

"Yeah, let's get over that shit. I really don't give a damn if you feel guilty or whatever." She shrugged. "All I want to know is if you meant what you said earlier, you know, that you're willing to help me."

"I stand by my word."

"Good."

They stopped next to John's Mercedes. "Then tell me how I can help you."

"I want to be part of Scanguards."

"In what capacity?"

She laughed. "I'm not interested in being a grunt. As a Stealth Guardian I was a warrior for several centuries, before I became a member of the Council of Nine. I paid my dues. I'm not going to pay them a second time."

"I'm afraid the top management positions are taken." Besides, his rank at Scanguards wasn't high enough to recommend anybody for a management position. Those were given out by merit, and by merit alone.

"You think I'm talking about being in management?" She shook her head vehemently. "How boring! Don't you get it? I want to feel adrenaline charge through my veins again. I want to fight."

He froze. "Fight?"

"Yes, I want you to get me a position at Scanguards that deals with the worst criminals, the most dangerous situations."

"You're crazy."

"No, not crazy. But I need a challenge. I need to prove that I can still do it." She pounded her fist against her chest. "That what's in here hasn't changed just because my body has changed."

"Is this about the actions that caused the Stealth Guardians to exile you? Because if it is, then I'm gonna tell you right now, you paid for that with your life. You paid for that on the battlefield when you took a dagger for Virginia."

Virginia, a Stealth Guardian, who was now the wife of Scanguards' resident witch, Wesley, had nearly lost her life in a battle with demons, had Deirdre not thrown herself into the path of the dagger meant for Virginia. Mortally wounded, Deirdre would have died, but Virginia had begged John to save her life by turning her into a vampire. Deirdre hadn't had a choice in the matter, and John kept wondering whether he'd done the right thing, or whether it would have been more merciful letting Deirdre die on the battlefield. It would have been an honorable death in her eyes.

"You've redeemed yourself," he added.

Deirdre shook her head. "Maybe in your eyes, maybe even in my brother's eyes. My standards are higher."

"Don't you appreciate that you've been given a second chance? Why risk this new life you've been given?"

"That's funny, coming from you."

"What's that supposed to mean?"

"Don't you do the same every day? Risk your life because you think you've got nothing worth living for anymore? You of all people should understand where I'm coming from."

He'd never talked about his own heartbreak. There was no way

Deirdre could know. "You don't know anything."

"No, you're right. I don't know what exactly it is that makes you think you've got nothing to live for, but every time I see you I can sense it. It's all around you. So don't deny me what you do every day. I need this."

John took a deep breath, filling his lungs with the cool night air, and sighed. "Very well, if that's what you want."

"I do."

"I'll talk to Samson."

"Thank you."

7

Savannah thanked the Lyft driver and got out of the Prius. It was mid-morning, and she hadn't actually wanted to come to the office, but she had responsibilities she'd been neglecting since Buffy's disappearance. And a few of these things had to be taken care of. She would only stay for two or three hours, make sure Alexi and Rachel knew what to do, and then she'd leave and do what she'd done the last few days: go to all the places in the city that Buffy liked, and speak to anybody who knew her in the hopes that somebody remembered something.

Savannah entered the office building in the SoMa district, where she rented a small suite for herself and her two full-time employees. There was no doorman, no security, which kept the rent at a reasonable level. She didn't bother with the elevator and instead took the stairs to the second floor. At the door to the suite, she stopped for a moment and took a deep breath, then entered.

The suite consisted of only two rooms: one large, open-plan office and a smaller, glass-enclosed room for meetings. There were several workstations with computers, one for her, one each for Alexi and Rachel, and another one, just in case she needed to hire additional help. Only one workstation was occupied.

Alexi looked up from his screen. "Good morning, Savannah." The blond, blue-eyed Russian still had a heavy accent, although he'd been working in the US for five years. His John Lennon glasses gave him a geeky look, one that was underscored by his slim frame and lack of fashion sense. But she hadn't hired him for his looks. Alexi was brilliant, his computer skills superior, his knowledge of algorithms and encryption second to none. Though he'd been working for her for only eight months, he'd already earned back double his first year's salary. With his help she'd landed a lucrative contract with a major bank, and Alexi was doing most of the work for it. A win-win.

"Morning, Alexi," she greeted him and placed her handbag on the desk opposite him, then glanced at the empty desk next to his. "Rachel not in yet?"

"She called in sick this morning." He scoffed. "Again."

"What do you mean by again?"

"She was sick yesterday, too. Left me hanging with the coding for the supermarket cashiering upgrade. I was here till eleven last night."

Annoyance boiled up in Savannah. She should have known that things would go sideways when she took time off. "I'm sorry, I should have been here. Why didn't you call me?"

Alexi tilted his head sideways and gave her a serious look. "You have enough to worry about. I shouldn't even have mentioned it. Forget about it. Tell me: have the police made any progress? Any leads?"

Savannah sank into her chair and automatically reached for the on-button of her computer to boot it up. She met Alexi's gaze and shook her head.

"I'm sorry," he said softly. "I wish there was something I could do."

"You're already doing it. You're holding down the fort. I'm grateful for that." At least she didn't have to worry about her business in addition to everything else. "So what's wrong with Rachel? Did she say when she'll be back?"

Alexi shrugged. "No idea. Her cough sounded a bit fake if you ask me. Maybe she thought she would play hooky while you're out."

"You don't know that. There's been a bug going around in the city. Maybe she caught it." After all, Rachel was a hard worker and not one to skip work on a regular basis.

Alexi grunted to himself, then said, "You're probably right."

"If she's not in tomorrow, I'll call her, okay?" Her computer booted up and she logged on. "Are the bank files ready?"

"They're in your folder for approval. There were a few issues with the encryption, but I fixed them. And I added a few lines of code, so that outage they experienced last week shouldn't happen again."

"Great, I'll check it out." She navigated to the folder and was about to open the file, when she heard the door open. Her gaze shot to it. Had Rachel decided to come to work after all?

But it wasn't Rachel who entered the suite. A blond man in his late forties, early fifties, dressed in a well-fitting business suit, entered, but when his eyes fell on Alexi, he hesitated. Had he come to the wrong place?

Savannah rose. "May I help you?"

The stranger's gaze landed on her. "This is Rice Communications, isn't it?" He spoke with an accent she couldn't place.

"Yes."

He smiled, a sign of relief filling his face. "Then I'm in the right place. I'm sorry I'm a little late, but I'm a little bit jetlagged, and I must have forgotten to set the alarm last night. I should have asked the hotel staff to wake me."

Confused, she looked at Alexi, who pulled up his shoulders in a helpless shrug.

"I'm sorry, you are…?" Savannah asked.

With an outstretched hand, he approached her. "Viktor Stricklund, nice to meet you."

"Stricklund?" The name meant nothing to her.

He hesitated again. "Yes, from Stockholm. Sweden." His forehead furrowed. "We had an appointment about half an hour ago. Again, I'm so sorry I'm late. I hope you'll be able to see me nevertheless. I traveled all the way from Sweden."

Savannah continued to shake her head. "But I made no appointment with you."

"Well, I didn't speak to you directly, that's correct, but I spoke to your assistant. Just a few days ago."

"Rachel?"

"Yes, yes, Rachel," he confirmed and reached for her hand. She felt obliged to shake it.

"Mr. Stricklund, there must have been a misunderstanding. Rachel knew I couldn't take any new appointments this week."

"But I got a confirmation from her."

Savannah looked at Alexi. "I asked Rachel not to make any appointments for this week and cancel everything on my calendar. Didn't she do that?"

Alexi looked surprised. "I'm pretty sure she did. At least she said she did."

Savannah turned back to the Swedish businessman. "I'm so sorry, Mr. Stricklund, I don't know what to say about this mix-up. Rachel should have never made this appointment."

"But, I'm here now. I traveled all the way from Sweden. Surely you can spare me an hour to discuss business."

She sighed. "I'm sorry, I just... I can't." She felt a lump in her throat. She couldn't deal with business now. She could barely hold herself together, let alone conduct a business meeting with a potential new client.

"I can come back this afternoon if that's more convenient," Stricklund offered.

"Mr. Stricklund—"

Alexi interrupted her. "I'll handle this, Savannah." Then he looked at Stricklund. "I'm afraid, Mr. Stricklund, Ms. Rice is dealing with a family emergency and can't conduct any business right now. We're sorry. I'll make sure we reimburse you for your travel expenses. But I'm going to have to ask you to leave Ms. Rice in peace now."

Stunned, the businessman's look bounced between her and Alexi. He appeared annoyed now. "Family emergency? What can be so important—"

"My daughter..." She didn't even realize that she'd spoken. She knew that she didn't have to justify herself, but the words just found their way over her lips. "...she has disappeared." Savannah's throat tightened like it always did when she spoke of Buffy.

Stricklund jolted visibly. "Oh my God! That's horrible! You must be beside yourself with worry." He put his hand to his chest. "I'm so sorry. I need to apologize. If I'd known..."

"I'm sorry that you've been inconvenienced," Savannah said, having found her voice again.

Stricklund made a dismissive hand movement. "Don't worry about me. Is there anything I can do?"

She shook her head, heartened by his sudden kindness and concern. "No, there's nothing you can do, Mr. Stricklund."

"The police, they are looking for her, aren't they?"

"Yes, yes, they are."

"It's not enough, I'm sure. I have many contacts, maybe I can find somebody who can help with the search?"

She forced a smile. "That's very nice of you, but there's no need. I've already hired a private firm to help with the search." And she hoped Scanguards would take the case and find Buffy. But she hadn't heard back from John yet. What was taking him so long?

"Oh good, that's good. One can't rely on the police alone."

She nodded.

"Well," he said, "then I'd better leave you." He took her hand and squeezed it. "I'm sure you'll be reunited with your child soon. I can feel it."

"Thank you, Mr. Stricklund."

He let go of her hand, nodded at Alexi, and left the suite.

For a few moments there was only silence in the office, and all she could hear was the sound of her own heart.

"Is that true?"

She looked back at Alexi.

"That you hired an outside firm to help with the search for Buffy. Or did you just say that to get rid of Stricklund?"

"No, it's true. I contacted Scanguards last night."

"Scanguards?" Alexi's forehead furrowed and he typed something on his keyboard, then pointed at the computer screen. "Thought I'd seen the name before. But aren't they just some sort of security company? You know, security guards watching office buildings at night?"

"I guess that's part of what they do. But they also do investigations."

"You mean like PI work?"

"Yes. The police recommended them."

"I guess then they must be good."

From everything she'd seen so far in her encounter with John and from the research she'd done on the company, plus Detective Donnelly's wholehearted recommendation, she was convinced that they were the best, if not the only, people who could help her find Buffy.

She met Alexi's eyes. "I hope so."

Alexi nodded. "They'll find her. They have to. Or it's going to get really boring here. Who else will annoy me with a million questions while I'm on a deadline if not Buffy, huh?" He smiled warmly.

"Yeah, she does that, doesn't she?"

He winked at her. "She's going to be as smart as her mother when she's all grown up. You'll see."

Savannah forced a smile. "Thank you, Alexi. You're the best."

8

John hadn't bothered going home at sunrise and had instead stayed at the office to continue working through the police reports on the abductions. Several hours before sunset, John showered in the gym in the basement and helped himself to blood from the tap at the V Lounge, Scanguards' recreation area accessible only to vampires. It was like a hotel lounge with comfortable seating areas, a bar, and a fireplace. During the day it was deserted, but his ID card gave him access to the restricted area.

He'd gulped down two full glasses of O-Neg and now leaned his head back against the pillow of one of the deep sofas, closing his eyes for a moment. He was too wound up to be able to sleep, but it felt good to rest his eyes after reading hundreds of pages of reports, trying to find a common denominator that connected the abductions. Without success. No wonder the police was stumped.

At the sound of the door opening, he blinked and recognized Oliver, a vampire who'd been working for Scanguards for nearly three decades, first as a human assistant to the founder, and later, after his turning, as a bodyguard.

When Oliver spotted him, he waved and approached. "Have you seen Blake?"

"Nope."

"You're in early."

John blew out a breath of air. "Make that late."

"You sleep here?"

"Didn't have much time to sleep." He motioned to the empty glass in front of him. "I just came to refuel."

"Heavy caseload?"

"You could say that."

"Did you hear that Gabriel is suggesting we put the hybrids on regular patrol duty?"

John pulled up one side of his mouth in a half-chuckle. Apparently, Gabriel was taking his words to heart. "Ran into Amaury last night. Apparently, I'm babysitting the twins tonight."

Oliver laughed and ran a hand through his shaggy black hair. "I wouldn't call that babysitting. Those two are the furthest advanced in their training. Besides Ryder."

"I notice you don't include Grayson on that list."

Oliver rolled his eyes. "Grayson is about as mature as my son."

"Your son is what, eleven?"

"Twelve."

"Well, then you'd better not let Grayson hear that you think he's no more grown-up than Sebastian."

"Don't worry, I can keep my mouth shut."

John nodded. "Can I ask you something?"

"Shoot."

"You were involved in that blood brothel case twenty-something years ago, right?"

Oliver stiffened, the memory clearly not a pleasant one. Long before John had joined Scanguards, the company had exposed a group of vampires who'd kept dozens of women as blood whores. Like pimps they'd sold them to other vampires to feed on.

"Yeah, I was. We rescued Ursula and all the others. Made sure all of the vampires involved were taken care of. I killed their leader myself." There was a satisfied glint in Oliver's eyes, which now shimmered golden as his vampire nature rose to the surface.

"Yeah, I heard about that. Are you sure that nobody of that outfit is left?"

"Absolutely. Why you asking?"

John sighed. "It's this case I'm evaluating for Donnelly."

"What's he sent you?" Oliver asked with interest and sat down in the chair opposite.

"Child abductions."

"Hmm."

"Yeah. They've got no leads. I went through the police reports to see if I could find similarities."

"And?"

"Nothing that I can see. Some of the kids were abducted during daytime, some at night." Which, in itself made vampire involvement doubtful. "No pattern that I can detect. And the kids come from different backgrounds. Some are black, some white, some Asian. Again no pattern. So I'm trying to figure out if something else connects them. I was thinking about the blood brothel case."

Oliver shook his head. "You can stop right there. All the victims were Chinese. Actually, when I looked up their backgrounds after we'd freed them, we found that all of them came from the Chinese Emperor's direct line. They all shared the same blood. That's why they were taken. I can't see how kids from diverse backgrounds could possibly have that kind of connection. I doubt it's their blood."

John knew the question had been a long shot, but he didn't want anything to remain unexplored. "Hmm."

"Did the parents get ransom notes?"

"No. Not a single one."

"How old are the children?"

"Between nine and twelve. All girls."

Oliver looked straight at him. "All girls?"

John nodded.

"Pretty girls? You know like JonBenet Ramsey pretty?"

John recalled the photos that had been attached to the police reports. "Yeah." He could see Oliver's mind working, and knew which direction it was going. He'd had the same thought many hours earlier, but he hadn't wanted to follow it to its conclusion.

"How many?"

"A dozen in the last five or six weeks alone."

Oliver sighed. "Bastards. Sick bastards."

"I was hoping that I was wrong. I was actually hoping that it's just another group of rogue vampires." It would be something he could handle easily. Because he knew how vampires thought, he knew how they acted, he knew their weak points. A vampire was after blood, first and foremost. Which meant while the kids would certainly be traumatized, they wouldn't be irreparably harmed. Not in the way these bastards would harm the kids. It was painful to give it a name. "It's a child sex ring."

Oliver pressed his lips together in a grim line. "That would be my best guess." He rose from his chair. "Sorry, man, but there are a lot of sick people out there."

"Yeah, very sick."

~ ~ ~

Two hours later, John walked into the small meeting room on the executive floor, where the offices of all of Scanguards' directors were located. Three people were already waiting for him: Samson, Gabriel, and Quinn, who was Oliver's sire and looked no older than twenty-five. With his attractive blond hair, he gave the air of a quintessential womanizer though he was happily blood-bonded to a vampire woman. They sat around the conference table talking and looked up at John when he entered.

Samson exuded authority despite his casual attire. His hazel eyes were alert, his black hair styled back, his shoulders relaxed.

"Evening, Samson." John nodded to the other two. "Gabriel. Quinn."

"Take a seat, John. Fill us in," Samson said and pointed to the chair opposite. He glanced at Gabriel. "I hear Donnelly is trying to get us to take on a case. What have you found?"

John sat down and placed his file in front of him, but he didn't open it. He didn't have to. He'd memorized every pertinent fact. And now he had to make a case for Scanguards to accept this assignment. He'd done this dozens of times before, but never with as few convincing reasons and as much heartfelt passion.

"Over the last few weeks, there've been a large number of child abductions in the Bay Area. All of them were girls between the ages of nine and twelve. None of the parents received ransom notes. The kids simply vanished."

"And you think vampires are involved in their disappearance?" Samson asked.

"Considering that some of the children were taken in broad daylight, no. However—"

"Then why are we even discussing this?" Samson asked. "Hand the case back to Donnelly."

"I don't think it's that clear cut," John protested. "This is big. Bigger than Donnelly's people are prepared to handle."

"That may be the case, but our arrangement with the SFPD is clear: we only get involved if we're dealing with preternatural creatures. We just don't have the manpower to do any more than that." Samson made a motion to rise.

John shot up from his seat. "Please, hear me out, Samson. I think we're dealing with child sex trafficking. These are little girls. If we don't help them, they might be lost forever."

Samson closed his eyes for a second and sighed. "Don't think I'm heartless, John. I'm not. I feel for the children and their parents, but we can't take on more than we can handle." He exchanged a look with Gabriel and Quinn.

Quinn patted the file folder in front of him. "Everybody's already taking on more assignments than they can handle. We're spread thinner than a Japanese paper screen. And since we had to dispatch some of our men to fulfill our obligations with the Stealth Guardians, we're short-staffed."

John knew about that. Only a few short months ago, Scanguards had allied themselves with the Stealth Guardians. They'd agreed to help each other battling evil, and as a result Scanguards had dispatched some of their staff to help the immortal warriors in their fight against the demons, while the Stealth Guardians in turn helped out whenever their skills were needed by Scanguards. At the moment, the Stealth Guardians' need for battling the demons outweighed Scanguards' need for assistance.

"But this is important. We're talking about kids. Innocents. I'm not confident that Donnelly's people can handle this. They have no leads."

"Do you?" Gabriel shot back.

John swallowed. "Not yet. But I can feel it. There is a connection between these children that will lead me to the culprits. I'll find it. I'll work day and night if I have to."

Gabriel shook his head. "John, be reasonable. As much as we all want to help these families get their children back, it would be at the expense of others that we've sworn to protect. If times were different, if we had more men at our disposal, there's no question that we'd take this case. But our hands are tied."

"And you can't work day and night," Samson added. "I appreciate your dedication. But if you work twenty-four-seven, you're going to burn out and you'll make a mistake. One that might cost you or someone in your care their life. I can't allow that."

"And if one of those children were your child?" John barked, realizing he was marching into insubordination territory.

Samson's eyes narrowed. "I'm going to ignore that question. Do you understand me, John? Hand the case back to Donnelly. This is their case. They have the resources. They will eventually make a break."

"Eventually? That might be too late for these children." Maybe it was already too late. Maybe some of them had already experienced horrors that would damage them for life.

Samson sighed. "If things change, if we can free up some men to help, we will. But as things stand now, I don't see that happening anytime soon. I'm sorry." He rose and marched out of the room.

John remained standing there, staring at Gabriel and Quinn. Both looked back at him with regret in their eyes. He cast a pleading look at Gabriel. "And the hybrids? Can't they be assigned?"

"They already are," Gabriel said and motioned to Quinn. "Quinn's already put them on the roster according to their level of skill and training. We're using them where we can. And much earlier than I would like to."

"You do know what those people will do to these girls, don't you?" John said, his jaw tight, his fists clenched. "What they've maybe already done."

Gabriel squeezed his eyes shut for a moment, while the scar on his face seemed to pulse. Then he rose. "John, you have your orders."

He left the room, while Quinn shuffled through his papers. "Damian and Benjamin are waiting for you in the V lounge. I suggest you get on with your work." He rose and walked to the door. There he looked over his shoulder. "I wish there was something I could do."

John grunted to himself and waited until Quinn had left the room. Then he sank back onto the chair, exhaustion and lack of sleep catching up with him. Or maybe it was just the knowledge that he had to face Savannah with bad news.

Scanguards wasn't going to help her find Buffy.

9

The twins were indeed in the V lounge, though they didn't seem to be too broken up about having had to wait for John. The rather lovely barmaid, a vampire female, made sure the handsome young hybrids weren't bored. Just like their father Amaury, Benjamin and Damian were dark-haired and blue-eyed, with broad shoulders and an abundance of charm. It was easy to tell them apart, even though they were identical twins. They wore their hair differently, Benjamin preferring a shorter, more cropped style, while Damian's hair grew over his ears and hugged his nape, though it was not as long as his father's. In temperament though they were quite similar.

John actually liked the two hybrids. They were intelligent and easy to get along with. More than that, they were fun to be around. They had great taste in music, a dry sense of humor, and weren't easily offended. Both loved fast cars and drove Porsches, the same model their father drove. And while they clearly adored their parents, they were the kind of kids who were self-contained, realizing that their parents were also a couple that needed their own space. Because of that they'd recently moved out of their parents' penthouse in the Tenderloin district, a rather seedy neighborhood in central San Francisco, and into another unit in the same building, which Amaury owned.

"Hey, John," Damian called out to him. "Want a drink before we head out?"

Having had plenty of blood earlier when the lounge had been empty, John shook his head. "I'm good. Drink up."

Benjamin downed the last inch of his glass, then wiped a drop of blood from his chin. Although hybrids drank blood—they had to if they wanted to maintain their vampire strength—they could also eat human food. Benjamin and Damian consumed plenty of both and had the physical strength to prove it.

Damian tossed the barmaid a charming grin and a promising wink, then placed his empty glass back on the counter. "See you later, babe. Gotta save the world."

She giggled and blew him an air kiss.

John refrained from rolling his eyes and waited for the twins to join him.

"Where to?" Damian asked and gave John a pat on the back as if they were buddies.

"You tell me. You're the one who wants to save the world," John shot back.

Benjamin slapped his brother over the head from behind and said, "Doofus!"

Instead of being insulted, Damian chuckled. "You would have said the same to her had I not been faster."

"Good thing you've always been a bit faster than me. Wouldn't want to get in the way of you making an ass of yourself."

"Shall we, gentlemen?" John interrupted and pointed to the door.

Both Benjamin and Damian made exaggerated curtsies as if they'd rehearsed it, then laughed at each other when they realized they'd both thought of the same comeback.

"Seriously, John," Damian said as he and his brother followed him to the elevators. "What's the plan for tonight?"

"Yeah, what can we help you with?" Benjamin added.

"Help?" He doubted that either of the two jokers could help him with what he had to do first. "You can get in your cars and follow me. I've got a quick visit to make."

"Great, who are we visiting?" Damian asked.

The elevator doors opened and John stepped in, the two hybrids on his heels. "You aren't visiting anyone. The two of you will stay in your cars and wait for me. It'll only take two minutes. Got that?"

"Yes, sir!" they said in unison.

Well, at least they'd learned to follow orders. It was a start.

Minutes later, John sat behind the steering wheel of his Mercedes and shot out of Scanguards' underground garage, two black Porsche Carreras following him. He took the most direct route to Lower Pacific

Heights, not wanting to drag out the inevitable. Sure, he could have made a phone call instead, but there was still the matter of his jacket. He'd lent it to Savannah and forgotten it at her place the night before. It was the only reason he was driving to see her in person.

And not because he wanted to see her one more time.

Yeah, not even he believed that. He couldn't care less about the jacket. In fact, it didn't even make the top ten when it came to his favorite pieces of clothing. If he lost it during a battle, he would certainly not go back for it. Yet, he was using his jacket as a convenient excuse to see Savannah. How pathetic! He should know better. Not only would she be disappointed and angry once he told her the news that Scanguards wasn't going to help her find Buffy, he was torturing himself by being anywhere near her. Yeah, he could admit at least that to himself. He had been thinking about inhaling her scent again ever since he'd said goodnight to her less than twenty-four hours earlier.

But nothing would come of it. Because he couldn't allow it. Couldn't allow himself to give into the need that had suddenly surfaced, the need to connect with a woman, not just for carnal pleasures, but to have another being touch his heart, just so he knew that he still had one. That it was still beating. That it hadn't died with Nicolette four years earlier. But to allow another woman in would mean to betray Nicolette, to betray her love. A love he'd vowed would last forever.

Yet here he was, bringing the car to a stop in front of Savannah's condo and turning off the engine. He sat there in silence. He didn't need the jacket, could just as easily pull his cell phone from his pocket and dial her number, tell her over the phone—in a businesslike, detached manner—that Scanguards had decided not to take her case. After all, he'd warned her about it. Told her in advance that Scanguards didn't take every case it was offered—though he'd lied about why. There was no evidence of vampire involvement in the children's disappearances. With each additional police report he'd read, his conviction about it had strengthened. And though he could have lied to Samson and Gabriel, could have pretended that there was some evidence that pointed to vampires, he knew it wasn't right. He couldn't even blame his bosses for their decision. In their shoes, he would have made the same choice.

And now it was his job to be the bearer of bad news.

He looked at the phone in his hand, then at the door handle. His heart beat like a jackhammer, and he could hear his blood rushing through his veins, the sound thundering in his ears like a storm overhead.

Decision time.

~ ~ ~

Savannah shot up from the couch. Had she nodded off? It wouldn't surprise her. After all, she'd barely slept the night before, and during the day she'd criss-crossed the city, visiting every spot she'd ever taken Buffy to. She knew it had been a long shot, but simply sitting around, doing nothing, waiting impotently, was worse.

There it was again, the sound that had woken her: the doorbell. She raced to the intercom. "Yes?"

"It's John Grant."

She buzzed him in and ripped the door open, watching him ascend the stairs to her floor. She couldn't see his face—the light bulb must have burned out after she'd returned home. When he reached the landing and the light from the hallway illuminated his face, she knew the news he was bringing wasn't good.

"No," she murmured to herself. "Buffy? Did you—"

He reached for her hand and stopped her with a quick shake of his head. "No news about Buffy," he said.

Her heart calmed by a fraction. But the solemn look on his face continued to worry her. "Something is wrong, isn't it?"

He shut the door behind him. "We need to talk."

She hated those words, because rarely did they mean good news. With a shaking hand she motioned to the living room and followed him. He didn't sit down, but turned to face her, meeting her gaze. He shifted, visibly uncomfortable.

"When you came to see me in my office yesterday, I mentioned to you that Scanguards doesn't take on every case that's presented to them," he started.

Her breath caught in her throat like a fat Santa Claus in a too-tight chimney.

John dropped his gaze to his shoes. "I'm sorry. But we can't help you."

She shook her head. Disbelief collided with the real fear that now she would never see her daughter again. "No. No. Please, don't say that."

She didn't recognize her own voice. High-pitched, pleading, borderline hysterical. Yes, she was all that. Because she was a mother, a mother who feared for her daughter. A lioness who was prepared to do anything to get her cub back.

"I'm sorry, Ms. Rice, I wish there was something I could do. But the decision has been made."

She shook her head, took a step closer to him. "Please, I'll pay more. Double of what you normally charge. I have money, you can check. I'll pay whatever it costs."

"It's not the money. It's not about that."

"Then what is it about? Please, tell me. What can I do to make you help me find my daughter? Please, you're my only hope!" She felt tears prick behind her eyes, but pushed them back. "The police haven't been able to find any of the other children, and they've been missing longer than Buffy. You know they can't help me. But I know you can." She didn't know where that confidence came from, but her instincts told her he would find her. If only he agreed to help her.

"You can't know that. There's no guarantee. Even if I could take the case. But I can't. My hands are tied."

There was compassion in his words, even though he stuck to his refusal. She'd seen that compassion before, when he'd first asked her about Buffy. Just like she'd seen something else that night. Something she would exploit now. For Buffy.

"If it's not money you want, then something else." She gripped his hand. "Anything you want." She locked eyes with him and moved closer, bringing her body to within inches of his much bigger one. "I'll give you anything if you help me. Anything."

There was a flicker in his eyes, almost like a flame igniting. She hadn't misjudged him the night before. Hadn't misjudged the stolen looks he'd cast her way. The looks of a man who wanted something. Wanted her—or at least her body.

Yet, he didn't react now. He stood as if frozen in place, his eyes the only part of him that seemed to be alive. But she wouldn't give up, not when she'd just discovered his weak point.

"I'll sleep with you as often as you want, however you want it. You can demand anything from me, no matter what it is, I'll do it. I'll fulfill all your fantasies without protest." She took his hand and guided it to her breast, making him cup one globe. His eyes seemed to shimmer, while his lips parted. "I saw how you looked at me last night. Undress me if you want to. Touch me. I know you want to." She grabbed his other hand and laid it on her other breast. Beneath his palms, though they were motionless, she could feel herself react. Her nipples were hardening, though she didn't understand why. This wasn't about her pleasure. This was about a deal she would make with him. Her body in exchange for his help.

"Ms. Rice," he ground out, his lips barely moving. "Don't—"

"Savannah," she coached and laid her hands over his, squeezing, so he was forced to squeeze her boobs. "Please, you can have all this. You can have me. Doing whatever you command. I'll make sure you'll enjoy it. I promise. You can fuck me now." She lowered her hand to his crotch. Hardness greeted her there. He wasn't as unaffected as his rigid stance suggested. "Or I can suck you. Would you rather have me do that? Do you want me on my knees, your cock in my mouth?" She didn't care what she had to do to make him help her. She had no pride left. Her only thought was her daughter.

His hands on her breasts were suddenly gone. Before she could say or do anything else, John's hands were framing her face, and his mouth was crushing her lips with a kiss that she hadn't expected. A kiss that could only be described as untamed. And to her surprise, not unwanted. By either party. She felt his need, a desire that she'd seen in his eyes and that he was now unleashing. And despite the reason why she was trying to seduce him, her body reacted to him. Reacted as if he was a man whom she desired.

He tasted of power and strength, and she'd forgotten what a man like that tasted. His mouth was punishing, his tongue demanding surrender. She didn't resist, couldn't have, even if she wanted to. She responded to his kiss, sliding one hand to his nape, the other to his waist so he couldn't escape, couldn't change his mind now that he'd accepted the deal she was offering. She pressed her body to his, and heard him groan in response. But he didn't free himself, instead, he pushed her back toward the wall, crushing her between it and his equally hard body.

She moaned, unable to hold in the unexpected pleasure this kiss ignited in her.

John seemed to become even more passionate as a result of her reaction, one hand now sliding down to her ass, palming it as if he had every right to do so. And he did. She'd given him that right by offering him carte blanche. By offering him her body to do with as he pleased. Though she hadn't thought it would please *her* as much as it did.

All of a sudden, she felt cool air on her lips and realized he'd severed not only the kiss, but their embrace too. He stood a couple of feet away from her now. She must have been so dazed from his kiss that she hadn't seen or felt him move.

He breathed heavily and stared at her, his eyes picking up the light from a lamp near the couch, which made them shimmer golden. There was something beautiful yet dangerous lurking in those eyes.

"I'm sorry," he choked out as if he could barely speak, his jaw tight as if he couldn't open his mouth. "I shouldn't have done that."

She suddenly felt naked, exposed. "John…" She didn't know what to say now, what to do, so she did nothing.

"This is wrong. I can't do this."

Her heart sank. He didn't want her. Which meant he wasn't taking her deal. He wasn't going to help her. She slammed a hand over her mouth to stop herself from sobbing. She'd humiliated herself, and for what? For nothing. She lowered her head, couldn't bear for him to see the despair in her eyes.

Why didn't he leave? Why wasn't he at the door already, hightailing it out of her flat? Was he enjoying her humiliation, her defeat?

"I can't take what you're offering. I'm not that kind of man. I'd never sink that low."

"Sink that low…" she repeated. "Yeah, you're right."

She suddenly felt his hands grip her biceps and snapped her gaze to him.

"You misunderstand me. I would never take advantage of a woman who's vulnerable. What I just did was a mistake, and I apologize for it. But I'm just a man, and there are moments when even I can't fight against my needs. When even I slip. It's not your fault. You did what you thought you had to do. It's my fault entirely. I should have resisted."

His fault? When she was offering herself to him? Begging him to take her? How could it be his fault?

"John, I—"

"No, please, I need to make amends." He swallowed hard. "I'll help you find Buffy. I'll do anything in my power, use all my skills, my connections, my resources, whatever it takes, to bring your daughter home." He let go of her arms and took a step back. "But I'm not going to take any form of payment from you. Not your money, and not your body. You should never have to sell your body to anybody. No matter the reason."

Her lips parted and a surprised puff of air escaped from her lungs. Had she heard correctly? "You'll help me? You'll take the case?"

He nodded.

"And you don't want…" She hesitated and searched his face.

Their gazes connected.

"I would never want what's not freely offered. You might think now that you won't mind sleeping with me, but you'll resent me for it later. Trust me on that. It's best if we never mention this again."

Pretend their passionate embrace had never happened?

Slowly, she nodded. Her respect for him had just tripled. She knew no man who would reject her offer and still help her. Only a saint would do that. Or a eunuch. And John was neither. He'd been aroused, and his kiss had been experienced and passionate. No, John was no saint. He liked sex. He found her attractive. And still, he'd said no, while at the same time promising to help her find Buffy.

No, John was no saint. He was a man of honor and integrity. A man she could trust.

10

John felt that his fangs had finally receded fully into their sockets. The danger was over. For now. But he was still in Savannah's flat, still in her presence. And he could still taste her on his tongue.

He'd acted impulsively, without thinking. And like an animal. But his control had snapped like a twig under the weight of an elephant, leaving him no choice but to do what his body commanded. What, in fact, Savannah had offered. Offered under duress. And that was the reason his mind had finally triumphed over his base needs, and he'd been able to wrench himself out of her arms. Not a moment too soon either. His fangs had already descended, readying themselves for the bite they craved. Savannah had no idea how close she'd come to finding out what he truly was. Not the hero she believed him to be, but the vampire who wanted to drink her blood.

"Thank you," she murmured.

He acknowledged her words with a nod. She was probably relieved that she didn't have to go through with her offer. After all, what woman would willingly submit to a stranger, giving him leave to do with her as he wished without even knowing how depraved the man might be? Not that John considered himself to be depraved, but he had his appetites, and those were insatiable. A quick fuck in the missionary position wouldn't be sufficient to slake his hunger. Particularly since he'd not engaged in that kind of activity in a while.

"I should go now," he said.

She nodded in agreement, but didn't move. "What are you going to do to find her?"

"I need to check up on all the people in her life and find out what Buffy has in common with the other children that disappeared. Things like going to the same school, having had the same babysitters, the same doctors, anything that ties them together. There has to be something."

"I understand. If there's anything I can do to help…"

"I received your email with the information about your employees. I'll start there." He didn't mention that he'd already looked into the babysitter's background and checked out her place. "I'll be in touch soon. But if you remember anything else, even if it seems insignificant, I want you to call me. Day or night." He pulled out a card and gave it to her. It only had his name and cell phone number on it. "This is my private line. Call me on this number only, no matter what time it is, even if you think I might be asleep."

She took the card. "I will."

With a last look at her, John walked past her into the hallway and out the door. Downstairs he opened the front door and stepped outside, glad to be able to breathe in the cool night air and rid himself of Savannah's delectable scent. A scent that was driving him insane with lust.

The twins were waiting for him, both leaning against one of the Porsches on the opposite side of the road. They exchanged a grin.

He crossed the street to join them.

"I hope we weren't rushing you," Benjamin said with a smirk.

"As I said before, it was a short errand."

Damian motioned back to the building. "Yeah, I could see that. Short, but clearly worth it."

John looked over his shoulder and stared up at the brightly lit second floor window. The living room, where he'd kissed Savannah. And the spot where he'd pressed her against the wall and kissed her was framed by the window as if a photographer had arranged it so. With hybrid vision, which was as perfect as vampire vision, the twins would have seen everything as clearly as if they'd been sitting in front of a television screen.

Shit!

He spun his head back to Damian and Benjamin and glared at them. "It's none of your fucking business. Not a fucking word. Is that clear?"

The two hybrids exchanged a quick look, then nodded.

"We didn't mean any harm," Damian said.

Benjamin added, "You're entitled to your privacy. We won't interfere."

"Good. Time for your hands-on-training."

"Excellent, what are we gonna do?" Damian asked eagerly, and both hybrids stared at him in eager anticipation.

It struck him then. It didn't matter that Scanguards had rejected the abduction case, because all he needed were a couple of guys who could do some snooping around for him. And two very eager—and rather capable—guys were right in front of him, willing to follow any order he gave, just to prove that they were ready for their final examination so that they could join the ranks of full-blown bodyguards at Scanguards.

But he had to make sure they knew the rules of this game. And the rules were whatever he decided. Because for the next few days he would be their superior, the one who decided how they spent their time.

"Listen up. I've decided that you're advanced enough to engage in a covert *super-secret* operation. Nobody, and I mean nobody can find out what this mission is. It's vital if you want to pass this test. Understood?"

Both grinned. "Cool!"

"During this mission, assume that anybody might be armed and dangerous, because they may be. This is a live-ammunition event. Anybody could attack you at any time, human or vampire. Their weapons will be real, as will their bullets and their intention to harm you. Trust no one, except me and each other. Everybody is a suspect until you can prove he's not."

They nodded eagerly, their eyes wide with excitement.

"Take the utmost precaution in whatever you do. Treat this as a real mission, not a training exercise. Keep your cover. Nobody can find out you're not human. Use every skill you might find necessary."

"Yes, of course," Damian said rather impatiently. "Come on, don't be so mysterious. What's the goal?"

John let out a slow breath. "The goal is to crack a child trafficking ring and save a dozen girls aged nine to twelve."

"Wow!" Benjamin exclaimed and bumped shoulders with his brother. "Awesome!"

"Who're the bad guys?" Damian asked.

"That's for you to find out."

"Got it," Damian said.

John motioned to his car. "I've got the facts in a file." He motioned them to follow him to his car. He'd brought the file with him to hand it back to Donnelly after telling Savannah that Scanguards wasn't taking the case, but all that had changed now.

It took a half hour to relay all the pertinent facts to the twins, and for them to photograph those pages from the police reports that they deemed important. Then he gave them their final instructions.

"The last girl disappeared four days ago. Buffy Rice. She's the freshest lead. That's why I want you to start with her. We need to look at her environment, at the people who know her. Her mother runs a cyber security company and employs two programmers, Alexi and Rachel. I want you to split up and take one each. Find out what they've been doing every minute since Buffy's disappearance. Look into their background, their finances, their habits. Anything odd, I want to hear about it. I've got their details here." He pulled out his cellphone to scroll to the email Savannah had sent him.

"Is Alexi a girl's name?" Damian asked.

"He's a guy." John suppressed a chuckle. Figured that Damian would want to investigate a girl. "Enjoy, he's all yours. Benjamin can take Rachel."

Benjamin grinned and winked at his brother. "Better luck next time, bro."

Damian shrugged it off.

John copied the names and addresses for Alexi and Rachel and texted them to the twins. Their cellphones chimed, and they both looked at their displays.

"Got it," they said in unison.

"Clock's ticking," John said. "Check in with me every couple of hours, whether you've got news or not. I want to know where you are at all times. Stay safe."

As he watched the twins saunter to their cars and get in, he could only hope that nothing bad would happen to them. Amaury would have his hide if harm came to his sons. But Scanguards had left him no choice. He had to help Savannah. Not because of that kiss or her offer of sex, but because his heart was breaking seeing her eyes tear up whenever she spoke of Buffy. She needed her daughter safely back in her arms. And once he'd achieved that, he would be at peace again, too. He would be able to go back to his lonely life and continue to live night by night. Do his duty to Scanguards. And maybe one day get over the loss he'd suffered.

Maybe by saving this little family, he could make up for having failed to save his own.

11

Outside of New Orleans, four years earlier

John stood at the door to the guard room and watched his men, a dozen well-trained and heavily-armed vampires, march past him after receiving their orders for the night. As leader of the king's guard, he was responsible for them, and for the safety of his king and queen, and their three hybrid children.

The triplets, David, Zack, and Monique were celebrating their sixteenth birthday, and tonight's celebration meant that a large number of guests were expected at the royal estate north of New Orleans. Which meant extra security was needed tonight. It also meant that he was required to remain here all night and most likely the entire morning, rather than return to his home in the Garden District, a home he and his blood-bonded mate Nicolette shared. A home that would soon hear the laughter of their first child.

John looked over his shoulder when he heard footsteps approaching from another corridor. Cain, his king, but also his best friend, walked toward him, a smile on his face.

"Evening, Cain," John greeted him. "You look relaxed."

Cain winked at him. "Faye has that effect on me. Besides, I might be able to get rid of those kids soon. When do you think I can ask them to move out? I mean, they're sixteen. They should be able to live on their own, right?"

John chuckled. "They cramping your style?"

"More than you know."

Despite his words, John knew that Cain was only joking. He loved his children, and if they lived separate from him and Faye, he would only worry. And then John would have to hire even more vampire bodyguards to protect them. Already now, each of them had a personal security detail.

Faye suddenly appeared from the corridor and joined them. "How's

Nicolette?"

John grinned. "Getting fatter every day." And he'd never seen anything lovelier.

Faye smiled. "Not much longer now, right?"

"Another month at least."

"I doubt it. When I saw her last week, she looked like it could be any day now."

Cain put his arm around his wife's waist. "Since when are you a doctor?"

"I'm not. But women know these things." Then she looked back at John. "You did tell her that she's invited to tonight's celebrations, didn't you?"

"Yes, I relayed the invitation. She wasn't sure how she was feeling, so I left it up to her to decide later. I know she wanted to take a nap. She might come later."

"And drive herself?" Faye asked, in surprise.

"Of course not. I made sure there's a car and driver available for her if she wants to join us later."

Faye let out a breath of relief. She was ever the doting queen. "Thank goodness. I really hope that she'll feel well enough to join the festivities."

"Me too," John said.

"You know, I was thinking," Faye added, exchanging a quick look with Cain. "Why don't you two stay at the king's guard cottage until the baby comes? Then we could keep an eye on her while you're on duty."

"That won't be necessary," John said and pointed to Cain. "Cain's ordered me to take a vacation starting as soon as the birthday celebrations are over." He would have never asked for it, but Cain had come to him the night before, announcing his decision in a tone that brooked no refusal. Not that John would have protested. Spending more time with Nicolette before she gave birth to their baby was the best gift his friend could have given him.

"Why didn't you tell me?" Faye said to Cain and slapped him on the shoulder. "I would have personally thanked you for being so nice to

John."

"Oh, you already thanked me earlier," Cain claimed and smirked.

A meaningful gaze passed between them, and John had to shake his head. They were still lovebirds, even after such a long time together. Just like John and Nicolette. Though he and Nicolette hadn't been lucky enough to be blessed with children in their first year of marriage, as Faye and Cain had been. But then, the king and queen had had help: since both of them were vampires, they had asked Maya, a vampire physician from Scanguards, to perform her ground-breaking stem cell treatment on Faye, so she could conceive. Something vampire females hadn't been able to do before Maya had made her discovery. Maya's treatment turned a vampire female's womb into a human womb. The resulting fetus was therefore half vampire, half human, incorporating some of the human DNA from the donor's stem cells into its genetic makeup.

The treatment had worked on the first attempt and resulted in triplets. Three tiny, screaming, and always hungry hybrids that kept everybody in the kingdom on their toes.

And now they were suddenly sixteen years old.

"Is everything ready for tonight?" Cain asked.

"The fireworks are being set up as we speak. The decorations are up. Very goth." John chuckled to himself.

Faye clapped her hands. "I don't know how to thank you, John! I can't believe you came up with the idea of hosting a vampire-themed birthday party. It solves all our problems with the kids' human guests. Since everybody's going to be in vampire costumes, nobody will blink an eye if one of us is seen drinking blood or exposing a fang."

"It's genius," Cain agreed.

John shrugged. "I figured with all those vampire books on the bestseller lists and that new vampire series on TV—which is, by the way, totally unrealistic—no human would find it strange that three teenagers requested a vampire-themed party."

"Just as well that those vampires on TV are nothing like us," Cain commented. "As long as they keep getting half of what we do and how we live wrong, we won't have to worry about them ever figuring us out. Our secret is safe."

"I hope it remains that way." John motioned to the door. "I'd better check that everything is ready for our guests."

"You do that. I'll have a word with the kids, reiterate the rules for tonight." Cain winked at him. "Just in case. You know how they are when they get excited."

John nodded at Cain and Faye, then walked outside. The mansion which housed the king and queen and their three offspring also contained quarters for the king's guard, highly trained bodyguards whose job it was to make sure no harm came to the family.

Outside, several small cottages, all retrofitted to be vampire-proof, dotted the expansive grounds. A long, broad driveway led to a public road several miles away. Along this driveway, tents and stalls had been erected, as well as a stage and a dance floor. It looked more like a carnival than a birthday party. Staff members were milling about, arranging last minute items, while early guests were already arriving, parking their cars in a designated area. From there, they would be led to meet the birthday boys and girl, while security staff discretely scanned them for weapons.

John surveyed the area, sweeping his gaze over the arriving guests. Everything looked good. There were no problems he could detect. There rarely were. His staff was extremely well-trained and dedicated, and the guests had been pre-screened before invitations had been sent out.

His cell phone buzzed. He pulled it from his pocket, and when he read the display, smiled. "Hey, my love," he murmured, answering it. "How are you feeling?"

"I'm feeling really well tonight," Nicolette answered. "A bit hot, but otherwise fine. And I'm bored."

He chuckled. "You are? Then why don't you text the driver and ask him to bring you here? Faye was asking about you. And I'd love to steal a dance if I may."

"I'm fat as a cow, John! You don't want to dance with me." There was a breathless quality to her voice, which reminded him of how she breathed whenever they made love. She'd sounded just like that when he'd made love to her two days ago, with her laying on her side to take pressure off her back and him behind her, gently thrusting in and out of her while he caressed her belly and her heavy breasts. "I'm too fat to dance."

He quickly glanced around. Nobody was on the terrace that surrounded the house. Nevertheless, he lowered his voice. "You're not too fat to make love, so if you won't dance with me, will you at least let me make love to you tomorrow morning?"

A soft chuckle came through the phone. "Oh, John. I honestly don't know how you can still find me attractive when I look like a balloon waddling around on two sticks."

He threw his head back and laughed at her description of herself. Then he murmured, "Don't you know how hard it makes me just thinking of you with your big belly and your heavy tits, and your gorgeous ass? If I weren't so concerned about your and the baby's health, I'd be fucking you like crazy every single day until you deliver our son. So, get your sweet ass into that limousine and come over here so I can at least put my arms around you and pretend to be civilized."

"I love you, John," she said. "I'll be there in an hour, just need to put some decent clothes on."

"I love you, too."

~ ~ ~

The arriving guests, a few complications regarding the planned fireworks, and a mix-up in the food tent kept him so busy that the next time John looked at his watch, an hour and a half had passed since he'd spoken to Nicolette. Had she taken longer to get changed into something suitable for a party, or had they run into traffic? He couldn't help but worry. He always did when he was away from her.

He called Nicolette's cell phone. It rang several times, then went to voicemail. He disconnected the call without leaving a message, and instead searched for the number of the driver he'd arranged for her. It rang once before the call was connected.

"Hello."

"Dean, it's John Grant. I tried my wife's phone. Is she with you?"

There was the sound of the car's engine, then the driver's voice again, "Oh, hi, Mr. Grant. We're on our way. Sorry for the delay."

"John." He heard Nicolette's voice coming over the speaker in the car. "Sorry, I must have forgotten my cell at home. I was trying on every dress I have, because nothing fit."

Just like he'd suspected. There was nothing to worry about. "Well, at least you're on your way now."

"We're only about ten minutes away. We'll be turning off the freeway in a second," she said. "There's our exit already."

"Great!" Then he added, "Thanks, Dean. I'll see you both shortly."

He was about to disconnect the call, when he heard Dean's voice again. "Oh fuck!" Then a high-pitched scream, coming from Nicolette.

His blood chilled. "Nicolette!" he screamed into the phone. "What's wrong? Dean? What's going on?"

But his voice was drowned out by screeching tires, metal-slamming-into-metal, glass breaking.

"Noooooo!"

Before he even knew what he was doing, he was running, the phone still pressed to his ear. There was another sound, as if a large object was being slammed against metal or concrete, something hard, and then everything went silent.

"Nicolette!" But she didn't answer him. Couldn't, because the line was dead.

There was only one other way to connect to her. *If* she could hear him. Their telepathic bond, a bond only blood-bonded couples had.

As he ran to the parking lot, he sent his thoughts to her.

Nicolette! Are you okay? What happened? Please talk to me!

Nothing. No reply.

No!

He reached the valet, snatched the key a guest was just handing him and jumped in the car, slammed the door shut, and took off.

John.

The word sounded so weak in his mind, but he heard it clearly.

Nicolette, I'm coming. Hold on, my love. I'm coming.

John. Again the message was weak. *Hurry.*

He raced down the narrow road and slammed the gas pedal down as far as he could.

I'm almost there, love. Almost there. Just a few more minutes.

He turned onto the public road, the tail of his borrowed car spinning out, but he kept the vehicle under control.

I smell something.

Panic hit him. No. Please, don't let it happen!

You've gotta get out of the car! Get out now!

There was silence for a few seconds, seconds that were too long. Then he heard her again.

Can't… seatbelt is stuck.

He tried to calm himself, not wanting to make Nicolette panic.

Try to wiggle the seatbelt. Try to loosen it. See if you can slip out.

I'm sorry.

No! he responded. *Don't give up!*

He came up on a curve. Behind it was the exit ramp from the freeway, the one Dean would have taken. He raced toward it, took the curve, and felt his heart stop.

I'm here, my love.

The front of the limousine was wedged against a low concrete wall and the tail of a big rig. A big rig that had taken the exit ramp at too high a speed and lost control.

The gas…

Nicolette didn't finish her thought.

A split-second later, the limousine's gas tank exploded, engulfing the car and its passengers in flames. John screeched to a halt only yards away from the inferno and jumped from the car. He ran toward the flames, despite the heat that felt as if it was melting the skin off his bones. But he didn't care. All he cared about was saving his woman and his child.

With supernatural strength he managed to reach the car. The windows had shattered, and flames were shooting out from them. But flames wouldn't stop him. Not now, not when he was so close.

His hands burned. Excruciating pain shot through him as he wrenched the passenger door open. He couldn't see anything but flames inside. Running on pure adrenaline, he willed his hands to turn into claws and reached inside. There, Nicolette. He felt her big belly, felt the seatbelt restricting her, and sliced through it with his sharp claws. All the while, the fire was burning the clothes off this body and the hair off his head.

He grabbed Nicolette and heaved her out of the car, brought them to the ground and rolled several times to extinguish the flames.

"Nicolette, I've got you."

But his vampire senses had already told him that it was too late. There was no breath, no heartbeat, no blood rushing through her veins. He laid his hand on her pregnant belly. No heartbeat from there either. All that was left was charred skin, singed hair, burned clothes. And unlike John, who would recover from his burns with sufficient blood and restorative sleep, Nicolette wouldn't. There was no life left in her. He couldn't even turn her into a vampire to save her; it was too late for that too. He'd failed. Failed to keep her safe, failed to save her. Failed her when she was at her most vulnerable.

Nicolette was no more.

He rose and looked at the car wreck, the flames still high, still burning hot. Hot enough to kill a vampire.

"Nicolette," he murmured, "I won't leave you." He walked toward the flames.

Strong arms ripped him back. The strong arms of another vampire.

"No, John, she wouldn't want that."

He turned his head to look at Cain. "I can't live without her."

"You'll have to learn to. She would want you to."

Forgive me, Nicolette. He swallowed back tears, standing there for what felt like an eternity.

And like a coward, he turned away from the flames and allowed Cain to help him.

12

Lack of sleep was finally catching up with him. After all, he hadn't slept a wink the day before, and despite consuming a larger amount of blood than normal, John knew he needed some shut-eye. But before he could go home and rest for a few hours, he had to make a few phone calls and pay somebody a visit.

He'd stopped at Scanguards' office in the Mission an hour before sunrise to use their system to run background checks on the babysitter and the neighbor, and made sure nobody saw him. He was supposed to be training Benjamin and Damian, not letting them run loose in the city. Explaining why they weren't with him wouldn't be easy.

His observations of the babysitter and the neighbor hadn't yielded any useful information yet, and he wasn't putting too much stock into the background checks either. But he needed to be thorough.

After shift change, when the vampires had left the building, he was able to get a few other things taken care of, before he snuck out of Scanguards' underground garage and headed for Cow Hollow and the Marina. The rays of the rising sun couldn't penetrate his car, so he was safe.

As soon as he'd merged into traffic, he called Benjamin, who picked up on the first ring.

"Hey, John, I was just about to check in."

"Good, give me an update."

"So this Rachel, she's a bit of a flake."

"How so?"

"She called in sick the last two days, but she isn't sick at all."

"Where is she?" John asked with interest. Had she fled after Buffy's kidnapping?

"Oh, she's home. But not alone. Looks like a private party involving drugs and sex. Not sure about the rock 'n' roll." Benjamin chuckled.

John grunted. "Sounds like somebody using her boss's absence to get away with skipping work, not like somebody involved in a kidnapping."

"Possible," Benjamin said, "but the shit they're snorting ain't cheap. I counted quite a few lines of coke. You said to check out anything odd. And considering that the guy she's with drives a rust bucket, I can't see where he got the money to pay for that stuff. She makes good money; I found her pay stubs, but from the credit card statements I saw, it looks like whatever she makes she spends just as quickly."

"You were inside her place?" John asked, not without admiration. Benjamin showed promise.

"Yeah, I picked the lock when the two were passed out. Nobody saw me. I made sure of it."

"Good work. Stay on her and follow her if she leaves the house today," John ordered. "Have you run her background check yet?"

"Sent it through the system a little earlier. Haven't got it back."

"Thanks. Call me when you have any news."

"Yep."

John disconnected the call and dialed Damian's number.

The older twin answered immediately. "Morning, John, still up?"

"Barely," John replied. "Anything I should know?"

"So I've been checking out this Alexi guy all night. Total geek. He's got every cliché down pat: gets home, orders pizza, and spends all night playing computer games or something. Boring as shit, I tell you. No girlfriend from what I could tell. No surprise there. But then I checked out his background, and listen to this."

John involuntarily straightened in his seat. "Yeah?"

"He's Russian. Did you know that?"

"I didn't." His last name, Denault, didn't sound Russian at all, though his first name certainly did.

"Yeah, parents are Russian, he grew up in St. Petersburg. Apparently the grandfather was French."

"Well, that explains the non-Russian last name."

"Speaks fluent French. Came to the US on a work visa five years ago, started working for Google, but left. Not sure yet why. I'll try to find out. But I digress. The point is he's Russian. And you said we're looking for a child trafficking ring. And who runs those kind of rings?" Damian made a dramatic pause. "The Russians."

"Bit of a stereotype, but let's go with it." It was at least a start. "What're your next steps?"

"I'll look into his connections, see who he meets, who he talks to, who he corresponds with. And I'll check out why he left Google and came to work for Ms. Rice."

"Good. If you need help, coordinate with your brother. And check if this Alexi owns any properties anywhere. You know, where he could hide the children."

"I was gonna do that," Damian quickly shot back a bit defensively.

"Uh-huh."

"I was. Honestly! You're not gonna use that as a minus point in my eval, are you?"

"Don't worry too much about your evaluation. Just get the job done. This is a team effort. Don't forget that. The goal is to find the girls. The methods don't matter. You find the girls, you pass the test. Even if you stumble on the way. Clear?" It never hurt to encourage Damian and dangle a reward in front of him.

"Absolutely."

"Okay, good work so far. Call me as soon as you've got something. I've got one more errand to run and then I'm gonna get a few hours of shut-eye. But if anything comes up, wake me."

"Sure thing." Damian disconnected the call.

At the next red light, John turned right, and only once he was halfway down the block, did he realize where his subconscious had taken him. He was outside of Savannah's condo. He let out a mirthless laugh. He was one sick son of a bitch. After practically mauling her the night before, he was back at the scene of the crime, hungering for more.

He brought the car to a stop and looked up at the windows on the second floor. Though it was still early, he saw a movement behind one of the windows. Was Savannah in the kitchen, making breakfast? What would it be like to be there with her, to watch her as she made coffee, perhaps still dressed in her bathrobe, naked underneath? Would she interrupt her task if he pulled her into his arms, opened the belt of her robe and touched her? Would she allow him to pull her onto his lap on a chair? Would she ride him right there, in the middle of the kitchen, impaling herself on his rock-hard cock, not stopping until he shot his seed into her?

His hand went to his crotch. Fuck! He was hard as granite. And confined to his car. There was no garage he could use to access Savannah's flat without exposing himself to the burning rays of the morning sun. Sexual frustration coursed through him. However, he knew it was better this way. Even if he could safely reach her flat, he shouldn't, even if there was a spark of attraction between them. Savannah was in a vulnerable position, full of fear for her daughter's safety, consumed with pain. He had no right to take advantage of a woman like that, even if he didn't want to harm her, but soothe her, give her comfort.

Before he could stop himself, he was already dialing her number. When she didn't answer on the second ring, he wondered if he'd only imagined the movement behind her window, his imagination playing tricks on him. He was about to disconnect the call, when there was a click on the line.

"Yes?"

He swallowed. He didn't know what he wanted to say. "Savannah, it's John. John Grant," he felt obliged to say. Who knew how many men named John she knew?

"John." There was a breathless quality to her reply. "Do you have any news? Did you find something?"

The hope he heard in her voice, the confidence she seemed to have in him, tore at his heartstrings. If only he could give her something that would help her believe that she would get Buffy back.

"Nothing much yet." He closed his eyes.

"Oh." Disappointment oozed from this one syllable.

"But we have a possible lead."

"What kind of lead?"

"It's too early to tell." He didn't want her to act awkwardly around Alexi, alerting him in any way, should he really have something to do with Buffy's disappearance. "My team and I are following up on it." At least that wasn't a lie. "This is just the start. We're looking at everything. We'll find her." He knew he was promising something he couldn't guarantee. But Savannah needed to hear it. Needed to believe it.

"Thank you, John. I…" She hesitated.

"What's wrong?" His gaze shot up to the windows of her flat, but he saw no movement.

"I'm scared. It's been four days now." There was a sniffling sound, as if she was trying to hold back tears. "I miss her. I miss my baby."

"I'm doing everything I can."

"I know that. I just wish there was something *I* could do. I feel so useless."

He could only imagine what that feeling must be like and hoped never to have to experience it himself. "I'm sorry, Savannah. I know it's hard. I know you love her. I *will* find her for you."

A slow exhale came through the line. If she started to cry now, he wouldn't be able to stop himself from running across the street, braving the sun to take her in his arms and comfort her.

"Please, Savannah, you have to hold it together. For Buffy." *And for me.*

"I will. Please call me as soon as you hear something."

"I promise."

John disconnected the call and set the car in motion, before he could change his mind and do something irresponsible.

He left Savannah's neighborhood and headed for Cow Hollow, a trendy neighborhood with high home prices and a large number of yoga-pants wearing yuppies, which had been his original destination before his subconscious had sent him in another direction.

The house was tucked away at the bottom of the Lyon steps, its

garden backing up to the Presidio. Facing the street and taking up half
the width of the lot, was a double garage. John stopped in front of it and
let the engine idle, while he scrolled through his phone directory until he
found the right contact.

He let it ring. Once, twice, three times. Finally, after the fourth ring,
just before it could go to voicemail, a sleepy voice answered.

"During the day? Really, John?"

Deirdre didn't sound too pleased about being awoken. He was
planning to change that.

"I need to talk to you. It can't wait. Open the garage for me."

"You're outside?"

"Yes."

"Fine." A few seconds later, the garage door lifted. When it was
completely open, he drove in and switched off the engine.

"I'm in," he said into the phone.

There was a click in the line, then the garage door lowered behind
him, shutting out the sun.

Moments later he entered the hallway that led to the living area and
the kitchen. He waited there, when he heard footsteps on the wooden
stairs leading to the second floor. He looked up. Deirdre, her hair in
disarray, dressed in a long black robe, walked down the steps.

"This had better be good," she said by way of greeting.

"It is," he assured her.

She motioned to the kitchen and he walked there ahead of her. He'd
been here a couple of times after she'd moved in, and had assured
himself that the place was vampire-safe. All the windows had been
retrofitted with UV-impenetrable film, blocking out the rays of the sun.
The house was huge. Deirdre had money, lots of it. It tended to happen
when one lived several centuries. Just a matter of compounding interest.
But with all her money she couldn't buy herself a purpose in her new
life. He was about to change that.

"You want a drink?"

He shook his head. "I'm good. I'll feed when I get home."

She sat down at the kitchen table and he took the unspoken invitation and did the same. "I need your expertise."

Deirdre raised an eyebrow, showing interest. Good.

"I'm working a case possibly involving a child trafficking ring. I've got a couple of people working on it besides myself, but there's something that's too sensitive to give to the others. So I thought of you."

"Don't trust your own men?"

It wasn't that he didn't trust Damian and Benjamin. He did. But this had to be handled by somebody else. Somebody with more experience.

"You're the better person for it."

"Shoot."

"I need you to do a thorough background check on the mother of the last girl that disappeared. Her name is Savannah Rice." He reached into his jacket pocket and pulled out an envelope. "I need to know whether there's anything about her that doesn't gel."

"You've met her?"

John nodded.

"So why not check her out yourself?"

He hesitated. There were plenty of reasons why he couldn't do it. And the fact that he'd kissed Savannah and wanted even more than that from her, definitely played into it. "Let's just say I'm too close to see everything. I need somebody who can look at her without prejudice." Without lusting after her. Because if he performed a check on Savannah he was likely to dismiss something as insignificant, because he was already on her side. But it wasn't how Scanguards worked. They always checked out their clients.

Deirdre reached for the envelope. "Too close, huh?" She cast him an assessing look.

John pointed to the envelope. "You'll find a temporary access card for Scanguards in there. As well as my login information for the various systems you'll need in the office."

"Temporary access?"

John shifted in his chair. It was all he'd been able to rustle up behind upper management's back. It was all the human staff that worked during the day had been authorized to issue without approval from the two co-chiefs of IT and Internal Security, Thomas and Eddie. Permanent access to Scanguards had to be vetted.

"If you do well on this case, I'll be able to get you a permanent position." What a lie. He hadn't even spoken to Samson or Gabriel about Deirdre's request yet.

Slowly, she nodded and opened the envelope, pulling out the access pass, a sheet with his usernames and passwords, and another one with the pertinent facts of the case and the person Deirdre needed to investigate. He'd briefly considered his actions when putting together the package, asking himself if he could trust Deirdre with all the sensitive information she would gain access to. But his gut had told him he would know if she betrayed his confidence. As maker and protégée they had a bond, albeit a tenuous one in their particular case.

The envelope also included a photo of Savannah, which he'd taken off her drivers license. Deirdre looked at it for a long while, and John couldn't stop himself from looking at the photo too.

"Beautiful." Deirdre suddenly lifted her eyes to him, and he wasn't fast enough to tear his gaze away from the picture. Something in his protégée's eyes flashed, and John realized that she was indeed a perceptive woman. A sly smile appeared on her lips. "Tell me what you want to know."

"Everything. Acquaintances, habits, financials, whatever you can get your hands on. Use my office at Scanguards. You'll find everything you need there."

"When do you need it by?"

"Yesterday."

She rolled her eyes. "Of course. Do I need a key to your office?"

"No. The access card will get you in. But make sure to be gone before sunset."

She raised an inquisitive eyebrow, but didn't comment. He appreciated that. She was discreet.

"I'll be getting a few hours of sleep at home. Call me on my cell the second you find something that gives you pause."

"Even if it means I have to wake you?" She smirked unexpectedly.

"You're going to work extra fast, aren't you, just so you *can* wake me? Isn't that right?"

"I'm very good at this kind of work, you'll see." She patted the envelope. "But you know you need to bring me in on the other stuff too, right?"

"What other stuff?"

"When you find the bad guys and are ready to take them down. I want to be there. I want to help destroy the assholes who're trafficking kids."

John rose. "Don't worry. When we get to that point—and I hope it comes soon—I'll make sure you're there and armed to the teeth."

Deirdre rose and pulled the belt around her robe tighter. "I'm glad we understand each other. Now get out of here so I can get dressed."

He nodded at her and left.

He knew he could trust Deirdre. She was a well-trained warrior, a woman who'd fought for her race for many centuries. She was no stranger to investigations, but first and foremost she had experience in reading people. She'd sat on a council for many decades, making decisions about life and death, and though one of these decisions had ultimately led to her exile, John wasn't going to hold this one decision against her.

Just like he hoped that Savannah wouldn't hold it against him that he was investigating her. It was only for Buffy's sake. Savannah was in no frame of mind to tell him everything about her life that could have something to do with the kidnappers. It wasn't even her fault. She wasn't trained to see connections the way he was. Certain things would seem too insignificant to her to bother mentioning them. But he and Deirdre would see those tiny grains that could lead them to Buffy and the people behind the disappearance of all these girls.

13

Savannah dried off after her shower and slipped into her robe. The warm water had soothed her somewhat, though it couldn't take away her worries or her fear. After the early morning phone call from John, she'd been at her computer, looking through pictures of Buffy to remind herself of the places they'd visited together in San Francisco. She'd made a list of those places, some of which she'd forgotten. After breakfast, which consisted of coffee and a cracker, her appetite still not having returned, she'd jumped in the shower.

Now, as she reached for the hair dryer, the ringing of the doorbell interrupted her. The sound sent her heartbeat into the stratosphere. She'd never been as jumpy as she'd been in the days since Buffy's disappearance.

Quickly, she wrapped a towel around her wet hair and rushed to the door. She hurried down the stairs and looked through the peephole at the man who stood outside. She didn't know him, but she noticed the messenger bag slung across his body. One of the many bicycle messengers businesses used to courier important documents around the city. Had Alexi sent her something from the office? Something she'd forgotten to sign?

She ripped the door open.

"Ms. Rice?"

She nodded. "That's me."

He handed her an envelope. "No need to sign anything. Have a nice day." He turned on his heel and rushed down the front steps to where he'd leaned his bike against the wall of the building.

Savannah closed the door, and walked upstairs into her flat, staring at the envelope. Her name and address were neatly typed on the front, confirming that the letter wasn't from Alexi: there was no typewriter in the office, and the smudges inside the occurrences of the letter *a* in Savannah wouldn't have been made by a printer.

Her heart beat faster now. There was nothing else on the envelope, no indication who might have sent it. But instinctively she knew who the sender was. Felt it in the drum of her pulse, the pounding of her heart in her chest. With trembling fingers, she ripped the envelope open and reached inside.

There were only two items in it: a folded sheet of paper and a smaller piece with a glossy surface on one side. She turned it over and froze. Her hand shot to her mouth to smother a scream.

"Buffy!" she choked out.

The photo depicted her little girl, eyes wide and frightened, sitting on a mattress, holding up a newspaper. Savannah narrowed in on it. It was today's San Francisco Chronicle. *Proof of life*, the police called these photos. The thought sent a chill through her. Even before she unfolded the sheet of paper, she knew what it was: a ransom note.

Two emotions collided within her: relief that the kidnappers were finally contacting her, and pain for what she saw in her daughter's eyes, the look of fear and desperation, the look of lost hope. Buffy didn't believe that her mother was coming to find her.

"Oh, baby, please hold on for me. I'm coming. Mommy is coming to bring you home."

Through the tears that started streaming down her cheeks, she read the letter. It was typed.

If you want your daughter Buffy back, bring two-hundred-and-fifty-thousand dollars in cash to the entrance of the Trocadero Clubhouse at Stern Grove at 7:30pm tonight. After you withdraw the money from your bank, don't go back home. Leave your cell phone at home. Come alone. Do not take a taxi, an Uber or a Lyft. Don't take your own car. Take public transportation to 19th Avenue, then walk. Don't tell anyone. If you involve the police, I will find out, and Buffy will die.

I trust you understand these instructions and will carry them out to the letter.

PS. Don't bother contacting the bicycle courier. The delivery of this letter was charged to an account that leads to a dead end. You won't find any fingerprints either except for those of the bicycle courier. So don't try to be smart, Savannah.

And before I forget: Don't contact that private investigator with the fancy Mercedes you hired, or I'll make sure he dies, too. And you wouldn't want that, would you?

She was shaking now. The kidnapper was watching her. He knew about John. He knew about her life. She hurried to the living room window and looked outside. Was he out there right now, watching her, making sure she was complying with his demands? The way he'd addressed her by her first name, as if he knew her, as if he had a right to call her by her first name, sent another shiver down her spine.

Sick bastard!

But it was useless to get upset now. She had to remain calm, decide on her next step. Hadn't she hoped for this? Hoped to receive a ransom demand so she could pay it and get her daughter back? And now it was here. In her shaking hands.

John had been wrong when he'd thought that Buffy's disappearance was connected to the other girls' disappearances. The other parents hadn't received a ransom note, at least they hadn't reported it to the police. But she had. And as much as she wanted John by her side to help her over this last hurdle, she couldn't risk contacting him. What if the kidnapper found out? Then she wouldn't only have put Buffy at risk, but John too.

Or was there a way to contact John without the kidnapper finding out? She glanced at her cell phone that lay on the coffee table. No, a cell phone conversation was always at risk of being overheard. Then maybe the landline. She still had one for emergencies, but what if somebody had bugged it? Was that how the kidnapper had found out about her hiring John as a private investigator? Because simply seeing John arrive at her condo wouldn't reveal why he was there. Or had John's license plate led back to Scanguards, and the kidnapper had put two and two together?

She let out a frustrated sigh. How could she know what mode of communication was safe, when she didn't know how the kidnapper had found out that she'd hired a PI? Who knew about it? She hadn't told anybody. Hell, she had barely spoken to anybody after hiring John.

Then it struck her suddenly: Alexi. She'd told Alexi. What if he was involved? He had the technical skills to do a full-scale surveillance of her home and office, her cell phone and landline, even her emails. Shit! And he knew her movements, knew when she dropped Buffy at school, knew her routine. Just like he knew that Savannah had sufficient money to pay a ransom. What if he'd gotten access to her account statements and seen that she could access several hundreds of thousands of dollars at a moment's notice and then formed his plan accordingly?

She cursed under her breath.

But there was nothing she could do. She couldn't tell John about her suspicions, because if Alexi was monitoring her communications, he would find out. And if he had somebody watching her, then he would know if she went to a payphone or an internet café to contact John from there. No, she couldn't take the risk. She had to do this on her own. She had to get her baby back.

Savannah dropped the letter and Buffy's photo on the coffee table and went back to the bathroom to dry her hair. She had to look perfectly normal when she showed up at the bank, so they wouldn't be suspicious and believe that she was under duress when she withdrew the ransom money. She knew that bank officials were trained to watch out for anything odd and would contact the police once she'd left the bank if they believed she needed help.

Savannah took extra care to dress as if she were going to a business meeting. She was glad that her even, dark skin hid the fact that she hadn't slept much and had been crying. All she needed was a little bit of concealer around the eyes, and nobody would know that she'd been going through hell the last few days. When she was ready, she sat down at the kitchen table and took a deep breath. She had lots of time to withdraw the money and make her way to the exchange point, but she couldn't sit around here. It was best to go to the bank early, make sure there was no hitch with getting that much cash, and then wait somewhere within a mile or two of the meeting point, until it was time to make her way there. On foot.

She understood why he didn't want her to take a taxi or another driving service: somebody would be able to trace her. Maybe that meant the kidnapper suspected that John would try to find her if he couldn't get a hold of her during the day. If she walked or took public transport, John would have no way of tracking her down, of coming to her aid and snatching the kidnapper once she had Buffy safely in her arms again. The kidnapper—and at this point she had to assume it was Alexi—had thought of everything. Maybe that was the reason it had taken him so long to send the ransom note: he'd had to set things up for a smooth exchange.

It was midday when she made her way to the bank. They knew her well; after all she was one of their more affluent clients and had banked with them for many years. When she asked to speak to the manager, she was immediately led to her office.

"Ms. Rice, what a nice surprise. Or did we have a meeting I forgot?" she asked, extending her hand.

"Mrs. Barnstable, so nice to see you." Savannah forced a smile. "I really should have made an appointment, but things moved a lot quicker on this deal I'm working on than I was expecting."

Mrs. Barnstable pointed to the chair in front of her desk, and although Savannah knew she wouldn't be staying long, she sat down and folded her hands in her lap.

"Well, how may I be of assistance?" the manager asked eagerly.

"As you know, I've got a substantial cash position in one of my accounts, and as it turns out, I've got the opportunity to invest in an multi-unit property in Cole Valley, which, as you know, is such a desirable area."

Mrs. Barnstable pressed a hand to her chest. "I love that area! Well, if you need a loan against your investments, I'll be able to approve you by tonight. No trouble at all."

Savannah pasted another fake smile on her face, when inside she wanted to scream. "Wonderful, wonderful! That can wait a week or so, but what I need today, this afternoon in fact, is cash for the down payment."

"You mean a cashier's check?"

"No, actual cash. Two-hundred-and-fifty thousand dollars."

"That's unusual."

"Isn't it?" Savannah said and leaned forward. "But I'm competing with an Asian buyer who's arriving with a suitcase of cash, and if I can't do the same and put down the cash this afternoon, I won't get the property." She shook her head. "I know it's crazy what these buyers are doing, but I can't let this property slip through my fingers. You understand, don't you?"

Mrs. Barnstable smiled. "Of course. It's not a problem at all, Ms. Rice. We're always happy to accommodate you." Then she laughed. "And it's your money anyway." She turned to her computer and typed something on her keyboard. "Let me just go in and authorize the withdrawal. And then I'll have one of my cashiers prepare the bills."

"Excellent." Savannah sighed a breath of relief. The money was almost in her hands, and the manager didn't suspect a thing.

"We can provide you with somebody to walk you to where you parked," the manager offered.

"I've got a car service waiting outside for me, so there's no need, but thanks," she lied. "And I brought my briefcase." She motioned to the leather briefcase she'd set on the floor next to her feet upon sitting down.

"Perfect." Mrs. Barnstable lifted her phone and dialed a number. A moment later, she said, "Heather, I just authorized a large withdrawal for Ms. Rice. Would you handle that, please, and bring the cash to my office when it's counted out?" There was a short pause. "Thanks, Heather." She put the receiver down. "It's going to be about fifteen minutes. Would you like a coffee or some water in the meantime?"

Though she wasn't thirsty, Savannah forced herself to accept a bottle of water and sipped the cool liquid, while sweat poured down her back and between her breasts. She was glad that her business suit disguised her bodily reaction.

Sitting in the manager's office, waiting for the cash, felt like the longest fifteen minutes she'd ever had to live through. When the knock at the door sounded, she almost jumped out of her chair, and had to clutch the armrests to force herself to remain seated.

In a few moments, she would have the money to pay the ransom. And in a few hours, she would have her daughter back.

14

John awoke mid-afternoon, too early to leave the house—and with a hard-on the size of California. No wonder: he'd dreamed of Savannah, of how her dark skin would glisten with perspiration when he made love to her until she could take no more. Continuing those kinds of thoughts while awake did nothing to bring down his erection.

Cursing, he jumped out of bed and walked into the bathroom. The house he'd bought shortly after joining Scanguards was located in Noe Valley, a family-oriented central neighborhood of San Francisco, conveniently located close to Scanguards' headquarters. It wasn't large: three bedrooms, two bathrooms, a small kitchen with dining area, and a decent sized living room.

He'd chosen the house because it was surrounded by a lush garden with mature trees and bushes, providing privacy and shade. In addition, the garage underneath the raised first floor had stairs leading directly into the living quarters, an essential feature for any vampire who wanted to have the freedom of coming and going during daylight hours.

In hindsight, he should have chosen a different neighborhood, one where he wouldn't hear as many kids playing outside in the afternoon, after they returned from school. Their voices and laughter were what normally woke him early, reminding him of what he could have had, a family of his own.

Today his sensitive hearing didn't pick up any kids' voices. It wasn't what had awoken him. He knew the vivid dream about Savannah was the culprit this time. Maybe a cold shower would bring him to his senses again.

Naked, John stepped into the shower and turned on the water. He turned into the spray and allowed the cold water to hit him. But no matter how much of it he directed toward his cock, the damn thing wouldn't deflate.

"Fuck," he cursed and slammed his fist against the tile wall, cracking one of the fifties era tiles. Well, he needed to update the bathroom anyway. No big deal. But letting his frustrations out on the bathroom tiles wouldn't help him with his current predicament. Only one thing would: taking the matter into his own hand.

So he succumbed to his primal need and gripped his cock with his right hand. Bracing himself against the shower wall with his left, he began to stroke himself, to pump his erection hard and fast. He let out a few breaths of air. He'd denied himself for too long, denied himself the pleasures of the flesh. That's why he was so on edge. That's why he had to do this now before he saw Savannah again, before he put his hands on her and pressed her against a flat surface to take her, to ram his cock into her sweet pussy and make her understand what he was: an animal, a beast, a vampire.

Yes, he wanted her to know, wanted to see the expression in her eyes when she perceived his fangs and the red glow in his eyes that surfaced only when the vampire inside him gained control.

Just like his fangs were descending now, while he ran his hand up and down his cock, squeezing and releasing, softer now, the way a woman would do it. The way Savannah would do it, pumping him with her soft hands before she would fall to her knees so she could swipe her moist tongue over the swollen tip of his cock and make him groan with pleasure.

Her luscious lips wrapped around him, bathing him in warm moisture. A hand cradled his balls, balls that had pulled up tightly, balls that were burning with the need to release their seed. A fingernail scratched gently against the tight sac, while her mouth took him deep, engulfing him in paradise. At first, she sucked on him almost playfully, but when he thrust harder into her mouth, she got the message and sucked him with more determination, harder and faster. The contrast of her dark skin against his white complexion was pure perfection. A perfect yin and yang, the dark and the light complementing each other, meant for each other. Interconnected, interdependent, indivisible. A duality, a oneness that nature had created. And man could never destroy.

He felt the pressure in his balls build, the hand on his cock squeezing harder, moving faster, the hand cradling his balls sending a tingling sensation through his body. His pulse was racing now, his heart beating faster than it ever had. He felt the approach of his orgasm, knew it was time to let go of his control, let go of the fantasy that had brought him to this point. He concentrated on one more image, on Savannah lifting her eyes to gaze up at him from her kneeling position, a look of love and lust in her eyes.

He came right there and then. His semen exploded from the tip of his cock and shot against the tile wall, running down in hot, thick streaks. He let out a sigh of relief. Maybe now, he would be able to get through the coming night and be able to concentrate on what he had to do.

He showered quickly, dried off, and got dressed. A look at the clock told him that the sun hadn't gone down yet. But it didn't matter. He would drive to his office anyway. Deirdre would still be there, and he could review the things she'd dug up in the meantime. The fact that she hadn't called him yet, probably meant that she hadn't found anything significant so far. Which was good and bad. Good, because it meant there was nothing in Savannah's life that raised any red flags, and bad, because it meant there were no leads to follow.

It took only twenty minutes to get to Scanguards' headquarters in the Mission, and another three to reach his office. He entered it without knocking.

Deirdre shrieked and shot up from the desk. When her eyes landed on him, she scolded him, "Damn it, you startled me. Could have told me you were coming!"

John shut the door behind him. "Didn't mean to." He stopped short of apologizing. After all, this was his office, not hers. Hell, she didn't have an office. She wasn't even really authorized to be here.

Deirdre sat down again. "I was gonna call you in a minute anyway."

Interest made him approach the desk and glance at the computer monitor. "You found something?"

"I think so."

His heart pounded. The way Deirdre was looking at him made him uneasy. As if she'd found something incriminating in Savannah's background.

"Come on, Deirdre, don't make me pull it out of your nose."

"Remind me not to choose you as my boss," she hissed.

He narrowed his eyes. "Like it or not, I *am* your boss. For now."

"Well, since you're asking so nicely…"

"Has anybody ever told you that your attitude stinks?"

"Has anybody ever told *you* that you're impatient?" she shot back, then smirked unexpectedly. "Though I can't blame you." She motioned to the computer. "I don't think you have any time to lose. Savannah Rice took a large amount of cash out of her bank account a few hours ago. It only updated in the online system a few minutes ago, that's why I didn't see it earlier. I was about to sign off, but when I saw how much money she's got, I wanted to keep an eye on it."

John stared at Deirdre. "How much money did she take out?"

"Two-hundred-and-fifty-thousand dollars."

"In cash?"

"Yes, cold, hard cash."

"Fuck!" he cursed. "There's only one reason why she would do that."

"That's why I was about to call you. She must have received a ransom note. And now she's going to pay the kidnappers."

John pulled his cell phone from his pocket and looked at it. "No missed calls, no text messages." Why hadn't Savannah called him? He pulled up her number and pressed the *call* button. It rang, once, twice, three times, then a fourth time, before it went to voicemail.

"This is Savannah Rice. I'm sorry I can't come to the phone right now. Please leave a message and I'll get back to you at my earliest convenience."

Beep.

"Savannah, where are you? I need to talk to you. I know about the money. Please call me!"

He disconnected, then sent her a text message with the same plea.

"Something's not right," Deirdre said.

He knew that already. "A lot of things aren't right. She shouldn't have received a ransom note. None of the other parents have."

"Then maybe her case isn't connected to the others?"

John shook his head. "No, they're connected. Somehow. I just haven't found out how yet." But he had no time to discuss this now. "I need to find Savannah. Now."

"Her cell phone is on, I'll see if I can get access to her GPS," Deirdre offered.

"Good," he agreed, already heading for the door. "I'm trying her flat. Call me as soon as you have a location for me."

He didn't even wait for Deirdre's reply and instead raced out the door and down the hallway. The thought that Savannah was meeting the kidnappers on her own, sent a chill down his spine. What if something went wrong?

Arriving at his car, John jumped in and raced out of the parking garage. It was rush hour traffic now. The Mission was a congested area at the best of times; during rush hour it was murder.

"Come on, you idiots," John yelled at the other drivers. But it did no good. All it served was to aggravate him even more.

Besides, what would he do once he arrived at Savannah's flat? The sun still had not set. He hated that it was summer, when the days were longer, giving him less time to move around freely. It would be another hour until the sun set and he would be safe to leave the protective cocoon of his specially modified car.

But he couldn't think that far ahead right now. First, he had to get to Savannah's place, or to wherever Deirdre found her cell phone. Impatiently, he activated the hands-free communication in his car and pressed Deirdre's number.

She answered instantly. "Yes?"

"Have you got the location?"

"I'm working on it," she said tersely. "You interrupting me isn't going to make it happen any faster."

A click in the line. Deirdre had hung up on him.

"Fuck!" But he wasn't even angry at Deirdre or her attitude, but at the circumstances he found himself in: stuck in traffic unable to get to Savannah any faster than a snail crawling across a patch of grass.

He tried Savannah's phone again, but it simply rang, then went to voicemail. He didn't leave a message this time.

He wasn't sure what was bothering him more: that Savannah was trying to meet with the kidnapper on her own, or that he hadn't seen this coming. It made him feel helpless, and he hated that feeling.

Knowing it would take him at least another fifteen minutes to reach Savannah's flat, he dialed Damian's number. It rang twice, before Damian picked up.

"Where are you?"

"Just getting to Glen Park. Why?"

"Shit!" Damian was even farther away from Savannah's neighborhood than he was. "Do you have eyes on Alexi?"

"Yep, he just stopped at a hardware store. There he is, coming out again. Why?"

"Stay on him. I have reason to believe Savannah just received a ransom note."

"Huh? I thought you said we're dealing with a child trafficking ring. Are you changing the rules on us?"

"This is real, Damian! A real case. Get that?" John slammed his hand against the steering wheel and honked at an idiot driver in front of him. "Don't lose Alexi. If he's behind the kidnapping, he'll be preparing for the money drop."

"Uh-oh," Damian let out.

"What?"

"He bought some rope and duct tape in the hardware store."

"Oh, shit! Follow him, no matter where he goes. Have Benjamin back you up."

"You got it."

John disconnected the call, saw an opening ahead of him and passed the indecisive driver blocking his progress. He managed to drive one block before he had to avoid another obstacle. At the next light, he turned left before the oncoming traffic had a chance to make it into the intersection, and finally, followed by angry honking, escaped the worst of the traffic jam.

He used his knowledge of the city's shortcuts to avoid more bottlenecks and finally reached Lower Pacific Heights.

A few more blocks, and he turned into the side street where Savannah's flat was located. All looked quiet from the outside. He saw no light in the front rooms, but then, it was too early to need light inside: the sun was still up, even though it was foggy here, foggier than in the Mission or his own neighborhood. He was glad for it, because at least the fog would help shield him a little.

John drove as close to the front steps of Savannah's duplex as he could and stopped the car. From the glove compartment, he retrieved a small leather etui and shoved it into his inside pocket. Then he checked behind his seat, and to his relief, the old blanket he'd tossed there a few nights earlier to give to the next homeless person he encountered, was still there. He pulled it out and wrapped it around his torso, covering his head and shoulders, and holding it closed under his chin.

"Here we go," he murmured to himself and opened the door.

He jumped out of the car as fast as he could, slammed the door shut and sprinted to the stairs. Already he could feel the UV-rays heating his body, though it was not as bad as being exposed on a sunny day. He reached the front steps and sprinted up to where two front doors were located. He now had a ceiling above him, but he wasn't out of the woods yet, because the sunlight could still penetrate the otherwise protected space from the street.

John hit the doorbell, but didn't wait for a reply. Instead, he pulled the leather etui from his pocket, took out a lock pick, and went to work. He hunched over the lock, making sure his head and shoulders were covered by the blanket and his broad body was shielding his hands from sunlight. But he could feel heat on the back of his calves, which were only covered by the thin cloth of his cargo pants. They didn't provide much protection, and he knew he would sustain burns there. But he didn't care. He would heal. He'd sustained worse burns before and survived.

Finally, the lock clicked. He shoved the door open, rushed inside, and slammed it shut behind him. Sighing a breath of relief, he paused for a brief second, letting the dark interior of the staircase soothe him.

He listened. No sound came from the flat above. Savannah would have heard the door being slammed, yet there was no reaction. It only confirmed what he already suspected. That he was too late.

John ascended the stairs and entered the hallway. He still wore the blanket around his shoulders, because the light entering from the windows in the kitchen and the front of the house, where the living room was located, could still burn him.

Without calling out for her, he moved from room to room, first the bathroom, then Savannah's bedroom in the middle of the house—the darkest room—then Buffy's room and the kitchen. Nothing. She wasn't there. He marched back to where he'd entered, then continued into the living room. It was brightest there. A large bay window let in the sun's UV-rays. John shielded his face as best he could, when his cell phone suddenly rang. He walked back into the hallway and the shade it provided and answered.

"What have you got for me?"

"She must be at home," Deirdre answered.

"I'm in her flat. She isn't here."

"Her phone is. Let me call it."

There was a brief pause, then John heard the ringing of a cell phone coming from the living room.

"I hear it." He marched back into the living room and saw the cell phone on the coffee table. Next to it lay several items: an envelope, a letter, and a picture. He grabbed all of them and hurried back into the hallway.

"Call you back," he said to Deirdre and disconnected the call.

He recognized the person in the picture immediately: Buffy. He also realized what the photo signified: proof of life. His gaze snapped to the letter. But before he read it, he drew it closer to his nose. He picked up a strange scent. Something pungent. A human might not smell it, but his enhanced sense of smell picked it up. Odd. But he had no time to think about it further. Instead, he read the letter, his heart pounding.

Shit! Why hadn't Savannah called him?

When he read to the end, he knew why. The kidnapper had made her believe he was watching her every move and would kill not only Buffy, but even John if she sought help.

He looked at his watch. "Oh God!"

It would take nothing short of a miracle to make it to Stern Grove in time.

15

Savannah entered Stern Grove from the northeast corner, after she'd gotten off the bus two blocks earlier. Her briefcase was starting to feel heavy, and her toes were hurting in her high heels. But she'd had to look professional for her visit to the bank, and there had been no opportunity to change into more comfortable clothes. In hindsight, she should have gone to the nearest clothing store and bought jeans and comfortable shoes. But that was just it: hindsight. It didn't matter now. She was almost there. It was just three more city blocks to the Trocadero Clubhouse. She'd never been there before, though she knew that the clubhouse was near the area where they held free concerts on weekends in the summer.

The path she was on led into a wooded area. The shade of the large trees together with the dense fog made the area darker. Once the sun went down, which would happen very soon, it would be pitch black here. Involuntarily, she shivered, whether from the cold that was seeping into her clothes or the fear that was growing now, she didn't know. Probably both.

She'd always been scared of the dark and the silence. And it was quiet here. The sound of the cars traveling on 19th Avenue which bordered the park on the East, and Sloat Boulevard on the South, seemed muffled. She couldn't hear any animals, but maybe that was good. After all, coyotes roamed freely in some of the parks in the city, though they were only a danger to dogs, cats, and small children. They stayed away from larger creatures. Nevertheless, nervousness crawled up her spine like a slithering snake, making her shudder.

It took her another ten minutes to reach the clubhouse. The old yellow Victorian structure with the wrap-around porch and the ornate white trim was dark. No light illuminated its surroundings or its interior. It was closed. The kidnapper probably knew that. He wouldn't want any witnesses to the exchange.

Savannah glanced around. She couldn't see any cars in the parking lot, though the dense fog prevented her gaze from penetrating all the way to its far end. Somebody could be parked there and she wouldn't even know it. She looked at her watch. It was two minutes before the appointed time.

In the distance she heard the engine of a car. She listened intently. Was it approaching, or were her ears playing tricks on her? She peered into the dark. The fog moved, creating eerie, shadowy figures in between the trees. As if the forest was alive with strange creatures. Her hands were trembling now. She wouldn't do well in the wilderness, that much was certain. She was a city person through and through. But she forced the fear down, knowing she had to get through this.

A beam of light suddenly pierced her dark surroundings. At first she couldn't tell where it was coming from, but then she heard a car and spun around. Two headlights were coming straight toward her. When the lights hit her, the car slowed. She squinted, trying to make out the make and model of the car, as well as its license plates. But the headlights blinded her. All she could tell was that it was a van or a large SUV.

It pulled to a stop opposite the stairs of the clubhouse, where she was standing, about eight to ten yards away from her. Now she could see it was a small white truck such as one a flower shop or a plumber might use. There was no writing on the side, nothing to identify it.

The passenger side door opened, and a man jumped out. Not only was he dressed in dark clothes, he also wore a ski mask. The driver remained in the truck, the engine idling. The masked man reached for the handle of the sliding door and slid it open halfway. Savannah tried to peer inside, but he was blocking her view.

Nervously, she watched him look to his left and right, perhaps checking whether somebody was lurking in the shadows. But she knew there was nobody there, nobody to back her up.

"Where is my daughter?"

"Where's the money?" he asked, ignoring her question.

She lifted the briefcase. "It's all here. Where is she? Where's

Buffy?" Her voice shook, and she knew it put her in a weak position. Hell, she *was* in a weak position!

The man motioned to the open sliding door. "In there."

Mustering all her courage, she demanded, "I want to see her."

"The money first." He motioned her to approach.

Slowly, she took a few steps. Then she stopped again, fear gripping her heart. "Buffy?" she called out. "Buffy, are you alright?"

There was no reply.

"She won't reply. She's gagged." Then he motioned to the briefcase again. "Give me the money."

She walked closer, until she was only a yard away from the kidnapper. He reached for the briefcase containing the money, and she let him take it. She pointed to the open van behind him. "My daughter. Give me my daughter."

"Of course." He turned around and placed the briefcase inside the van. "You'll see her shortly."

He swung around all of a sudden and grabbed her with both hands, lifting her off her feet and yanking her forward, so the upper part of her body landed in the van. She slammed onto the bare floor, and in the last second managed to turn her head to the side to spare her face any injuries. At the same time she got a view of the interior of the van. It was empty. Buffy wasn't inside.

"Nooooo!" she screamed. Adrenaline shot through her veins, and she kicked back with her legs, managing to slam her spikey high heels into the kidnapper's stomach.

"Ugh!"

She rolled over and kicked again, but this time the bastard managed to grip her ankles, preventing her from doing any damage.

"Fucking bitch! You'll pay for that," he threatened.

She didn't waste her energy screaming for help, because she knew nobody would come. Instead she pulled herself up, rocked forward and threw a punch at his face. He dove to the side and twisted her legs, attempting to turn her back on her stomach again.

"Get the fucking bitch in the van!" the driver yelled from the cab.

For a second, her aggressor seemed distracted, and she used the moment to jerk her legs up. This time she was able to free one leg from his grip and swung it in the direction of his head. But before it could connect, the asshole twisted her other leg, causing her to cry out in pain. She felt him shove her deeper into the van, but she managed to grip the side of the door with one hand and held on for dear life.

"Jump in, you idiot," the driver yelled. "We've gotta get outta here!"

Her attacker jumped into the van and would have landed on her, had something not jerked him sideways at the last second. What, she couldn't see immediately, but she could hear it: a ferocious growl accompanied the thud and a painful howl sounded as the kidnapper slammed against the rough metal interior of the van.

"Fuck!" the driver screamed.

The van jerked forward, as a dark figure reached for her.

"Savannah!"

She recognized the voice instantly and let go of her grip on the door frame. John yanked her out of the van, which was already in motion. With his arms securely around her, they tumbled, landing on the hard ground, rolling for a few feet, before coming to a stop on the grassy shoulder of the dark road.

The van's engine revved, and when she whirled her head in its direction, she could only see faint taillights disappearing in the distance. She squinted in an attempt to read the license plate, but couldn't make out any letters or numbers.

Tears ran down her cheeks.

"Are you hurt?" John's voice was full of concern.

She shook her head and tried to sit up, but searing pain shot up her side where she'd landed on the hard surface of the van.

"You *are* hurt!" John helped her sit up.

"Just some bruises." Then, for the first time she looked at him and met his eyes. "She wasn't in the van, John. They didn't bring her. I gave them the money, and they didn't bring Buffy." Sobs tore from her chest. "Why?"

John helped her up. "I don't know, Savannah, I wish I did. But we have to leave. There's nothing for us to do here. They're gone."

"I couldn't read the license plate."

"I'm surprised you had the wherewithal to even try to read it." He put his hand on her elbow. "I got a look at the plate. I'll have my people run it, but I don't have much hope. Thugs like that don't use vehicles registered to them." He motioned in the direction the van had disappeared. "My car is over there."

She sniffled, trying to stop her tears and allowed him to lead her to his car. He helped her into the passenger seat, then shut the door and got in on the driver's side. A moment later, the engine hummed, and the car was in motion. The smooth ride should have soothed her, but it didn't. She was still shaking, still in shock. She'd done everything the kidnappers had asked for, and they hadn't given Buffy back to her.

While she went back over the events of the day to try to figure out if she'd done anything that could have warranted the kidnapper's change of mind about handing over her daughter, John made a phone call, reciting a license plate number and requesting it be checked out immediately.

If he hadn't gotten there in time, she would now be in the van and would have disappeared too, and then who would save Buffy? But John had found her.

"How?"

He gave her a sideways glance. "What?"

"How did you know? How did you find me?"

16

John looked at Savannah's tearstained eyes. His heart had almost stopped when he'd seen the thug trying to drag Savannah into the van to abduct her. He'd arrived at the same time as the kidnappers, which was good timing, as it meant that neither Savannah nor the kidnappers had heard his car engine. He'd already switched off his headlights before he'd stopped the car. His superior vampire vision had allowed him to drive without the lights, once he'd entered the park—just as the sun had set.

"When I couldn't reach you, I broke into your flat and found the kidnapper's note."

"Why did you come?"

"I had to make sure you were safe. I was fully prepared to watch without interfering. I didn't want to put you or Buffy in danger, but when I saw that thug toss you into the van, I had to act. I knew then that Buffy wasn't inside."

He noticed her swallow hard, then she continued, "I think I know who's behind this."

Surprise shot through him. "You do?"

"Alexi, my employee. You read the note, you saw what it said—not to involve you, my private investigator. Alexi knew that I'd hired you. In fact, I think he's the only one who knew. I hadn't said anything to my neighbor or to Elysa or the teachers. Yet the kidnapper knew. It has to be Alexi. He would also have the technical knowledge to watch me constantly. That's why I couldn't contact you." The words fairly tumbled over her lips, while her chest heaved. "We have to follow him. He'll lead us to Buffy."

John contemplated her words for a moment. He'd had the same suspicion. "I've got two men on his tail already. They're under orders not to let him out of their sight. I spoke to them less than an hour ago. Alexi was in Glen Park at the time."

She shifted in her seat. "That's plenty of time to get to Stern Grove."

"The kidnappers wore masks. Did they speak?"

She nodded, then her shoulders dropped. "Alexi has a strong accent. Both of those guys sounded American." She let out a breath. "But that doesn't mean anything. He could have hired them to do his dirty work, while he kept watch on Buffy."

It was a possibility. John nodded, but decided not to tell Savannah that Damian had seen Alexi purchase duct tape and a rope. "Let me check in with my guys to see where Alexi is now." He pulled out his cell, and instead of letting the call go via the hands-free speaker system in the car, he brought the cell phone to his ear and waited for Damian to pick up.

"Hey, John."

"Damian, any news? Where's Alexi now?"

"At home."

"You sure?"

"I'm right outside his place. Yeah, I'm sure."

"Did he stop off somewhere on his way home?"

"Actually, he went across the street from his place and knocked at a neighbor's door."

"Did he go in?"

"No. Just handed the old man the shopping bag."

"With the stuff he bought in Glen Park?"

"Yep. The old dude thanked him and gave him the money for it."

The rope and duct tape were a dead end. But that didn't mean that Alexi was off the hook yet. He could still be involved. "Stay on him. I'll call you later."

"Okay."

John disconnected the call and looked at Savannah. "Alexi is at home. No sign of Buffy or of him having contact with anybody that could lead us to her." For a split-second he thought about the old man Alexi had given the rope and duct tape to. Could he be holding Buffy for him? It was a possibility, but Damian had mentioned that the old man had paid Alexi for the purchase, and he wouldn't have done so if he was Buffy's jailor.

Savannah turned her head and looked out the passenger side window. In the reflection of the glass he saw the effort with which she kept herself together, the energy it cost her to stay strong in the face of this setback.

He was glad that they were turning into her street now, and even more relieved when he saw somebody pull out of a parking spot outside Savannah's condo. John took the spot and brought the car to a stop.

Before he opened the car door, he looked around using his mirrors. He'd done the same while they'd driven to her place, but hadn't noticed anybody following them. And he was trained to notice. It was safe. For now.

John exited the car and walked around to the passenger side to help Savannah out. When they reached the front door, she stared at it for a moment then looked up at him. "I don't know what happened to my handbag. I must have lost it in the struggle."

"It's okay." He reached inside his jacket and pulled out his lock pick again. Within seconds, the door was open. He ushered her inside.

"You do this a lot?"

He shrugged and closed the door behind them. "Comes with the job."

She didn't smile, her facial expression one of pain and resignation. When he followed her up the stairs into her flat, he noticed her favoring her left side, pressing a hand to the ribs on her right side. She was still hurting, though she put on a brave face.

He knew what it felt like to put on a brave face. He'd done that too after Nicolette's death, when he'd lain there in a dark room in Cain's palace for a week to recover from his severe burns. Fresh human blood had seen him through the worst and aided his healing process. But it hadn't soothed his emotional wounds. He saw both in Savannah now: the physical and the emotional pain. He could do nothing for the latter, but he had a way of healing the former.

In her flat, he led her to the living room and made her sit on the couch.

"I think you need a drink," he said. "Red wine?"

She nodded and was about to get up, when he pressed her back down gently.

"In the kitchen?"

She looked up at him, a grateful expression in her eyes. "On a shelf underneath the island."

"I'll get it."

He walked to the kitchen and found the bottle, opened it and poured half a glass. Then he glanced down the hallway, assuring himself that Savannah hadn't left the living room. She hadn't. He brought his hand to his lips, extended his fangs and pricked the pad of his thumb. When blood oozed from the tiny wound, he held his thumb over the glass and let it drip into the red wine. He squeezed his thumb, causing the blood to flow more freely. Then he brought his thumb to his lips again and licked over the incision. His saliva closed it instantly, leaving neither a scar nor any sign that there'd ever been a wound. With his finger he mixed the liquid so the color of the wine hid the blood. Savannah wouldn't be able to taste it; the quantity was too small, and the wine would mask its flavor.

Savannah still sat at the same spot where he'd left her, but was now holding the picture of Buffy in her hand. John stared at it, his heart breaking for the scared little girl in it. He felt like he knew her, though he'd never met her in person. But when he looked at her, all he wanted was to protect her. Protect her like his own.

John sat down next to Savannah and reached for the picture, while handing her the glass of wine. "Here, that will make you feel a little better." It would, at least physically. Vampire blood had healing properties that humans responded to very quickly. It didn't take much to take care of a few bruised ribs. "Drink," he encouraged her softly, took the photo from her hand and placed it back on the coffee table.

Savannah took several sips, then a few more, as if she realized that the alcohol was helping calm her nerves. In truth, it was her body's primal instinct to crave the healing vampire blood, without actually knowing it. It was nature, the perfect symbioses between the two species. Another yin to a yang. Because just like his vampire blood could heal her, her human blood could heal him.

A moment later she set the empty glass on the table and looked at him. "What now? What am I gonna do now? I gave them the money. Why didn't they return Buffy to me? I don't understand it. I followed the instructions."

"I don't understand it either." He motioned to the kidnapper's note. "This shouldn't have happened. The ransom note. None of the other parents received one."

"Then maybe Buffy's disappearance isn't connected to that of the other children. Maybe it's personal. It must be Alexi. It has to be him." She looked at him, her eyes pleading with him to agree with her assumption, as if that would make everything alright.

He took her hands in his and squeezed them. "We don't know that it's him. But I agree that something isn't right. They weren't after the money. They were after you tonight. Why only ask for two-hundred-and-fifty thousand dollars when they could have asked for a million, knowing you had that kind of money in the bank?"

She drew back a little, stunned. "How do you know that?"

"I ran a background check on you. It's standard. We do it with all our clients," he explained, though he still felt as if he needed to apologize. "That's how I learned that you took out a quarter of a million dollars today. Had I not seen that, I don't think I would have realized something was wrong."

She seemed to contemplate his words, then slowly nodded. "I understand." She sniffled. "You think the money was just a pretense to get me to meet them?"

"Yes. They wanted to make sure you were alone. They knew you wouldn't risk Buffy's safety."

"But why? If Alexi wanted to kidnap me, there are easier ways. He knows where I live, he knows my routine."

"We have to consider that it's not Alexi, though, believe me, I'm not discounting him entirely. But there's something else going on. And I'm going to figure out what it is. Buffy's disappearance is connected to the other children. I can sense it." And his instincts were rarely wrong.

Savannah pressed one hand to her mouth, choking back a sob. "I don't want to believe that. I just don't." New tears welled up in her eyes. "Because believing that she's been taken by a child trafficking ring means the chances of ever seeing her again, of ever holding her again…" A sob choked off her words. But he still knew what she was thinking. That she would never see Buffy again.

It hurt him to see her like this, to see her lose hope. He gripped her shoulders. "Please, Savannah, trust me. I will bring Buffy back to you. I know I will." He had leads. Alexi was one of them. The strange smell on the ransom note was something else he could follow up on. And maybe the license plate of the van would lead to something after all.

"I want to believe you. I do. But I miss her. I miss her so much." Her hands clung to his jacket now as if she needed to hold onto something to keep herself from collapsing. "I'm scared for her. I'm so scared. She's everything I have."

He pulled her to him, wrapped his arms around her and held her tightly. "I know what she means to you. That's why I'll get her back for you. I'll work tirelessly until she's back in your arms. Until she's safe again." He pressed a kiss to the top of Savannah's head.

It felt good to have Savannah in his arms, to know she was safe now. "When I saw that man drag you into the van, my heart stopped." He rubbed one hand over her back, while the other found its way to her nape, without him directing it. As if the need to feel her skin, her warmth was just too strong to resist.

Savannah suddenly lifted her head and looked at him, her eyes still wet with tears. But there was something else in them, too. Awareness. Awareness of him, of him touching her, holding her. He should have released her in that instant, should have risen and moved away from her as far as he could, but he didn't.

"You saved me," she murmured. Her lips were red and wet with her tears.

He could smell the salt, wanted to taste it too. He knew he shouldn't. Nevertheless, he dipped his head toward her face. "You have to stop me."

She didn't honor his plea, didn't pull back. Did she want this? Maybe even need this? To feel close to another being so she would know that she wasn't alone? He tried to justify what he was about to do by answering yes to those questions, when he knew, or at least suspected, why she wasn't putting up any resistance. It was the vampire blood in her. Even though the quantity was small, to a human unaccustomed to it, it was potent. It couldn't really make her do anything she absolutely didn't want to do, but together with the alcohol she'd downed so quickly, it was the perfect mixture to loosen anybody's inhibitions. If those inhibitions had even previously existed. From Savannah's response to his kiss the previous night, he knew that she didn't carry around a lot of inhibitions with regard to physical love.

As for his own restraints, he had none left, not after what had nearly happened tonight. He could have lost her. And that thought was the straw that broke the vampire's back.

"Savannah, please," he groaned in a last attempt to make her push him back and reject his advances, when he knew it was useless.

He knew it was happening. And this time it wouldn't end with just one kiss.

17

John's lips came closer, and as much as Savannah knew that it was wrong to accept the comfort he was offering, she couldn't resist it. She should be thinking of Buffy, of how to save her, but in this instant, she was selfish. She'd never been as scared in her life as in the moment when the thug had pushed her into the van and she'd realized that Buffy wasn't inside. She was still shaking with fear and the knowledge of what could have, would have happened, had John not gotten there in time. Was it therefore so wrong that she now sought comfort in the arms of her rescuer? That she wanted something that would drown out the fear and the desperation, if only for a short moment?

She moved her head only slightly, until her lips brushed against his. It was as if something ignited between them, because a second later, they were embracing so fiercely, with such urgency that not even an earthquake hitting San Francisco could have separated them.

His lips were demanding, pressing firmly against hers, his tongue sliding between them with such certainty, such self-confidence, as if he'd never been denied. Just like she wouldn't deny him—or herself—tonight. She allowed the invasion, welcomed it with eager anticipation, knowing he would whisk her away to a world where no fear, no pain, no evil existed.

He tasted of virile man, of strength, of power. His hands were on her, touching, squeezing, exploring… undressing. He was already pushing her jacket off her shoulders, freeing her, temporarily preventing her from touching him. But when she was free of it, she brought her hands back to his chest, this time not just gripping the lapels of his jacket, but sliding underneath. Through his shirt, she felt heat emanating from him. If she wasn't careful, she would burn herself. The taut muscles under his shirt flexed beneath her touch, but before she could explore them further, she felt his hands on her naked skin, her naked breasts. She hadn't even noticed that he'd unbuttoned her blouse, under which she wore nothing. She hated bras, always had, and whenever she could get away with it, she went without.

John moaned into her mouth, while his hands played with her naked flesh, alternately squeezing her boobs, then tenderly stroking her, then pinching her nipples lightly. She let out a sigh in response and pressed her breasts into his hands, begging him silently to continue. She didn't dare speak, couldn't voice what she wanted, not because she was shy, but because she was afraid that speaking would destroy the magic that was unfolding between them and wake them both from this fantasy they were indulging in. And she didn't want to return to the real world, didn't want to face reality.

John's kiss turned molten. His lips didn't tire, nor did his tongue as he rubbed it against hers, every stroke more insistent, every exploration more intimate. His hands freed her of her blouse now, tossing it somewhere. Cool air blew against her back, but her chest was on fire. John had a masterful touch. His large hands were rough at times, yet she liked feeling them caress her, feeling his skin slide against hers. She liked his fingers dancing on her breasts, liked his palms squeeze them to explore their firmness.

She responded to each of his touches, pressing hard against him when he squeezed her boobs in his hands, and shivering when he teased her nipples and turned them hard as rocks. She'd always thought her nipples weren't very sensitive, but John proved her wrong. His fingers teased reactions from her that she didn't realize she was capable of feeling. And all the while, he continued kissing her.

She wanted to explore him too, to feel his skin underneath her palms. Though it was difficult to concentrate with John turning her to putty, she managed to unbutton his shirt. Finally, she could slide her hands onto his chest. When she did, a visible jolt went through him, and at first she feared she'd done something wrong, but then his kiss turned even more passionate, and she knew he wanted her to touch him.

Savannah rid him of his jacket, then did the same with his shirt. Underneath her fingers exploring his chest, she felt only a whisper of hair. Otherwise his chest was smooth, just how she liked it. She would have loved to plant kisses on his chest, but she couldn't interrupt the kiss they were still sharing. She didn't want to break this magical moment, so she contented herself with caressing his chest and exploring his hard muscles, just as he explored her much softer flesh.

She wasn't sure how long they'd been touching like this when she suddenly felt herself being lifted up, and realized that John was carrying her out of the living room, his lips still on hers. Her breasts felt cold all of a sudden, but the knowledge that he was carrying her to her bed where they would continue their explorations, forced her to be patient.

She felt her soft duvet beneath her back. Only now did John let go of her lips and release her. She stared up at him, scared at first that this might be the end, that maybe he'd come to his senses, when her eyes fell on his pants. A definite bulge was stretching the fabric over his crotch. When she lifted her lids to look at his face, he was staring at her, his eyes not the chocolate color they were normally, but instead suffused with a golden hue. Before she could wonder about it, he reached for her and quickly peeled her out of her pants. She'd kicked off her high heels earlier in the living room.

She wore only bikini panties now. Black, lacy panties. He stared at them and growled low and dark in his throat. The sound sent a shiver down her spine and made her entire body tingle pleasantly. Not taking his eyes off her, his hand went to his pants, and he unbuttoned them, then slid them down his hips. He had to bend down to undo his boots and kick them off, before freeing himself of his pants. When he stood up straight again, her eyes fell on the boxer briefs he wore. The gray fabric stretched tightly across his front. A drop of liquid had darkened the fabric at one spot. She involuntarily licked her lips. She'd done that to him. Everything female awoke inside her at that thought, the thought of arousing John.

With a groan, he hooked his thumbs into the waistband of his boxer briefs, then pushed them down completely. His cock sprung to attention, the long thick shaft heavy and hard, its tip glistening with pre-cum. Pre-cum she wanted to taste, to lick.

She sat up and scooted to the edge of the bed so she could reach for him. He didn't stop her when she placed her hand around his erection and brought her face close to it. Slowly she looked up and saw him watching her, his jaw clenched as if what she was about to do would hurt him.

Without breaking eye contact, she licked over the tip of his cock, tasting the salty liquid and swallowing it. John threw his head back and groaned. At the same time his erection rocked forward and slid into her mouth.

"Fuck!" he cursed.

She locked her lips around the hard shaft and sucked him deeper. She loved his response, loved how he fisted his hands at his sides as if he needed to restrain himself not to grip her and thrust deep and hard into her mouth. And she loved his taste, loved how he was at her mercy, loved that she could make him come like this if she wanted to. She loved that power, it made her strong. And she needed to feel strong right now. So she sucked him harder, took him deeper. She cradled his balls in one hand and held his cock at the root, squeezing him in her palm, up and down, while she licked and sucked him until he finally gripped her shoulders with both hands. At first she thought he'd start fucking her mouth hard and fast, but then, on a groan, he jerked back and withdrew his erection from her mouth.

Moments later, he pushed her back into the mattress, and gripped her panties. He pulled, and the lace ripped, tearing the garment into pieces. He didn't seem to care, and neither did she, because he was already rolling over her, already pushing her legs apart to make space for himself. Before she could take another breath, he was thrusting into her pussy, plunging deep. His balls slapped against her flesh and his pelvic bone grazed her clit, when he seated himself to the hilt. She nearly came right there and then, but he instantly withdrew, before plunging back in.

When he began to ride her, deep, hard, fast, his lips were back on hers, and he kissed her with the same wildness with which he plunged in and out of her. She'd never been with a man who loved like this, as if the world was going to end and this was the last time he would ever be with a woman. As if he had to make it count. It was new to her. New and addictive. Was this what she'd always craved, but never dared to ask for? A man who loved without restraints, without basic civility? A man who took what he wanted and gave her what she needed? Why had she never experienced this?

She felt it now, felt the heat that was singeing her body, the excitement that shot through her veins, the air that rushed from her lungs in a race that she wanted never to end. She felt it in the way their bodies connected, dark skin sliding against light, perspiration making every movement even more erotic.

John's long hair caressed her torso as he continued kissing her. She slid her hand to his nape, caressing him there, making him shiver, while with her other hand she clasped his ass and urged him to take her harder, to thrust deeper. She moved with him, loving the sparks that ignited in her body each time John rammed her with his cock. And he was ramming her, hard and relentless. She didn't understand why she wasn't hurting, why she wasn't getting sore from the rough treatment, but she was glad she wasn't, because she needed this, needed to feel this man taking her with almost animalistic passion. He even sounded like an animal: his grunts and moans more like the roar of a lion than the voice of a man.

Everything felt more intense than she'd ever experienced during sex. Her heartbeat echoed in her ears, her body seemed hypersensitive, reacting to every touch by sending tiny shudders over her skin. Her chest was heaving, her heart pumping more oxygen into her blood. She could feel it already, feel her orgasm approaching. And as if John could feel it too, he shifted his angle slightly so with every thrust, he rubbed against her clit until she couldn't hold back the waves any longer.

Like a massive explosion, she climaxed, while a cry of release ripped from her throat. She'd never been a screamer, never made sounds like that, but John had unearthed something in her that she didn't think she could ever put back into a box again. Something entirely primal.

18

John felt Savannah's muscles spasm around his cock as she came, and let himself go. He climaxed hard and long, shooting his semen deep into her welcoming sheath. As if marking her as his. As if by doing so he could prevent another man from laying claim to her.

Seconds passed, before his body's spasms subsided, and his brain started to function again. Slowly, he rolled off her and came to rest on his back next to her, his eyes aimed at the ceiling.

What had he done?

If he could flog himself, he would. Because he deserved a severe beating. He'd taken advantage of Savannah, of her vulnerability. And not only that, he'd fucked her like an animal, without finesse, without tenderness, without concern for her likes or dislikes. He hadn't whispered tender words to her, goddamn it, not even dirty ones, when he'd made love to her. Made love to her? He shouldn't be allowed to call it that. Because he hadn't behaved like a lover, he'd behaved like a caveman, like a wild animal engaged in rutting. Shame flooded him. This wasn't how he'd imagined things playing out.

Sure, he could blame the fact that she'd almost been kidnapped tonight and that he'd needed to reassure himself that he hadn't lost her. But it was more than that. It went deeper. Savannah had gotten under his skin, appealing to that part of him that he kept hidden. The part of him that was all vampire, all animal, all alpha. And had he not kissed her during the entire time, had he dared lay his lips onto her neck or any other part of her, he would have bitten her. And lost her. Because she would have pushed him away in horror. Because what could be more frightening than realizing that the man she was in bed with was a dangerous creature who lusted after her blood?

Had he been a gentle, tender lover, maybe then he could eventually have revealed what he was and shown her that she didn't have to be frightened of him. That a bite could be a loving experience. But the way he'd behaved tonight, the way he'd fucked her with almost brutal passion, had made that impossible. She would be crazy to believe that he was capable of tenderness and love.

With a sharp intake of breath, he sat up and swung his legs out of bed. He couldn't allow this to happen ever again. Or his chances of winning Savannah were equal to nil.

Winning her? Was that his plan? When had he made that decision?

He let out a shaky breath. He had no reason to believe that Savannah was even interested in him. She was probably already regretting having slept with him. Or why else wasn't she saying anything or reaching for him? Why else was there this awkward silence between them? He didn't dare look back at her, not wanting to see the look of regret on her face. Instead he reached for his boxer briefs and stood up. He pulled them on, keeping his back to her, while he looked around for the rest of his clothes.

His eyes fell on the chest of drawers. On top of it stood a framed photo of Buffy. He froze in his movements. He'd seen pictures of Buffy before, but this one was different. This one was taken by a professional, it was posed. And there was something about it that drew him to it. Something about the photograph was familiar. He'd seen it before, even though he knew with certainty that this photo hadn't been in the police file. Not in Buffy's.

"This is it," he murmured to himself. The connection.

"What?" Behind him, he heard Savannah sit up in bed.

He turned around to her, his eyes taking in her naked body. God, she was gorgeous. Her hair was tousled, her body glowing with perspiration, and her eyes were full of passion. But then she pulled the duvet to cover herself, as if embarrassed. Regret. Yes, he saw it now. But for the sake of Buffy, he had to push that disappointment aside.

He reached for the photo and showed it to her. "When did you get this photo of her taken?"

Surprised, Savannah stared at it for a moment, then she said, "Two or three weeks ago, why?"

"Because I think this is the connection. This is the missing link I've been looking for." He put the photo back on the dresser then reached for his pants. "Get dressed."

"Where're we going?"

"To my office. The other police files are there. I need to look at them to confirm my hunch."

She jumped out of bed, suddenly not concerned about her nudity. "What hunch? John? What do you see?"

But he didn't want to give her false hope, in case he was wrong. Though he didn't think he was. "I'll explain when we're in my office, and you can see it for yourself."

While they got dressed, they didn't speak. However, John couldn't help but steal glances at her as she dressed in jeans and slipped into a tight turtleneck sweater. Again, no bra. Did this woman not realize what she was doing to every healthy man by wearing no bra? Could she not see that when she moved, her breasts would bounce ever so slightly, tempting every sane man to touch them, to squeeze them? Could she be so innocent that she didn't realize that even a turtleneck sweater that revealed no cleavage, no skin, couldn't hide her sexiness? Couldn't hide her delectable curves. Couldn't hide that body that was made for sin. For sex. For him.

Savannah didn't bother freshening up her makeup or wasting time in front of the mirror to fix her hair, instead, she simply combed her fingers through it a couple of times, and then looked at him. "Ready."

He'd never seen any woman get ready this fast, particularly not after sex. He was more than just a little impressed.

"Let's go."

"You're not wearing a shirt," she said.

Fuck! He felt like an idiot. He motioned to the bedroom door. "Living room." Then he pointed to the picture. "We need to take that with us."

While Savannah took the picture out of the frame, John finished dressing. Moments later, he was ready.

They drove in silence. Traffic was much lighter now, though it got busier when they reached the Mission. Many popular restaurants, bars, and nightclubs were located in the neighborhood, making driving challenging at any time of the night.

John drove into the parking garage underneath Scanguards' headquarters and parked in his assigned spot. He knew it was against the rules to take a client into the building this way, since he was bypassing security where she would have to sign in. But there was no time for formalities right now. Besides, she wasn't a client. Not an official one, and the less people knew of her presence, the better.

They reached his office without incident. John opened the door and ushered Savannah inside, glad to see that Deirdre had left. However, she'd stuck a post-it note to his computer.

You could have called me back. D. P.S. You're welcome.

Apparently Deirdre was a little miffed that he hadn't let her know whether he'd been able to reach Savannah in time. He grabbed the note and crumbled it up, but not before Savannah had seen it and managed to read it.

"A problem?"

"No. Just a colleague." Or rather a passive-aggressive protégée. He'd deal with Deirdre later. Maybe a little thank you for her help would smooth things over.

He pulled out the police file he'd stashed in his top drawer and opened it. Then he leafed through it, and pulled out the photos of all the missing children, lining them up along the edge of his desk. Savannah watched him wordlessly.

When he was done, he looked at her. "Put Buffy's photo next to them."

She pulled it out of the handbag she'd brought—not the one she'd had with her during her meeting with the kidnappers, but another one.

When Buffy's photo lay next to the pictures of the other children, John took a moment to look at every photo. Not all of them had the same background, or were staged like Buffy's. Some hadn't been taken by professionals, but clearly by the family. But seventy-five percent of the pictures were like Buffy's: professional, posed in the same fashion, and, most importantly, they showed one thing in the background that had drawn his attention in the first place.

He pointed to it now. "See this?"

Savannah leaned closer. "What am I looking at?"

John tapped at a spot in the right hand corner of Buffy's photo, then did the same on several of the others. "They all have the same blue background color, which I suppose is a popular background for staged portraits, but look closer."

Savannah's gaze switched from Buffy's photo to those of the other children, then she suddenly stared at him, her mouth agape. "A tear."

He nodded. "Yes. Photographers store different backgrounds on rolls, then roll them down behind the person they're photographing to change the backgrounds. What are the odds of more than one photographer having a blue background that shows a little tear at the same spot?"

Savannah pulled up straight. "All those kids... they had their pictures taken by the same photographer."

John nodded. "That's the connection."

Savannah pointed to the other photos, the ones that looked like snapshots. "What about these children?"

"I bet, once we call all families, we'll find out that they all saw the same photographer, but just like you, they didn't give the police the professional photos and gave them snapshots of their kids instead."

Slowly Savannah nodded. "I never thought of giving the police the framed photo. I had so many of Buffy that I'd taken myself."

"Exactly."

"So what now? You think it's the photographer?"

"We'll find out. You remember the name and address?"

She nodded quickly. "Of course."

"Good, then let's start with him."

"Her. The photographer was a woman."

"Okay." It didn't matter. A woman could just as much be involved in a child trafficking ring as a man. In fact, it was an even better front.

The parents wouldn't have seen her as a threat. "I'll get one of my guys to call all families and find out if they all went to the same photographer. Can you write down the name and address for me?"

She pulled out her cell phone. "I should have it in my calendar." She started scrolling through her phone, but before she got to the entry on her electronic calendar, the door was ripped open.

John's gaze shot to it. Samson stood in the door frame, annoyance in his expression. And the fact that he'd stormed down to the second floor, rather than called to summon John to his office, wasn't a good sign either. Something had just hit the fan.

"Samson."

When Samson saw Savannah, he stopped in his tracks. "Excuse the interruption." He nodded at Savannah, a tight smile on his face, then looked at John. "Do you have a minute, John?"

It wasn't a question. It was an order.

John walked around the desk and followed Samson out. He looked over his shoulder at Savannah. "Back in a second." Then he pulled the door shut.

Samson walked to the end of the corridor, where he stopped and turned around. John joined him a moment later.

"What the fuck, John?" Samson snapped.

Though he could guess what Samson was upset about, he wasn't about to volunteer any information. He had to assume that his boss didn't know the entire score, so it was best not to give him any more reason than he already had to chew him out.

"What are you referring to?"

Samson pushed him against the wall, his face only inches from John's. "Did you really think I wouldn't find out?" He let out a huff. "Using the twins to work a case Scanguards sent back to SFPD, and making them believe it's their final practical assignment? Are you out of your fucking mind?"

"How did—"

Samson moved a step back. "Oh please! You do know that Damian and Benjamin are in constant competition with Grayson, or don't you? You didn't stop to think that they would rub it in the moment they got a chance? And you know what Grayson did? He came running to me, complaining that he wasn't getting nearly as interesting a case to solve for his assignment as the twins." Samson put his hands on his hips. "Imagine how surprised I was when I heard what the twins were working on: a child trafficking ring. And the person who gave them the assignment: you!" He jammed his index finger into John's chest. "Care to explain what the fuck you're up to?"

John cleared his throat, trying to buy himself time. Apparently Samson wasn't having any of it.

"My patience is wearing thin!"

"Listen, Samson, I know you didn't want this case, but I couldn't just turn it down."

"Couldn't you? That wouldn't have anything to do with that woman you've been fucking, would it?" Samson sniffed, making it clear how he knew.

Maybe he and Savannah should have taken the time to take a shower after sex, but there just hadn't been any time. Following this lead was more important than worrying about what his boss and his colleagues thought.

"It's about the children. About little girls who're vulnerable. Little girls who'll go through hell if we don't find them in time. I can find them. I can bring them home." He clenched his jaw. "And if I have to quit Scanguards to do that, then that's what I'll do."

Surprise flashed on Samson's face. For a moment, he stood there in stunned silence. "You're serious, aren't you? You're willing to leave us for a case?"

"It's not just any case." It was about a little girl he was starting to care about as if he had a right to do so.

"It's a case that has nothing to do with us." Samson suddenly lowered his voice. "There're no vampires involved. You said so yourself. Even Donnelly didn't think this had anything to do with preternaturals."

"That may be the case. But these people are monsters nevertheless. So they don't have fangs, they don't bite, they don't suck their victims dry, but, by God, these people have less humanity in them than any of us." He kept his gaze steady, meeting Samson's eyes. "I found a lead. I know I can take them down. Please, Samson, you know what it's like. You've been in their shoes. When your daughter was kidnapped—"

"Stop!" Samson raised his hand. "Not another word." He took a few deep breaths, the memory of his own daughter's ordeal reflecting in his eyes. He ran his hand through his raven-black hair. "You're not playing fair, John. You know we don't have the manpower."

When John opened his mouth to protest once more, Samson continued quickly, "But because I know what these parents are going through, and because I know you mean well, I'll give you forty-eight hours to take care of this."

Forty-eight hours wasn't enough time to solve this case, but he'd take it, and then ask for more later. "Thank you, S—"

"Under one condition," Samson interrupted.

John held his breath.

"Grayson and Ryder will join you and the twins."

Fuck!

John swallowed. "Grayson?"

Samson pulled one side of his mouth up. "You left me no choice. If I don't put Grayson on this case, I'll never have peace in my home again." He made a motion as if wiping one hand on the other, ridding himself of an issue. "He's your problem now."

"Samson, you can't—"

"I can and I will," he said and pivoted. He was already marching toward the elevators, when he added, "And John, if Grayson gets into trouble, I'll hold you responsible."

Samson disappeared in the elevator. John heard the doors close, while he stood in the corridor, frozen. The good news was that he had two more bodies on his team. Ryder was a very capable young hybrid and would come in handy. The bad news was he'd have to deal with

Grayson, the boss's son. He was arrogant, entitled, and manipulative, which made being his supervisor a pain in the butt. Had those been his only defining characteristics, he would be hated by everybody. But Grayson had also inherited his father's charm, and could wrap anybody, man or woman, around his little finger if he wanted to. Which made it hard to be mad at him for very long.

When it came to women, Grayson was like a modern-day Casanova—he hadn't yet met a pretty face he didn't like. And it wasn't just women his own age who were susceptible to his advances, older women fell prey to him too. Which meant John had to keep him on a tight leash so he wouldn't put his paws on Savannah. Otherwise John would have to teach the pup a lesson about coveting another man's woman.

19

Alarmed by the appearance of Samson, whose name Savannah had recognized as that of the owner of Scanguards, she stood at the closed door, listening. She couldn't make out many individual words or phrases, but the timbre of the two men's voices left her with no doubt that they were arguing. She picked up words like *case* and *children*, indicating that they were talking about *her* case, *Buffy's* case. But then their voices suddenly dropped to a volume where she couldn't hear anything anymore. And she couldn't very well open the door to listen.

Worried that whatever Samson had an issue with might impact their search for Buffy, she wrung her hands and started pacing. She wasn't sure how long she was alone in John's office, when the door suddenly opened. She spun around and watched John walk in. She was about to ask him what was going on, when she saw two younger men enter behind him.

Both were dark-haired, tall, and good looking. And both stared at her, one with a polite smile on his face, the other in a more assessing manner. Was this kid checking her out? And why did he look so familiar?

"Savannah," John suddenly said and pointed to the two men. "This is Ryder Giles and Grayson Woodford. They've been assigned to me to aid in the investigation. Guys, this is Ms. Rice, our client."

Ryder extended his hand. "Ma'am, pleased to meet you." She shook his hand, surprised at his polite manners.

"Likewise," she answered.

Then Grayson took a step toward her, also extending his hand. "I hope I may call you Savannah." Charm oozed from him. She knew now who he was. His last name identified him as the owner's son.

Why had Samson assigned his own son to this investigation when only minutes earlier he'd had an argument with John?

"Very nice to meet you," she said, noncommittal.

John looked at her. "I've quickly filled Grayson and Ryder in on where we are with this, and they'll dig into more details later. But right now we've got to check out that photographer."

She nodded. "And what about Alexi? I still don't—"

"Don't worry," John interrupted. "Damian and Benjamin are tailing him. Wherever he goes, they'll be on him. He won't go anywhere without us knowing about it."

She felt relief wrap around her.

"In the meantime," John continued, addressing Grayson and Ryder, "you'll go through the police file, call every family and ask them if they took their daughter to a photographer before her disappearance. Take down the photographer's name and when they visited the studio. I expect the photographer to be the same in all cases. Savannah, you have the name and address?"

She pointed to a post-it note on the desk. "I wrote it down."

"Thanks." John took it and showed it to the two Scanguards employees. "This is the photographer."

Both pulled their cell phones from their pockets and snapped a quick picture.

"I don't want you to pose leading questions. Don't tell them the name, otherwise we might get false positives. Understood?"

Ryder nodded. "Yes, John."

"You don't need both of us making these calls. It's only a dozen or so, right? Ryder can handle that by himself." Grayson slapped Ryder on the back. "Right, buddy?"

Ryder grimaced. It appeared he was used to Grayson taking over.

"I'd rather come with you guys to put the screws on the photographer," Grayson said, grinning.

"Nobody's putting screws on anybody. We're going to ask some questions, that's all," John said firmly, authority coloring his voice. "And if you step out of line, it's desk duty for you all the way. Understood?"

Grayson grunted to himself, but then, after a few seconds said, "Of course, John, you're the boss."

John nodded, then looked at Ryder. "You know what to do?"

"Sure thing." He walked around the desk and took the seat behind it. "That the file?"

"Yep. Have at it." Then he pointed to the snapshots of the children. "Call those families that gave the police these snapshots rather than the professional photos first. Call me and give me the results as soon as you've confirmed that they saw this photographer."

"Will do. See you guys later." He reached for one of the photos, checked the name and dug into the file.

Instinctively, Savannah liked the young man. He seemed diligent and reliable, and he would do as John ordered. She was a little less sure about Grayson. While the owner's son was charming, he also had a rebellious streak. Maybe he needed to be that way to forge his own way. Or did he think because he was the boss's son, he didn't need to follow the rules? She didn't really care, as long as he could produce results. As long as he would be of help in finding Buffy.

"Let's go," John ordered. "Savannah, you're riding with me. Grayson, take one of the vans and follow us."

"Rock 'n' roll," Grayson replied and followed them to the elevators.

When minutes later, they shot out of the garage in John's Mercedes, Savannah looked in the mirror to make sure Grayson was following them. But she didn't see a van following. The only other car exiting the garage behind them was an Audi sports car.

"He's not behind us yet," she said with a sideways glance at John.

"Oh, he is," John grunted in displeasure. "But as usual he's decided to ignore my orders and taken his own car." He glanced in the rearview mirror. "The R8 behind us is his. Showoff."

"Can't be easy working with the boss's son."

John shrugged, but remained silent.

"Were you arguing with your boss about the case earlier?"

He whirled his head in her direction. "What did you hear?"

Taken aback by his abrupt tone, she fidgeted. "Uh, nothing. I mean, not much. But it was evident that you two had an argument. He seemed furious when he stormed into your office."

John seemed to relax and concentrated on the traffic again. "It was nothing. Just some administrative issues. Nothing for you to worry about."

She could tell that he was lying. But she didn't press him for more information, knowing that it wasn't her business. Just because they'd had sex didn't mean she was entitled to know everything. By blowing her off like this, he'd made sure she knew not to cross that line again. She wasn't his girlfriend or lover, she was just a client who he'd had sex with in a moment of madness. And that was all there was to it. His silence afterwards had already made her suspect that he regretted what had happened, and his evasive answer now was confirmation.

Savannah turned her head to look out of the window. It had been a mistake to sleep with John, to indulge in a few minutes of pleasure. Now that it was over, she felt guilty for having allowed herself a few moments of sheer and utter bliss, while her daughter was locked up somewhere, scared and alone.

She was a bad mother.

A terrible mother for having sought a few moments of happiness in the arms of a man she barely knew. Arms that had felt comforting and soothing. Arms she longed to feel again.

And that thought made the guilt she felt even worse.

20

The photographer's studio was located in a live-work loft in the South of Market district only a ten minute drive from Scanguards' headquarters. The converted warehouse contained eight such lofts, and according to Savannah, the photographer, a woman named Kerry Young, occupied one unit on the top floor.

John pulled to a stop in front of the building, blocking the entry to the common garage, since there was no parking spot in sight. Knowing that the police would take at least a half hour from the time a resident called to complain, there was no chance that he'd get towed. They'd be gone by then. And if he really needed to stay longer, he could rely on one other failsafe: once the arriving officer from parking enforcement ran his plates, he'd get a notification that the car was being used for official police business. He wouldn't tow it, and John would get a text message, alerting him that he needed to move his car. It was a perk Samson had negotiated with the police chief to make it easier for Scanguards staff to patrol the city.

John got out of the car, as Grayson pulled up next to him, double parking the sportscar. John closed the car door, then walked around the front. He didn't get a chance to display his old-fashioned Southern manners by opening the door for Savannah, because she'd already hopped out of the car and was shutting the door. John clicked his key remote, locking the car.

"Ready for this?" he asked her, meeting her eyes.

"What are we gonna say to her? I mean, we can't just storm in there and accuse her of having kidnapped Buffy and the other girls," Savannah said, with a doubtful look on her face.

"Don't worry, I'll handle this. All you need to do is get us into the building." He pointed to the entry system, a rectangular box with buttons, a speaker, and a camera, which allowed the residents to see who wanted to gain entry. "Ring her flat and tell her you need to come up to see her urgently. Grayson and I will stand to the side so the camera will only show you."

John moved aside, out of the camera angle and motioned for Grayson to do the same. He watched Savannah punch in a few numbers. A ringing sound emanated from the box, then a crackling, accompanied by a female voice.

"Yes?"

"Ms. Young, I'm Savannah Rice. You remember me? I came with my daughter Buffy to have her picture taken a couple of weeks ago."

"Oh yes, now I recognize you. Is there a problem?"

"Yes," Savannah said, "I need your help." She looked around herself as if she heard something. "My cell phone's battery is dead, and—" She whirled her head around and then back to the intercom. "Oh God, no! That man, he's still following me. Please! I need to get off the street and call for help."

"Quickly!" Kerry Young said. The buzzer sounded at the same time.

Savannah pressed against the door and held it open.

John walked to her. "That's quite some acting." He gripped the door, let Savannah enter ahead of him, then walked into the foyer with Grayson on his heels.

"You can always count on a woman to help another woman if she believes a man is chasing her," Savannah said and pressed the elevator button. The doors opened immediately.

Savannah stepped inside, while John pointed to the stairs. "Grayson and I will take the stairs. Give us about ten seconds before you press the button for the top floor, so we can get upstairs before you reach the top."

She nodded.

John ran up the first flight with Grayson following him close behind. The building had only four floors, including the entry level, and since both he and Grayson used their vampire speed to ascend the stairs, they were just around the elevator shaft when it pinged, announcing that Savannah had reached the top floor.

A door opened right opposite the elevator just as Savannah stepped out of the cab.

"Come on in," John heard the photographer say.

"Thank you so much, I'm really grateful."

When he heard Savannah's footfalls on the concrete floor, John charged around the corner and reached for the door, gripping it, so Ms. Young couldn't slam it in his face.

She cried out in shock and stumbled backward. John followed her into the flat, Grayson behind him.

"Help!" the woman screamed, cold fear in her eyes.

John raised his hand and motioned Grayson to step back. "Easy, Ms. Young. We don't mean you any harm. We're just here to get answers to some questions."

The woman edged farther back until her back hit the dining room table. "Get away from me." She glanced past him and Grayson. "You! I was trying to help you!"

Savannah stopped between John and Grayson. "Ms. Young. It's not what it looks like. I swear, nobody's going to hurt you. But we have questions. Regarding the photos you took of my daughter, of Buffy. She was kidnapped five days ago. And the pictures you took are our only lead."

The woman tossed a look between Savannah, Grayson, and John. "They're not the police. Or they would have said so."

"We're private investigators," John offered. "Unfortunately, most people don't let us into their homes voluntarily, so we have to fall back on a ruse or two. My apologies."

She still hesitated, still looked at them with doubt and fear. "I want you to leave now, and I won't call the police."

John shook his head. "We'll leave—after you've answered our questions."

"I don't understand. I'm just a photographer."

John reached into his jacket pocket. Ms. Young shrieked, as if she expected him to retrieve a gun. "Calm yourself, Ms. Young." He pulled out Buffy's picture and held it up so she could see it. "Did you take this picture?"

She stared at him for a moment, then diverted her gaze to the photo. Slowly, she nodded. "Yes, I remember her. She's very photogenic. A pleasure to work with." Then she looked at Savannah. "You said she was kidnapped? Is that true, or just another ruse so you could get in here?"

A sad expression on her face, Savannah shook her head. "She was taken five days ago. Just like a dozen other kids."

Stunned, Ms. Young looked back at the photo, then at John. "What does this photo have to do with it?"

"Every single girl that disappeared came to you for a photo session before her disappearance," John said calmly, even though he hadn't received confirmation from Ryder yet.

The photographer's eyes widened in shock. "No, that can't be. B-b-but that's impossible," she stammered. She pressed her hand to her chest, her gaze bouncing back and forth between Savannah, Grayson, and John. "You think I've got something to do with it?" She shook her head and then pointed to Savannah. "But you were here with her. You know nothing happened here. You took her home with you."

John cleared his throat. "We're not saying that you were the one who took the girls. But you're the common link. The *only* thing these girls have in common is that you took their pictures."

"But that doesn't have to mean anything," she protested.

"It does," John said. "That's why we're here. We need to know what you did with the digital files, who saw them, who could have copied them, who had access to them."

"Nobody does. My files are secure." She pointed to a desk in the corner, where two large computer monitors stood next to each other, a keyboard in front of them, and a docking station with a laptop in between. Various pictures were displayed on the screens.

John motioned to the desk. "Grayson."

The hybrid walked to it and plopped into the chair, then touched the mouse.

"Hey, you can't just use my computer." But Grayson didn't even turn around, so she addressed John instead. "What if he deletes something? That's confidential stuff."

"Don't worry, he's trained," John said calmly and approached the desk, as Grayson swiveled around in the chair.

"Safe, huh?" Grayson huffed. "Then why are there pictures of all these kids on a publicly accessible website?" He pointed to several of them. "Look at this, John. I recognize this one, this one, and these two. They're the ones from the police reports."

"Fuck!" John spun around. "You call that secure? Every pervert in the country can see those pictures."

"No!" Ms. Young protested and approached, looking more pissed off than frightened now. "The only reason you can see them on this site is because I'm logged in." She pointed to a spot in the top right-hand corner of the screen. "I was working on it earlier, that's why I'm still logged in. Nobody can access the site without a login and password." She turned around to look at Savannah, who'd also stepped closer. "You know that. I told you that I give a separate login and password to each client so they can see the proofs online, but they can only see their own, not the pictures of any other client."

Savannah nodded and looked at John. "It's true. Ms. Young gave me a password to choose which pictures I wanted from the shoot. And it only worked for a week."

Ms. Young nodded eagerly. "The logins expire after seven days. And unless a parent shares them with their friends, there's no way anybody else could have seen those photos."

"Actually," Savannah said slowly, "there is."

Everybody's gaze snapped to her.

"How?" John asked.

"Somebody could have hacked the system. It's not that hard."

The photographer opened her mouth to protest, but Savannah lifted her hand. "I know what I'm talking about. You're not a government agency, nor a high-powered tech company. You don't have the kind of security measures in place those companies do." She pointed to the computer. "If somebody wanted to get in there, they could."

"I don't believe it," Ms. Young ground out.

"It doesn't matter if you believe it," John said. "I believe it. Tell me, where do you keep the names and addresses of your clients?"

Ms. Young tipped her chin in the direction of the computer. "On a database."

"And I assume that you somehow link the addresses with the photos?"

She shook her head. "No, I don't. The database is separate."

The clicks of the computer mouse sounded behind him, and John looked over his shoulder and noticed Grayson clicking on the pictures and revealing the file names. He turned, grinning triumphantly at the photographer. "Last name, date, and sequential number? That's your naming convention for the photo files, really? And you think the person who hacked into your computer and swiped the database wouldn't be able to match the photos to the names and addresses?" Grayson clicked his tongue. "Amateur move."

A gasp came from Ms. Young, and John saw her press her hand to her mouth. Her eyes took on a pleading look. "But why would somebody…"

"Because child sex traffickers are—"

"Shut up, Grayson!" John wanted to bare his fangs at the hybrid, instead, he just glared at him.

Grayson grunted something unintelligible, which could be an apology, but it was too late. John shifted his gaze to Savannah, and saw the tears in her eyes. Fuck! Did Grayson have to remind her what fate was awaiting Buffy if they couldn't find her in time? Insensitive bastard!

Even though he knew that Savannah had to already have suspected that a child trafficking ring *was* a sex trafficking ring, there was no need to spell it out and make the pain worse. It was better to leave certain things unspoken. He wished he could comfort Savannah, but this was neither the time nor the place.

Instead, John addressed the photographer again. "We need to take your computer with us. We'll have our IT team comb through it to find any evidence of hacking."

"But I need this for work. Without it—"

"If you'd rather I'd take you down to the police station and have you booked as an accessory for thirteen counts of kidnapping and child trafficking, that can be arranged," John thundered.

Ms. Young shrank back, visibly intimidated, and wrapped her arms around her torso as if she was cold. "Take it, please. I'll cooperate. Whatever you need. Logins, passwords. Just ask for it."

John nodded, somewhat appeased by her compliance. "My IT team might call you if they need anything else." He pointed to a stack of business cards on her desk. "Is your cell number on there?"

"No, just my business number."

He took a card and a pen and handed both to her. "I need a number where we can reach you 24/7."

She quickly scribbled a number on the back of the card and handed it back to him.

"One other thing: what happened here tonight, anything we told you, or you told us, not a word to anybody about it. Not to your mother, your father, your sister, your brother, your best friend. Do you understand? If you tell anybody about what we suspect, I'll have to assume you're trying to warn them. And then I'll have to come after you."

"Yes, I understand." Ms. Young nodded quickly, her lower lip quivering.

He hated scaring women, but in this case it was important to make it clear to her that she couldn't tell anybody that they were following this lead. Any leak might tip the people behind this off and they would disappear before he could snatch them.

21

Upon exiting the building, John turned to Savannah. "Grayson can take the computer to our IT team at headquarters, while I take you home."

She stared at him. "I'm not going home. We finally have a lead, and you expect me to sit at home and twiddle my thumbs?" Sure, she was a little shaken by how John had intimidated the photographer to secure her compliance, but it had produced the right results. Now she knew why the police had suggested she hire Scanguards: they weren't bound by the laws the police had to operate under. Scanguards could enter somebody's home without a warrant and threaten people to make them answer their questions.

"Figures," John said finally and exchanged a look with Grayson, who was carrying the laptop. "Meet us in the computer lab and check with either Thomas or Eddie, see if one of them can look at the laptop right away. Don't have them delegate this to one of their staff. I want the best."

"Understood," Grayson said and got into his car.

Savannah walked to the passenger side of John's car and reached for the handle.

"I don't suppose I can change your mind," he said.

She looked over her shoulder and saw him approach. "No. Frankly, I don't know why you even need to hand the laptop over to your IT guys. I can just as easily figure out if it was hacked."

"I know you can, but just as a heart surgeon doesn't do surgery on his own heart, I'm not going to have you do this. We don't know what we might find. And I don't want you to, uh—"

"Fall apart?" she finished his sentence.

His look told her that it was exactly what he'd wanted to say.

"Because of what Grayson said?" She shook her head, though hearing somebody actually say it out loud had chilled her. "Do you really think that this thought hadn't crossed my mind? From the moment you told me that Buffy wasn't the only little girl who'd disappeared and that all the others were girls her age too, I knew what it meant." She sighed. "It was considerate of you not to say it, but we both know why children are trafficked, what these bastards intend to do to them."

John put his hand on her forearm and squeezed it. "Doesn't mean somebody has to remind you of it constantly. And I have good reason to believe that they haven't touched her yet."

"You don't have to lie to me." She made a motion to turn away, but he didn't let go of her.

"I'm not. The picture they sent you. She looks frightened in it, yes, but she hasn't lost her innocence yet. I've seen children who've been through this. You can see it in their eyes, see the horror they experienced. I don't see it in Buffy."

A glimmer of hope blossomed in her heart. "You're not just saying that?"

He shook his head lightly. "Trust me. If this is a child trafficking ring, it means they'll have to transport the children to a secure location where whoever bought them will take possession of them. And these people want their…uh… want them in pristine condition. Not damaged. The traffickers are generally not the end users. Their job is to deliver the kids, nothing more."

"I hope you're right. I hope we're not too late."

John let go of her arm and opened the car door to let her get in. Moments later, they were driving back to Scanguards, back into the parking garage. But this time they didn't return to John's office. Instead, they remained on one of the basement levels, where John led her through a maze of corridors, until they reached a large room with a multitude of computer workstations. To one side, behind a glass wall was a smaller room, most likely climate-controlled, were rows of servers were located. On another wall, dozens of screens were mounted. Together, they formed one large screen, the kind one would find in the control room at NASA.

To Savannah's surprise, virtually every workstation was occupied. She glanced at her wristwatch. It was almost midnight, yet this room was humming with activity like a freeway during rush hour. Several of the men and women working here turned their heads and stared at her as if she'd entered a place she shouldn't be at. But when their gazes fell onto John next to her, they turned their attention back to their computers.

"There's Grayson," John said and pointed to a workstation toward the far end of the room.

As they walked to join him, Savannah noticed that he'd already set up the laptop, booted it up and was speaking to a tall, blond man wearing leather pants and a white shirt, whose sleeves were rolled up to his elbows. She couldn't help but notice how well those pants fit him, and how physically fit he appeared, when he suddenly looked over his shoulder as if he'd sensed her eyes on him. Piercing blue eyes scrutinized her—but not in the way she was used to being eyed up by a man. He didn't linger on her breasts or check out her legs, but kept his gaze locked on her face, before he shifted it, seemingly satisfied, to John.

"Hey, John," the man said.

"Thomas, thanks for coming so quickly," John replied and shook his hand. "This is Savannah Rice. Savannah, this is Thomas Brown-Martens, Chief of IT at Scanguards."

She'd never seen an IT guy who was as muscular as this one. And she'd met a lot of computer geeks. How had he made it to the top and still had time to work out?

She offered her hand, and he shook it. "Pleased to meet you."

"Likewise."

"Did Grayson get a chance to fill you in on what we're looking for?" John asked.

"The basics, yeah. I'm sure anybody on my staff could handle this." Thomas tossed a quizzical look at John. "Care to explain to me why you need me for this?"

"Because you're the best and the fastest," John said, emphasizing his Southern accent.

"Flattery, I see. How about you teach Eddie that accent, and we've got a deal?" Thomas sat down in front of the laptop. His hands flew over the keyboard with a confidence that stunned even Savannah. She'd always thought that she was good, that she knew her craft well, but watching Thomas unlock bits and pieces of information from the photographer's laptop made her feel like an amateur in comparison.

She turned her head to look at John and caught his gaze on her.

"Do you want anything to eat or drink?"

She shook her head. "I'm fine."

"Did you have dinner?" John added.

"No, but that's okay."

"It's not." He looked at Grayson. "Call my cell the moment you guys have something. We'll be in the H Lounge."

"But I'm not hungry," Savannah protested.

"Give me thirty to forty minutes," Thomas said, glancing over his shoulder, his eyes meeting hers. "You can't do anything here right now anyway."

John took her arm and led her outside. "You might not think you're hungry, but I can't have you collapsing for lack of energy. You've been up all day, you've been through a terrible ordeal tonight, and then—" He stopped himself as if he'd been about to add something he knew he shouldn't mention: what they'd done earlier.

"Fine, I'll eat," she said quickly to prevent an awkward silence.

She didn't want to be reminded that only a couple of hours earlier she'd had wild, hot sex with John, a man she barely knew. Surely he didn't want to be reminded of it any more than she did. After all, it had been a mistake. A lapse of judgment on both their parts. Entirely a product of the danger they'd been in.

John led her to a large room on the first floor and closed the door behind them. They were the only people here. Savannah looked around. The place looked like a first-class airport lounge. She didn't really know what she had expected. Maybe a cafeteria? But this was much more than that. There were comfortable seating areas, dining tables, a bar, and along the walls, refrigerated shelves with pre-packaged food of all sorts, as well as fresh fruit, chocolates, and other sweets. There was something for every taste.

"This is the cafeteria?" she asked, giving John a surprised look.

He shrugged. "We just call it a lounge. Employees come here between their shifts or on their breaks. It can be a stressful job, and there are days we don't have time to go home. Management knows how to keep everybody happy." He pointed to the food. "Take whatever you want."

When she walked toward the shelves stacked with yogurts and fruit, she noticed that John sat down on one of the comfortable sectionals. "Aren't you having any?"

"I had dinner earlier. But don't let that stop you. You need your strength."

She chose a yogurt, a bowl of mixed fruit, a bottle of water, and a bar of fancy looking chocolate, and joined John on the sofa, sinking into the corner at the other end.

"That doesn't look like a lot," he said with raised eyebrows.

"It's more than I can eat right now," she assured him and dug into the yogurt. Only when the food hit her empty stomach did she realize that she was famished. She'd polished off the yogurt, the fruit and most of the chocolate, when she looked up and realized that John had gotten up and fetched more of the same.

"Eat," he simply said and put the items in front of her. "I'll be back in a minute."

She nodded and watched him leave the room. The soft music coming from speakers in the ceiling felt soothing, and for a short moment, she leaned back into the comfortable cushions and closed her eyes to relax.

John and his colleagues at Scanguards had impressed her. They were efficient and extremely capable. Thomas was clearly an IT genius, and John knew how to get information out of anybody. She knew she was in the right hands. Scanguards had achieved more in a few hours than the police had in the weeks since the first child had gone missing.

She sighed. Would this nightmare be over soon? Would Scanguards be able to keep its promise to her? Would they bring Buffy home?

22

John quickly popped into the V Lounge to get a glass of blood. Being in Savannah's presence made his need for blood stronger than usual. He knew he had to take precautions in order not to lose his head around her, so he quickly downed two glasses of O-Neg. Just as he left the lounge, his phone rang. He looked at the display.

"Ryder?"

"Hey, John. Your hunch was correct. All kids that disappeared had a photo shooting session at Kerry Young's studio."

"Thanks, Ryder. We were just there. It's possible that her site was hacked. Thomas is looking into it right now. I'm back at HQ."

"Anything you want me to do?"

"Follow up with Damian and Benjamin and see if they know yet whether Alexi Denault owns any property where he could hide the children. At this point he's our number one suspect. He had opportunity and the right technical knowledge."

"Yeah, and he's Russian. I've been looking through the police reports. If it's him, he has to have quite a few accomplices. They'll need several people to watch the kids. This is not a one-man operation."

"No, it's not. But it seems he's very careful. Damian said he keeps to himself. We just have to catch him off guard."

"Are you sure the photographer isn't involved?"

"Pretty sure. She was genuinely surprised when I confronted her. Hard to fake that." He sighed. "Anyway, thanks, Ryder. Stay at HQ for now in case I need you for something else."

He disconnected the call and walked back to the human lounge.

Savannah was still seated at the same spot as before, but her eyes were closed and she was leaning back against the sofa cushions. He sat down quietly, not making a sound and watched her peaceful face. No wonder she'd nodded off. She'd been through a lot, and she wasn't used to the hours he and his vampire colleagues kept. He didn't have the heart to wake her, and at present, there was no need, so he simply sat there in the other corner of the sofa, his body turned sideways, one leg angled, one braced on the floor, and watched her sleep.

Had they been real lovers, two people in a relationship, he would get to see her like this often. He knew he'd enjoy seeing her like this. Safe under his watchful eye. Trusting him as she slept. Yes, he would like that. But he also knew that the chances of that happening, of a relationship developing between them, were doubtful. Wrong place, wrong time. Wrong species—not hers, but his. Because would a woman like her, a woman who had responsibility for a child, really risk bringing a vampire into her home? Wouldn't she always fear that he would hurt her daughter, even if he told her that he would treat Buffy like his own? But why would she believe him? All she would see was the bloodthirsty creature, not the man with the capacity to love and protect innocents.

His cell phone pinged softly. A text message from Thomas. He read it.

Good news and bad news. Come to the lab.

John shoved the phone back into his pocket. He looked at how peaceful Savannah slept, and for a brief moment, he contemplated not waking her. However, he knew she would be upset if he didn't. She had every right to be involved in this, and if he excluded her, how could she ever truly trust him?

Gently he put his hand on her shoulder. "Savannah."

She shot forward, shaking off his hand in the process. "What?" When her eyes landed on him, she pressed her hand to her chest, drawing his gaze to her rapidly rising breasts, as she drew in calming breaths. "How long have I been asleep? Did something happen?"

"Everything's fine. You nodded off for only a few minutes. Thomas has news. We should go back to the computer lab." He offered her his hand to help her up, but she either didn't see it, or didn't want his help. He tried not to take it personally, nevertheless, the rejection only emphasized that she wanted to forget the intimacy that they'd shared earlier.

When they arrived in the computer lab a couple of minutes later, Thomas was still seated in front of the monitor, while Grayson had hopped on the desk.

"So what did you find?" John asked without preamble.

"First the good news", Thomas started, and Savannah sucked in a breath. "There is indeed evidence that somebody hacked the photographer's server, and accessed the picture files and the client database."

"You said good news," Savannah said, her voice shaking a little. "So there's bad news?"

Thomas looked straight at her, a serious expression on his face. "The hacker is good. Very good indeed. He was able to wipe out his footprint. I can't trace him. I have no idea where he is. He could be in the next building, or he could be all the way around the world in China, for all I know."

"Fuck," John cursed.

"Yeah," Thomas agreed. "But that's not all." He swiveled in his chair and clicked on a window. "We also found this in Buffy's client file." Pictures of Buffy together with Savannah appeared on the screen.

John shot Savannah a look. "You didn't mention that the photographer took photos of you, too."

She shrugged. "We just took a few, because Buffy wanted one with me and her together. And the photographer didn't mind adding a few extra shots for the same price. Why should it matter?"

Grayson hopped off the desk. "It matters because they tried to kidnap you too."

Surprised that Grayson knew about this, he gave the young hybrid a questioning look.

"I spoke to the twins. They filled me in."

"I still don't understand," Savannah interrupted.

John turned to her. "What Grayson is pointing out is that whoever kidnapped all these children, saw your photo, and for whatever reason decided to kidnap you too."

Thomas pointed to the screen. "I can think of a few reasons why."

Savannah spun her head to him, but Thomas didn't elaborate.

"But…" She pointed to the picture, but didn't finish her sentence.

John sighed. "Whoever wanted Buffy, saw you and decided he wanted you too." And now he remembered something that would explain why the kidnapper hadn't taken them both at the same time. "Do you remember you telling me that on the day Buffy disappeared, you were running late, and instead of picking her up from school, you had to send the babysitter?"

Savannah nodded, then pressed her hand to her mouth when she seemed to realize what this meant. "They intended to kidnap us both. Together. And when I wasn't there, they took Buffy and came back for me later."

John nodded. "I'm afraid so."

"We have to find this bastard," she pressed out through a clenched jaw.

John sighed. "Thomas, is there any way you can find the hacker?"

Thomas shook his head. "I wish I could, but unless he makes another attempt at accessing the site, I can't trace him."

"That's it," Savannah said suddenly.

"What?" John asked.

"We have to make the hacker access the site." She looked at Thomas. "We can put a tracing code into the site and follow it to him. You know how to do that, right, Thomas? If not, I can—"

Thomas lifted his hand. "I can do it, no problem, but we have no idea how long it will take for the hacker to come back to the site to access it."

"Then we'll have to give him a reason," she said.

"What do you have in mind?" Thomas asked the question that was also on John's mind.

"We have to assume that he has a spider monitoring the site and knows when new material is uploaded."

Thomas nodded. "Yeah, but—"

"We'll just need to upload new photos, embed a tracing code in them, and create a new client file in the database so it looks legit," Savannah continued undeterred.

"Brilliant," John praised, then addressed Thomas, "Can you do that?"

"Nothing easier than that. Only thing is, we need pictures of a pretty girl aged between nine and twelve," Thomas replied.

"Easy," Grayson claimed. "Let's use the aging software that Eddie purchased a couple of months back. We can use photos of one of our female staff members and age her down to about eleven."

If it worked, this was the best idea the hybrid had ever had. John nodded at him. "Do it. Who do you think will give us permission to use their photo?"

"Permission?" Grayson asked with a frown.

John scowled at him. "Yes, permission."

"I do," a female voice said from two desks away.

John turned his head in her direction. "Isabelle?"

The twenty-two year old hybrid approached. "Sorry, couldn't help but overhear you guys."

"Savannah, this is Isabelle, Samson's eldest. Isabelle, this is Savannah Rice, our client."

The two women exchanged greetings.

"You can take my picture. The software works best the less years you have to shave off somebody. Eddie showed me how it works," Isabelle said.

"You would do that?" Savannah asked.

Isabelle smiled. "I was kidnapped once myself, and I know how frightening it is. Anything I can do to bring your little girl home, I'm happy to do."

Savannah reached for Isabelle's hand and clasped it. "Thank you, thank you so much."

"Well," Thomas said and turned back to the computer. "Let's get to work."

23

It took the team at Scanguards a mere thirty minutes to create several pictures from Isabelle's original photo, upload them to the photographer's site and add a client file with a fake address.

"Now we wait," Thomas said.

"How long?" John asked.

"No idea. It's the middle of the night. Not sure if the hacker is up right now monitoring his spiders. If he is, it may be just a few minutes. If not, it could be hours."

"Okay. I guess you don't need us right now," John said and upon Thomas's confirmation looked at Savannah. "There's something I need from your flat. And you need to pack a bag."

"A bag? Why?"

"Because you can't stay at your place anymore. Knowing what we know now, I don't think it's safe. They'll try again."

"Okay."

To Thomas, he said, "I'll be back soon. If you get a location on the hacker before that, call me."

He led Savannah out of the computer lab and back to his car.

After leaving the garage, Savannah said, "Isabelle seems to be a very well-adjusted young woman, despite what's happened to her."

John gave her a sideways glance, guessing what she was thinking. "With the right help and support a kidnapping doesn't have to leave permanent scars. Isabelle went through a traumatic experience, but she's come out of it a strong young woman."

It had helped that all of Scanguards had been mobilized to find her. During her capture, she had held onto the belief that her father would move heaven and earth to save her. And he had. Buffy didn't have a father to protect her. Instead, John would now move heaven and earth to save her.

"It's given me hope," Savannah admitted. "And your colleagues…

they are all amazing. Smart, and skilled. Without them—"

"Don't sell yourself short. Your idea to upload new pictures was brilliant. I'm confident that it will lead us to the hacker. And once we have him, we're almost there."

"I hope you're right." She sighed. "You said you wanted to get something from my flat. What is it?"

"The ransom note."

"Why? There's nothing on it. And I believe the kidnapper when he says there are no fingerprints."

"I agree. He wouldn't be so stupid. He would have worn gloves, but there's a strange smell to the paper. It's very distinct."

"I didn't smell anything."

And she wouldn't have, because it was too faint for a human's nose. But his vampire sense of smell had picked it up. "I'm going to have our forensics guys check it out. It may help us in narrowing down where our kidnapper is holing up." Because if the paper had been kept in the same location as the kids, its smell might give them clues as to the type of building the children were in. "I meant to bring the ransom note earlier, but—" Crap! He didn't want to remind her of what they'd done in her flat earlier. "—when I saw Buffy's photo, I forgot all about it."

Had she noticed his pivot? He cast her a quick sideways glance, but couldn't detect what she was thinking about. Maybe he was the only one who couldn't get their passionate encounter out of his mind.

Once they were inside her apartment, John said, "Pack only what you need for a couple of days. I'll get the ransom note."

"Okay." She walked toward her bedroom, when she suddenly looked over her shoulder. "Do I have time for a quick shower?"

He nodded. "Go ahead."

When she disappeared, he walked back into the living room, pulled out a small Ziploc bag and put the ransom note as well as the photo of Buffy the kidnapper had sent in it. Maybe his team could find out where the photo was taken, though at first glance the room Buffy was in looked too generic to provide any clues. But maybe somebody else had a better eye.

John pulled his cell from his pocket and scrolled through his contacts, then pressed Benjamin's number.

"Hey, John. What do you need?"

"How far are you from Savannah's flat?"

"About five minutes, why?"

"Is Damian still watching Alexi?"

"Yep."

"Good. I want you to come to Savannah's flat. I've got something for you to deliver to HQ."

"Be there in five."

A click in the line, and the hybrid was gone.

He listened for Savannah, who was opening cupboards in the bathroom, and then heard the water of the shower running. He pressed another number, walking farther away from the door to the hallway.

A sleepy male voice answered his call.

"John, what the fuck?"

"Hey, Wesley, I need a favor."

"At three in the morning?"

"You know the hours I keep. Can't be avoided."

"Yeah, whatever. Make it snappy."

"I need you to take in a guest for a few days."

"What kind of guest?"

"A client, a woman."

"Did her place burn down or something?"

"No."

"You need me to protect her?"

"Yep."

"I'm assuming there's a reason you can't do it yourself."

One reason? Hundreds of reasons. "Yep."

"I'm assuming that's all the information you're gonna give me," Wesley said dryly.

"Afraid so. Can you do it?"

"Sure. When's she due to arrive?"

"In about half an hour."

"Gee, thanks for the advance notice."

"Oh, and Wes," John added, looking over his shoulder to check that Savannah was nowhere near. "She doesn't know who we are."

"Okay, I'll keep things under wraps."

"Owe you one."

"Don't worry, I'm keeping track."

John disconnected the call and slipped the phone back into his pocket.

A few minutes later, Savannah was ready. John walked to the window and looked outside. A black Porsche was just turning into the street. Perfect timing.

"Let's go."

He took Savannah's travel bag and walked downstairs ahead of her. As he exited, Benjamin was already coming up the steps.

"Hey, John," the young hybrid said. His gaze fell onto the bag in John's hand, then drifted past John to Savannah who was exiting behind him and pulling the door shut.

She let out a gasp when she saw Benjamin stand there as if blocking their exit.

"This is one of my colleagues," John said. "Benjamin LeSang. He's been checking up on Alexi and Rachel and some of the other people Buffy had contact with."

Savannah seemed to breathe a sigh of relief. "Hi, Benjamin."

"Hi, Sav—I mean, Ms. Rice."

Savannah made a dismissive gesture. "Savannah is fine."

Benjamin nodded politely. "You had something for me, John?"

John pulled the plastic bag with the ransom note from his inside pocket and handed it to the hybrid. "Have this analyzed right away. I smelled something really pungent. Some sort of chemical. It's faint, but I think it's significant. It could lead us to where the children are kept."

"Alright. Not a problem."

"And once you've got the results for it, let me know. And contact Detective Donnelly. He might be able to help us find where in the city this chemical is used, if indeed it is a chemical." And if the kids were indeed being held in San Francisco and hadn't already been transported somewhere else.

"I'll be in touch," Benjamin promised and, with a nod to Savannah, walked back to his Porsche and got in.

John motioned to his Mercedes, unlocked it and put Savannah's bag behind the seat, while she sank into the passenger seat. He joined her seconds later and drove off.

"Where are we going?"

"I'm taking you to a friend's house where you can stay until all this is over."

"A friend's house?"

There was an edge to her voice that made the hairs on his nape rise. Why did he suddenly have the feeling he had to tread carefully? "Yes, Wesley and his wife will protect you."

"I see."

She might as well have said *fine*, because it sounded just like it. *Fine*, when a woman used it, meant anything but. It meant she didn't agree, didn't like what he'd arranged. He felt he had to explain.

"Listen, Savannah, you can't stay at your place. I thought you understood that. The kidnapper knows where you live, and now that we're certain that he wants you too, I can't risk you being without protection. Wesley is a fully-trained bodyguard." And a witch to boot. And he had a wife who could make people invisible. He and Virginia were the perfect people to watch over Savannah.

"And what's wrong with you protecting me? I hired you."

"Please understand, I can't."

It was too risky. If she stayed with him, how could he resist the temptation to touch her again? And who knew what would happen this time? For both their sakes, he couldn't allow it.

24

"I understand fully," Savannah said.

Because it was so obvious: John wanted as little to do with her as possible, because he regretted sleeping with her. And if she were smart, she wouldn't bring the subject up, but she couldn't bear that this tension between them might impede the investigation.

"I'm sorry, John. I know you regret having slept with me."

He spun his head in her direction. "Regret?"

She didn't want to look at him and stared out the window instead. "Yes, please don't pretend it's otherwise." She tried to find the right words to continue. "We're adults. And just because one of us wanted something and dragged the other into it, doesn't mean it has to continue. I don't expect anything from you. I'm not going to hold it against you that you did what most men do when a woman comes on to them."

"You came on to me?"

She couldn't tell whether he was mocking her or not, but it didn't matter. Her pride was long gone. All she wanted was a clean slate between them. "First, when I offered you my body for helping me. You can't have forgotten that. And then, after you rescued me, I practically threw myself into your arms. I don't blame you for…for—"

"—for giving into temptation?"

She shrugged. "If you want to call it that. In any case, I see now that you don't want anything further, and that's fine. I'm not going to tempt you again." As much as she longed for his arms again, for the comfort they gave her, the strength they lent her.

"I don't think that'll work, Savannah," John said.

She spun her head to him. "Please, John, I promise."

John suddenly slowed the car and pulled to the curb, where he stopped. Then he turned sideways in his seat and stared at her. "I don't think you understand what I'm trying to say."

Alarmed by the odd tone in his voice and the fact that he'd stopped the car, she asked, "What are you saying? That you're giving the case to somebody else?" Her heart was thundering now.

John let out a deep sigh and ran one hand through his hair, pushing the long strands back behind his shoulder. "What I'm saying is that no matter what you do, no matter how you behave around me, I'll always be tempted. I'm tempted right now."

The words slammed into her like a freight train coming out of nowhere.

"But I can't allow myself to act on it again. Don't you see that? You were vulnerable, and I took advantage of you. And instead of being gentle with you, I fucked you like an animal. I used you for my own pleasure, when I knew you didn't really want me. You went along because of the situation you were in. You'd gone through a horrible experience, and you needed comfort. And instead of giving you comfort, instead of reassuring you, I fucked you."

His confession stunned her into silence. Did he really believe that he'd taken advantage of her?

"Now you know. You should stay away from me, for your own good. I can't trust myself with you. If I take you to my house, if I let you stay there, I can't guarantee that it won't happen again. It's been too long since I've…" He stopped himself. "You don't need somebody like me. And you know it deep down. I could sense it afterwards. After we had sex. You couldn't even look at me."

Her heart beat into her throat. John was afraid of hurting her. He thought that he was imposing himself on her. That she hadn't acted upon her own free will. That he'd steamrolled her.

Slowly Savannah shook her head. "I think you're the one who doesn't understand, John. I wanted you. Being in your arms, feeling you make love to me, was better than anything…" She dropped her lids and sighed. "But the guilt I felt afterwards, the guilt of having allowed myself to feel pleasure, to take something that was just for me, while Buffy is still in danger… that guilt is crushing me. I felt so ashamed afterwards. So ashamed that for a few minutes I was only thinking of myself." She lifted her eyes again and met his gaze. "That's why I couldn't look at you. That's why I couldn't tell you how good it felt to be in your arms."

"Goddamn it!" he cursed and hit his fist against the steering wheel. "You're not supposed to say that. You're not supposed to tell me that you want this, that you want me. How am I going to resist you, when you tell me you want this?" Torment shone from his eyes.

"You don't have to resist. We're adults. Nobody is preventing us from—"

"I feel like I'm betraying her, because I desire you."

Shock charged through her veins like acid. "Her?"

"My wife." He closed his eyes and breathed heavily. "I owe you an explanation." He turned back in his seat and gripped the steering wheel. "But not here. This is not a conversation I want to have in the car."

Savannah sat there in stunned silence. John had a wife. Yet he'd slept with her. Desired her. And why had he said it *felt* like he was betraying his wife? By sleeping with her, he *had* betrayed her. But a sideways glance at John told her that he wasn't going to say another word until they'd reached their destination, wherever their destination was.

Ten minutes later, John pulled up to a small house in Noe Valley and pressed the garage door opener on his visor. The garage door lifted and he drove inside.

"Where are we?" Savannah finally asked.

He switched off the engine. "This is my house."

Before she could protest or ask him anything else, he was already getting out of the car, taking the bag with him.

She didn't move. He couldn't possibly intend to introduce her to his wife. That would be madness. He opened the car door for her.

"You coming?"

A lump in her throat, she got out of the car and followed him into the interior of the house. John flipped a light switch in the corridor and set her bag down next to the door through which they'd entered. Ahead of her was an archway into the living room. John motioned to it.

"In here." He flipped another light switch, and subdued light flooded the small but comfortable living room. "Take a seat."

She followed his invitation and sat down on the couch. John sank into a broad armchair opposite her. Savannah listened for sounds in the house, but there were none. Nobody apart from the two of them was here. They were alone. Which begged the question: where was his wife? Visiting relatives? Was that why he'd slipped, why he'd slept with her earlier tonight, knowing his wife was out of town?

Not able to bear the suspense any longer, she asked, "Where is your wife?"

He met her eyes. "Nicolette is dead."

A gasp burst over her lips and she pressed her hand to her mouth as if she could take her question back, but it was too late. "I'm so sorry, I'm—"

"You don't have to say that. You didn't know her. What happened to her happened four years ago. But sometimes it feels like it was yesterday."

The pain in his voice was palpable.

"You see, you're not the only one who feels guilty for having experienced pleasure. I know how you feel. I know how guilt tastes, how you try to deny yourself any kind of pleasure because of it. That's why I'm determined to find Buffy, so you won't have to go through this any longer. Because it will eat away at you."

"Tell me what happened to her. To Nicolette," Savannah said, because she could feel that he needed to talk, that maybe, he'd never talked about it before. That he'd kept it all inside.

For a long moment John was silent, and it looked like he wasn't going to respond, but then suddenly, he started to speak in a voice that sounded as if he was talking to himself. "She was pregnant with our first child. A son. We were living in New Orleans, and I was working as a bodyguard. There was a big party that night. I was overseeing the festivities. My boss had invited Nicolette too, and I'd made sure she had a limo and a driver to pick her up so she wouldn't have to drive herself in her condition. She was almost eight months along. So close to giving birth."

Savannah noticed him take a deep breath as if to steady himself. As if to collect his strength so he could continue.

"When she didn't arrive when she was supposed to, I called the driver. They were just reaching the exit ramp of the freeway. They were only a few miles away. The phone line was still open when a big rig slammed into them. Later we found out that the truck driver had been driving for ten hours straight and had nearly missed the exit. He took it too fast. Lost control of the truck. It fishtailed."

Savannah pressed her hand against her mouth, suppressing a sob, while tears stung in her eyes. She knew how this story would end, but she knew John had to tell it.

"I heard it all, and I heard Nicolette. She was still alive. I jumped into the closest car and raced to her. I got there within minutes. I was so close to saving her. So close. But the crash had punctured the gas tank." He lifted his head to look straight at her, though Savannah wasn't sure he saw her. "The limo exploded into a ball of fire in front of my eyes. It was an inferno. But I couldn't give up. I ran toward it. Somehow I managed to pull her out of the burning car. But it was too late. She was already dead. And so was our son. I wanted to die then too. I wasn't that lucky. My boss had followed me and stopped me."

"You must have loved her so much," Savannah choked out.

"I still do." John rose and walked to the fireplace.

Savannah followed him with his eyes and saw the photo that stood there in a gilded frame. Instinctively, she rose and walked to join him. When she was close enough to get a good look at the photo, she froze. The woman in the picture was a black beauty, her eyes shining with love, her smile infectious.

John turned toward her. "You remind me of her, even though in so many ways you're different from her. She was Creole; her mother was from the West Indies, her father from France. And she accepted me with all my faults. Because she loved me." He sucked in a breath. "And now I'm betraying that love. I'm betraying her because I crave you. I've desired you from the moment you walked into my office. I yearn to have with you what I had with her. And I feel guilty because of it. And scared. More scared than ever in my life." His eyes locked with hers for the first time since they'd entered his home.

"Oh, John." She could barely believe what she heard. So much pain, so much anguish.

He shook his head. "I can't go through that again. I can't survive it a second time." He let out a bitter laugh. "What am I saying? Most people don't even find this kind of love once in their lives. How can I hope to find it a second time?" He turned away abruptly. "I'll take you to my friend's house. I think it's best for you. At least you'll be safe there. You won't have to worry about me coming to your bed and trying to force myself on you."

"You're not capable of forcing yourself on a woman, John," she said. She was convinced of it. A man who could love so deeply, a man who experienced guilt so profoundly, wasn't capable of hurting a woman he desired.

"You can't be sure of that. Please, Savannah, please let me take you to Wesley's house."

She took a step toward him and put her hand on his shoulder, making him turn toward her. "I want to be here with you. For you. You were there for me when I needed comfort. When I'd nearly lost all hope of finding Buffy. Now I'm here for you. Nicolette would want me to stay to give you the comfort she can't give you anymore."

"You know what will happen if you stay," he warned without malice in his voice.

She lifted her hand to his cheek and brushed her knuckles over it. "Yes, I know what will happen. Because we both want it to happen. We need each other. I don't know whether what's between us right now will ever have a chance to flourish. Nobody knows that. All I know is that right now, I need you, and you need me."

"Savannah," he murmured, and this time he wasn't pleading for her to leave. He leaned in, put one hand on her waist and slid the other to her nape. "I'm going to be gentle this time. I promise."

"I don't care how you take me, John. As long as you take me."

25

John slanted his lips over Savannah's mouth, and, deliberately slowly, he kissed her. This time he wouldn't allow himself to act like a beast. She was putting her trust in him, offering him a second chance, and he wasn't going to throw that away. The guilt he felt about betraying Nicolette's memory was still there, but having shared his story with Savannah gave him a sense of relief. His shoulders felt lighter now, as if some of the burden of his past had been lifted.

Savannah's lips parted under light pressure, and her breath rushed into him. She tasted sweet and welcoming. She was right when she'd said that he needed her. But she had no idea to what extent. He needed her not only in his bed to satisfy the desire he felt for her, he also needed something else from her. Her blood. And while she offered her body so freely, he doubted that she would part with her blood as easily. So for now, he had no choice but to content himself with what she was willing to share with him.

When the kiss grew more passionate, and she pressed herself to him so his chest crushed her breasts, and his hard cock rubbed against her soft stomach, he drew his head back.

"Easy, Savannah, we're going to take it slowly this time."

Her lips were wet, her cheeks flushed, and her eyes dilated. Just one kiss, and she looked like the most enticing tableau of lust and desire he'd ever encountered.

"You don't have to go slow on my account," she claimed and ran her hands down his torso.

Before she could reach his groin and play havoc with his good intentions, he imprisoned her hands with his.

"A woman like you deserves to be loved slowly and thoroughly. It'll give us both more pleasure." He lifted her into his arms and carried her out of the living room.

In the bedroom at the end of the short hallway, he laid her onto the large bed, then flipped the light switch. The soft light of the bedside lamp cast a golden glow over the room.

He bent over Savannah and reached for the seam of her sweater. She lifted her back and head off the mattress and allowed him to rid her of the garment. Beneath it, she was naked. He ran his eyes over her breasts, then cupped them both, enjoying the feel of them in his palms.

"Tell me, Savannah, why don't you wear a bra?" He lifted his head to look at her face.

"I don't like the feel of it, of the tight strap around my chest confining me. It's like a prison."

"Hmm." He dropped his gaze back to the two large globes in his hands and squeezed them, eliciting a soft moan from their owner. "Don't you know what you're doing to a man seeing you without a bra underneath your sweater? Don't you know how tantalizing it looks when you move and your breasts bounce with every step you take? Or do you love it, knowing you're making our cocks stiff when we see your nipples turn hard in the cold air?"

And just like that, her nipples stiffened in his palms, and uneven breaths left her lips.

"I didn't know," she claimed. "It's just more comfortable."

"Is that so?" He dipped his head and licked over one nipple then the other. "The moment you walked into my office, I knew I had to lick these breasts. You can't tell me you didn't know that. Didn't you see how you turned me on?"

"Not at first," she said finally.

"That's why you made me touch them, didn't you? Because you knew my weakness." He sucked one nipple deep into his mouth and licked it vigorously.

Savannah moaned and arched her back, thrusting her chest toward him in open invitation. "Yes, oh! I knew you'd like them."

John switched to the other breast, gave it the same treatment: long, wet licks and hard sucking.

"Oh, yes, more!"

"I wanted to press you against the wall of your living room, strip you bare, and take you right there. I could barely keep it together. When I got home that night, when I stood in the shower…" He looked at her face and met her eyes. "I took my cock into my hand and imagined it was you touching me."

Another moan rolled over her lips, and her hips moved as if she wanted to rub herself against him. He could smell her now. She was wet, her arousal drenching her soft petals. Soon, he'd take care of her need, but he'd promised himself not to rush this.

"But it wasn't enough. There's no substitute for you."

"I'm here now." She reached for his shirt and started opening the buttons.

Happy about her eagerness to undress him, he helped her and tossed his shirt to the floor a moment later. Her hands were on him then, touching, caressing, exploring.

"I love the way your skin feels under my hands," she murmured, kissing his chest. "And my lips."

"I love your lips on my skin." And he remembered what her lips had felt like wrapped around his cock. But tonight, he wouldn't allow her to do that. Tonight was for her. Tonight, he had to show her that he could be gentle and selfless.

He pulled back and reached for the waistband of her jeans. Quickly, he popped the button open, then lowered the zipper. Savannah was already pushing the pants down over her hips, and John pulled them farther down, freeing her of them, pulling her shoes off at the same time.

She wore black bikini panties and reached for them. But he stopped her. "Allow me." There was something about helping a woman out of her panties, because it gave him the feeling that she was at his mercy, because he was the one deciding when to undress her.

She lay down again, her head supported by the pillow. "Go ahead," she whispered, a seductive glimmer in her eyes. "Do what you desire."

The way she said it, the way she offered him carte blanche made his balls tighten and his cock jerk against the confines of his pants. His zipper cut into the hard root and made him bite back a groan.

Gently, he slid his fingers underneath the silky fabric and caressed her skin there, ran his fingers through the neatly trimmed hair at her center, and delved lower. Her hips lifted toward him, inviting him. But he withheld what she was asking for and instead took hold of her panties and pulled them down over her hips, then her legs. Then he ran his hands back up her legs until he reached her thighs. He nudged them apart, and Savannah spread them wider.

When he moved into the space between her legs and dipped his head, Savannah's chest rose, the pert nipples even harder than before, and she pulled her lower lip between her teeth.

"I should have done this earlier, but when you sucked me, I could barely hold on to my sanity."

Before she could react, he brought his head to her pussy and inhaled deeply. Her scent filled him, sent more blood to his cock, and made his fangs itch. But he pushed back that particular need. Instead, he licked over her slick cleft and lapped up the juices that oozed from her. Immediately, she writhed beneath him, but he put his hands on her hips and held her motionless.

"Easy, darlin'," he murmured. "This will take a while." Because tasting her, licking her, pleasuring her in such intimate fashion felt too good to rush.

"Oh, John," she said breathlessly.

John lowered his lips to her warm folds again and continued exploring her. It had been a long time since he'd done something like this. Too long. He'd missed this intimacy, missed pleasuring a woman like this, missed feeling her react to his gentle caresses. Savannah's hips were moving under his hold, and he eased up and allowed her to move, allowed her to rub herself against his tongue for more friction. He indulged her and moved farther up, bringing moisture to her clit, which was plump and throbbing. Demanding attention. He licked over the sensitive nub and felt Savannah jolt beneath him. He eased off for a moment, then did it again. And again.

Her moans and sighs bounced against the walls of his bedroom, mingling with his own groans and sounds of pleasure. He couldn't get enough of her, couldn't stop, because feeling her let go and enjoy a few moments of bliss, was what he wanted to do. She deserved it. She needed it. Just like he needed to feel that he could give this woman what she craved.

With every second of their lovemaking, he sucked her harder and faster. He could feel her heartbeat accelerate, hear the pounding of her blood in her veins, the drumming of her pulse against her skin, and knew she was close. He sucked her clit into his mouth and pressed his lips together.

Savannah cried out, just as her body began to spasm. He loved the vibrations that hit his lips as her orgasm engulfed her. It took minutes until she finally stilled, and he lifted his head from between her thighs and looked at her. A tiny rivulet of sweat ran down between her breasts that rose and fell in a rapid rhythm, while she panted, her eyes closed.

He loved that look on her. Relaxed, satisfied, happy. That's how he wanted to see her all the time.

He slowly rose, not wanting to disturb her bliss, when she suddenly opened her eyes and looked at him.

"John." Her voice sounded lazy and so familiar. As if he'd heard her say his name like that a million times.

She reached her hand out to him now. "We're not done." She pointed to his pants where his cock had created a definite bulge. "Take those off. Now."

John chuckled. "Detective Donnelly warned me you were a little bossy."

"Then he's a good judge of character." She pointed at his pants again. "And don't try to change the subject."

He complied with her order, taking off his shoes and pants, then pulling down his boxer briefs. Just like earlier in the evening, she stared at his cock and licked her lips. But before she could sit up and repeat what she'd done to him during their first encounter, he was already rolling over her. He brought his cock to her center, and gently drove into her. This time he savored every inch of his descent into her heavenly sheath.

"Oh God, it's even better the second time," he said to her, gazing into her blue eyes. "I'm sorry I was so rough with you the first time. It's just…" When she put her hand on his cheek and stroked it, he continued, "…it's been a long time since I touched a woman. Since…"

Understanding glimmered in her eyes and told him he didn't have to say it out loud.

"I know," she murmured.

And because there was nothing else to say, he dipped his head to her face and kissed her. She responded to him, kissing him back with tenderness and passion, kissed him as if she knew everything about him, knew everything that mattered. Because now there was an understanding between them. They would be there for each other, give one another what they needed without any other expectations. Because for now, it was enough.

He relished every second their bodies were connected, moving in perfect harmony, coming together and pulling apart. There was no rush, no hurry this time. No frantic fucking. Instead, they were making love, getting to know each other's bodies.

Whenever he was getting too close to his climax, or Savannah to hers, John slowed down and drew back until the danger of coming too early was past. Then he started again, first with tender kisses and caresses to her neck and chest, then with leisurely thrusts, before he picked up the tempo and allowed himself to take her harder.

But when he suddenly felt her fingernails dig into his back, and her heels drive into his upper thighs to urge him deeper, he couldn't resist any longer.

"You wanna come with me, darlin'?" he asked.

"Oh, yes, John, yes, please."

Thrust for thrust he delivered, drove deeper and harder now, faster too. He could feel her respond, understood her body's reaction so acutely that he knew how to adjust his angle, how to rub against her, how to touch her.

She didn't have to tell him how close she was, because he could feel it, could sense it in the way her heart beat against her ribcage and her breath rushed out of her lungs. When she crested, he was right there with her, releasing his seed into her in hot, eager spurts as her interior muscles squeezed his cock like she wanted to milk him of every last drop.

Breathing heavily, he rolled to the side with her, then onto his back, so she came to lay on top of his chest. For a moment neither said anything, but this wasn't the same silence that had descended upon them after their first encounter. This silence was different, companionable.

John stroked his hand over her hair and brushed several strands from her face. "Savannah?"

"Mmm?" She lifted her head and looked at him.

"I want you to know something."

"Yes?"

"Whatever happens in the next few days, trust me when I tell you that everything I do will be so I can bring Buffy back to you. There may be things I have to do that you won't like or that might scare you."

"You mean like how you barged into the photographer's place and scared her?"

"Things like that and worse. The work I do can be violent. But I promise you that I'll never hurt you or Buffy. I'll do everything to protect you and her. Even if that means I have to hurt other people."

"Why are you saying that, John?" She lifted herself farther up. "Are you talking about killing somebody?"

He didn't avoid her scrutinizing look. He wasn't ashamed of the kind of actions his work sometimes demanded. "If it comes to killing whoever is behind this, I won't hesitate."

Savannah shivered visibly, while she appeared to contemplate his words. "Have you killed before?"

"When I had to protect those who relied on me. Does that disgust you?"

"No. I'm relieved. It means I won't have to kill the bastard who's behind this myself."

John reached for her, put his hand to her nape and pulled her head to his. "You're an amazing woman. So strong. So brave."

He could love a woman like that.

26

It was around noon when John's cell phone rang. He'd already showered and gotten dressed quietly, but had let Savannah sleep in. After all, she needed her rest—as had he—and there wasn't much they could accomplish during daylight hours. He'd been about to snatch a bottle of blood and gulp it down in secret, before Savannah was awake to catch him at it, when the call came. He put the bottle back in the refrigerator and shut it, before answering his phone.

"Grayson?"

"Got some news, John," Grayson started.

"Let me have it."

"We got a location on the hacker. Name's Otto Watson. We traced his IP address to a flat in Marin City. We're picking him up now."

"You're what?"

"We're going in."

"We?"

"Yeah, Ryder, the twins, and I."

"And who the fuck made that decision? Your father's gonna rip my head off if anything goes wrong." And so much could go wrong when four inexperienced hybrids ran a mission on their own. They'd taken part in many missions before, including a very successful one not too long ago against a bunch of demons, but those missions had always been directed by somebody with more experience, with the hybrids following orders.

"Relax, John, we're not novices. The four of us can handle it."

That's when it struck him. "Four? One of you guys is supposed to be tailing Alexi."

"Damian said nothing's happening with that guy. Alexi doesn't own any properties anywhere that we can find. He's a dead end. So I pulled Damian off his surveillance."

"You can't just do that."

"Yeah, well, I made an executive decision."

"Who the fuck made you boss? Last time I checked, your father told you to follow my commands and not the other way around."

Grayson huffed. "Yeah, and last time I checked, you were a full-blooded vampire who burns in the sun. So, would you rather we wait till this evening so you can grab the hacker yourself and waste valuable time, or would you prefer to trust that we can do the job?"

Grudgingly, John had to admit that Grayson had a point. He just wished they would at least take a fully trained vampire with them, even if that person had to stay in the blackout van and monitor the operation from there.

"I want you to take every precaution. We have no idea who this guy is and whether he's got backup, is armed, or—"

"Yeah, yeah, I know the drill. See you at HQ in a couple of hours."

"Grayson—"

But the headstrong hybrid had already hung up.

John cursed.

"Something wrong?"

He spun around. His anger toward Grayson vaporized instantly.

Savannah stood at the entrance to the kitchen, wearing one of his shirts and nothing else. Her hair rumpled, an expression of concern flashed over her face. Despite that, she looked way too tasty for a vampire with an empty stomach.

"We found the hacker. My guys are on their way to pick him up."

"That's great news." She hesitated, scrutinizing him. "But you don't seem to be happy about it."

"I'm not thrilled that they're going in without me."

"But they're trained like you, right?"

If he allowed her to doubt this, her hope would be crushed, and he couldn't risk that. "Of course they are. They're the best." He forced a smile. "I'm just a bit of a control freak." Then he walked to her and drew her into his arms. "How about you shower and get dressed, and we'll drive to Scanguards to meet them when they bring the guy back for interrogation?"

"Sounds good." She glanced around the kitchen. "I wouldn't mind a cup of coffee if you're making some."

"Sorry, I just noticed that I ran out of coffee. Haven't had time to go grocery shopping," he lied. "But I'll get you a full breakfast once we're at HQ. Their coffee is better than mine anyway. Can you wait that long?"

"Sure." She smiled at him and eased out of his arms, then sashayed down the short hallway in a manner so sexy that he wanted to follow her and press her against the nearest flat surface to bury his cock in her.

But there was no time for that now.

While Savannah showered and got dressed, John consumed two bottles of blood, double his normal ration. And he needed it, because the more time he spent in close contact with Savannah, the more his hunger for her blood grew.

After washing out the bottles and disposing of them in the recycle bin, he made sure the kitchen counter was clean and he hadn't left any traces of his feeding behind.

Again Savannah was ready to go faster than he'd expected. "I'm ready," she announced from the entrance to the kitchen.

He turned to her and smiled. "Let's go."

Her forehead furrowed and she approached. "Did you hurt yourself?" She reached for his chin. "You're bleeding."

Fuck! He quickly turned before she could touch him and reached for a kitchen towel, wiping his chin and pressing it to the spot where apparently a drop of human blood had dripped when he'd been drinking greedily. "Must have cut myself shaving." He pretended to press the towel against the spot a little longer as if he was trying to close the cut, when he knew there was none.

"No wonder." She motioned behind her. "You don't have a mirror in your bathroom."

Crap! He'd forgotten about that. Since vampires didn't have reflections, there was no need for mirrors. And since he never had human visitors, he'd never felt the need to install fake mirrors. They were in fact large computer monitors with a mirror-like surface and lenses behind it to record in real time anything in front of the monitor, making it look like a mirror. Many of his colleagues used them and found them practical.

"Oh yeah," he said slowly, trying to buy himself some time, "it broke a couple of weeks ago and I haven't had a chance to get the contractor in to get it replaced." He grimaced. "Crazy work hours, you know."

She seemed to buy it. "Let me see your chin."

Reluctantly, he removed the kitchen towel.

She stared at the spot. "Looks like it's fine."

"Great. Let's go. You must be starving."

Eager to get Savannah out of his house before she found something else strange, John led her back to the garage and helped her into the car. Moments later they were on their way to Scanguards. Once there, he ushered Savannah back to the human lounge, which was much busier this time of day. But he knew he couldn't stay, or Savannah would find it strange that he wasn't eating.

"Can I leave you here for a half hour while I take care of a couple of things in my office?"

"Aren't you hungry?"

"I'll grab something later." He kissed her on the cheek before she could protest. "Stay here. I'll come pick you up when the team gets back with the hacker."

"Promise?" She looked straight at him and he knew what she was asking.

"Don't worry. I'll let you watch while I interrogate him. From a safe distance."

"What does that mean?"

"You'll be in a room looking into the interrogation room. Same as in a police station. But I can't let you into the interrogation room itself, in case the guy goes berserk and attacks you."

"Okay."

"Now eat something." He brought his mouth to her ear. "'Cause I love your curves. Wouldn't want you to lose any weight."

Then he pivoted and left the lounge, and her enticing scent, behind him.

27

Savannah had finished her breakfast and a second cup of cappuccino, when the young man who'd come to her flat to collect the ransom note, approached her.

"Ms. Rice?"

"Oh, Benjamin, like I said, it's okay if you call me Savannah."

He grinned. "I'm not Benjamin. I'm Damian."

Confused, she stared at him. She remembered the name clearly, or was she going crazy? "I'm sorry, I guess I'm bad with names."

Damian chuckled. "Benjamin and I are twins. Happens all the time." He pointed to his hair. "If you wanna keep us apart, just look at the hair. Mine is longer than his."

"Oh, I didn't know there are two of you."

"John asked me to get you. He's starting the interrogation."

"They came back with the hacker?"

Damian's chest puffed up proudly. "Oh yeah, piece of cake. We snatched him. He had no idea we were coming." Then he motioned to the door. "I'll take you to the observation room."

"Thank you."

She followed him as he led her to the elevator, which they took back down to the basement. When they arrived at one of the sub-levels, he ushered her down a long corridor, then used his access card to open a door. He held it open for her.

"Go ahead. Take a seat."

She walked inside and saw Ryder sitting at a computer in front of a big window that looked down into another room.

"Hi," she said.

Damian entered behind her and closed the door.

"They just started," Ryder said and pointed to the chair next to him. Then he pressed a button on a microphone. "We're all here."

Savannah sat down and looked into the room below. Several people were assembled: John, Grayson, and Benjamin. At Ryder's announcement, they'd turned their heads briefly. There was one man she didn't know: the hacker. He sat on a chair while the three Scanguards employees stood several feet in front of him, their backs now turned to the window from which she was observing.

"Let's try this again, Otto," John said, his voice coming through loudspeakers in the small observation room as clearly as if she was sitting in the interrogation room with him.

"I know my rights. You can't keep me here. And you're not the police," the suspect said with a defiant upward jerk of his chin.

"You're right about that," John acknowledged. "If we were police, you'd get a phone call and a lawyer. Guess what? We're not that generous."

A flash of fear passed over the hacker's face, but then he reined himself in again. "I'm gonna sue you!"

John exchanged looks with his two young colleagues, who were flanking him. "You hear this joker, boys? I don't think he knows who he's dealing with."

Unexpectedly John took several steps toward the suspect, almost jumping at him. Otto's eyes widened, and he tried to get out of his chair, but John gripped the armrests, and got right in his face.

"Let's talk, Otto. Let me explain how this is gonna work: I ask questions, and you answer them. Simple. Do you understand?"

The suspect nodded, his eyes still filled with fear. She knew that John could look intimidating, but clearly sitting in a chair in a bare room with three tall and muscular guys bent on getting answers scared the living daylights out of the man. Savannah clasped her hands in eager anticipation. Her heartbeat accelerated.

"You hacked into Kerry Young's database and photo files to get access to photos and addresses of young girls aged nine to twelve. What did you do with the data?"

"I don't know what you mean," Otto said. "I didn't hack into anything."

"We have proof you did, so let's not quibble about that. Thirteen girls were kidnapped in the last few weeks, all after photoshoots at Miss Young's studio. If you don't answer my questions, I'm going to have to assume that you're the kidnapper. And I'm not very kind to people who hurt little girls."

Savannah thought she could hear a growl coming through the speakers, but it was probably static in the line.

"I didn't kidnap anybody. I didn't. I swear."

"Then who did?"

"I don't know. I swear."

"You swear a lot. You'd better search your memory, because if I think you're no use to me anymore, I might just discard you." He turned his head slightly. "Boys, why don't you tell our guest what I mean by discard, since he clearly isn't familiar with my vocabulary."

Grayson stepped closer. "I believe the correct translation for discard is being beaten to a pulp."

The hacker gasped in fear.

"Thanks, Grayson," John said politely. "Now, Otto, how about I repeat my question and you search your memory really hard and tell me what I want to know?"

"Please don't hurt me. I didn't know." Suddenly tears shot to the hacker's eyes.

"You didn't know what?"

"I didn't know what would happen to the girls. All I did was provide access to the website, and then, when my client liked a girl, I sent over her details, you know, from the database. I swear. That's all I did."

"Who's your client?"

"I don't know."

"I'll ask you again: who's your client?"

"I don't know." The hacker started crying. "I really don't. He emailed me a few months ago. I never met him. He pays me via a dead drop. Cash."

"Liar!"

"No, it's the truth."

"So some mystery man just contacted you out of the blue to hack into some random photographer's website and database, and you expect me to believe that? How stupid do you think I am?"

"She's not some random photographer. Kerry and I dated a while back."

John drew back, giving the hacker some space now.

Savannah couldn't believe what she was hearing. The hacker and the photographer knew each other. Did this mean that the photographer was involved after all?

"Go on," John said, his voice now more controlled.

"I might have bragged to some of my buddies that I had a really successful girlfriend and what she was doing. You know, taking kids' portraits, and that the kids were really cute. Anyway, after we break up, I get this email, and I suppose I was a little pissed at Kerry for dumping me, so I wanted to screw with her and her business." He sniffled. "I had no idea what the guy really wanted. I thought maybe he was a rival and just wanted to steal clients or business or whatever. What do I know?"

"Yeah, what do you know?" John shook his head. "Then what?"

"There were reports in the papers about a few girls disappearing, and I recognized three of them from the photos. So I got suspicious. So the next time he contacted me, I said I wanted out. He said there was no out. I was scared." He tossed a glance at Grayson and Benjamin, then looked back at John. "You see, I couldn't stop. He wouldn't let me stop."

"How do you contact him?"

"Only by email."

"You're a hacker. Have you tried to track him?"

"I did. After I realized he wouldn't let me quit, I sent him an email with the usual link to the photos, but this time I embedded malware into it, so that once he clicked on it, it installed a small program on his computer that let me track his location."

Savannah nodded to herself. That's what she would have done. The hacker was smart.

"But he moves around a lot," Otto continued. "Whenever he contacted me, he did it from a different location. He never used the same location twice."

"So you're telling me you have no idea who he is or where he is?" John leaned in again. "None at all?"

Savannah noticed how the hacker lowered his lids, an indication that he was hiding something. John must have noticed too, because he added, "Otto?"

"He's gonna kill me."

"Not if I kill him first," John said.

Otto's eyes widened. Then he swallowed. "A couple of weeks ago, I gave him the name and address of another girl he requested. But this time I followed the girl, and I saw when she was taken."

Savannah gasped, her heart beating frantically into her throat now.

"I followed them. Two guys in a van."

Just like the two guys who'd tried to grab her. Savannah shivered.

"Where to?" John asked.

"The port of Oakland. They brought her there."

"Do you know where exactly?" John asked.

Otto nodded. "I know the dock number and which building. I can write it down for you. Show it to you on a map if you want."

"Why didn't you go to the police after you saw them take the girl?"

Otto shook his head. "He knows who I am, where I live. He would have killed me."

John straightened. "Fine." Then he turned to Grayson and Benjamin. "Get the exact location from him." A moment later he left the room.

Savannah turned to Ryder and Damian. "What now?"

The two young bodyguards exchanged a look.

"What'll happen to the hacker?"

"Oh," Ryder said, shrugging, "he'll be handed over to SFPD when we're done with him. He's an accessory. He'll do time."

Savannah nodded. "Good. I guess your work is done."

Damian shook his head. "Time to suit up. We're going in."

"What do you mean?" Savannah asked. "Aren't we gonna call the police?"

Ryder winked at her. "And let them screw this up? Trust us. This is what we do best." Then he smiled. "Now let's get your little girl back."

And those were the best words she'd heard in five days.

28

It was still daylight when two blackout vans left Scanguards' headquarters and headed for Oakland. Samson had authorized three more men in addition to the hybrids for this rescue mission: Zane, Quinn, and Oliver. Zane had volunteered, clearly itching for a bloody battle. The three vampires were riding with Damian, while John was in the van with Benjamin, Grayson, and Ryder, who was driving.

Everybody was armed to the teeth. In addition, John had donned the spare Kevlar suit and visor that Luther kept in Scanguards' basement in case of emergency. It was the uniform of the prison guards at the vampire prison in the Sierras, where Luther, Wesley's brother-in-law, consulted on security issues. The suit would enable John to help the hybrids gain access to the building the kidnappers were keeping the girls in, and open the gates so the remainder of the rescue crew could drive in and get out of the rays of the late afternoon sun.

As they were approaching the location Otto Watson had given them, John said, "You know what to do?"

"Sure thing," Grayson said confidently. He patted the thermal vision goggles in his lap. "We should be able to figure out pretty quickly where in the building they're keeping the girls, and how many men we're dealing with."

"Shouldn't be too many," Benjamin guessed. "There're only thirteen girls. I doubt they'll have more than three or four guys watching them."

John had to agree with that assumption, though he wasn't relying on it. But what he was relying upon was that the men they were dealing with were human. And eight vampires and hybrids could easily defeat a small army of humans.

"We're here," Ryder announced, slowing the vehicle. "I'll get us as close to the entrance as possible without them being able to see us." Ryder pulled the van alongside a few dumpsters and a row of pallets.

John peered outside through the darkened windows of the van. The building was a warehouse like so many on the docks. In the large yard that opened to the water, shipping containers were stacked up, narrow walkways between them. The building itself looked dilapidated and unused, but then so did many of the buildings on the docks, even those that were regularly used by legitimate businesses. There were two oversized garage-door style gates which were closed, and a smaller door next to it. Above it John noticed something.

"Ryder, can you see, is that a camera over the door?"

Ryder hesitated, then said, "Yep. Looks like it." He reached for his gun and screwed a silencer onto the nozzle. "I can take it out. Give me a few seconds." He opened the car door and slid out of his seat.

John lost sight of him for a moment, then Ryder appeared between the pallets and a dumpster and aimed. Despite the silencer, John's sensitive hearing picked up the sound of the shot. The camera lens shattered and pieces of it rained to the ground, but John doubted that anybody inside the building would have heard anything. Cranes operating in the vicinity provided sufficient background noise to drown out the breaking lens.

John pressed his earpiece, through which he was connected to all members of his team. "Ryder took out the camera. Team one is going in. Team two, stand by. We'll get you access through the gate. Team one, we're on the move."

He motioned to the two hybrids in the van and slid the side door open, then jumped out, Benjamin and Grayson behind him. Using the pallets and the dumpster for cover as much as possible, John approached the door. Ryder had waited for his sign and was now trying the handle. The door was locked.

It wasn't a big hurdle, not for a hybrid trained in all manners of breaking and entering. It took Ryder only twenty seconds to pick the lock. Then he nodded.

"Lock is open," John whispered into his mic. "Grayson, what do you see on the thermal images?"

"Nothing in the front of the building. You're good to go in."

"And farther back?"

"Can't reach that far. Too blurry. There's something, but it could be just a heater. Not sure yet. I'm going in with you."

"Wait! Benjamin, I want you to go around the building, see if you can penetrate the walls with your thermal goggles from the other side. We need to be sure."

"I'm on it."

The wait seemed to last forever, though it probably only took thirty seconds, until Benjamin reported back. "Only a few heat signatures in the back of the building. Northeast corner. Either two or three. Most likely adults. Can't get a reading on the kids, though it looks like there might be another wall I can't get through."

"Thanks, Benjamin. Any other exits back there?"

"One door, but it looks bolted."

"Good. Come back."

John made a sign to Ryder. "On my mark, Grayson and I will go in. Ryder, you'll open the gate for team two, and Benjamin will cover us."

Ryder nodded.

"We're going in."

Ryder swung the door open, and John slid into the interior as soundlessly as possible, his gun ready. Grayson did the same, weapon drawn.

The warehouse was only half full with pallets of boxes and crates. Despite that fact, John couldn't see all the way to the back of the building. But that fact also gave him an advantage: he could use the crates as cover while moving toward the area where Benjamin had detected people.

John motioned to the two hybrids, and alternately, they covered each other as they made their way toward the back of the building. When they reached the end of the crates, John peered past them. There were several doors, two to the right of him, one in the northeast corner of the building. The door there was next to a window, which allowed him a clear view into the room beyond. It appeared to be an office. He heard faint voices coming from it.

"Only heat signatures I'm getting are from that office," Grayson whispered via the mic.

"Nothing behind the other two doors," Benjamin confirmed to John's right.

"Okay, I'm going into the office. Stay behind me," John ordered and charged forward.

It was only a few steps to the door. He kicked it open with his foot, his gun aimed at the men inside. There were only two. Both jumped up from their chairs where they'd been lounging with bottles of beer in their hands. The bottles now clattered to the floor and shattered.

"Fuck!" one man yelled.

"Shit!" the other grunted and lunged for a gun that lay on the desk.

He didn't reach it. John was faster, and in a second the nozzle of his semi-automatic was pressed into the man's forehead. "One move, and I'll splatter your brains all over the floor."

The thug froze. The other man didn't make a move either. Grayson had his gun pointed at the man's head. From the front of the building, John heard the van enter, then the sound of the gate lowering again.

John turned his head toward the door. "We got two guys in the office," he told his colleagues over the mic. "Check the rooms next to this one."

He heard somebody acknowledge the order, then looked back at the two men. "Where are the girls?"

Both men's eyes widened.

"Talk. One of you," John ordered, his jaw clenched. When neither of the two opened their mouths, he pressed the nozzle of his gun harder against the forehead of his victim. "I'm not the police. So I don't have to adhere to any laws regarding use of lethal force against a suspect. I could kill one of you, maybe then the other one will talk. Shall we try that?"

"Don't shoot," his victim begged. "I'll talk."

"I'll talk, too," the other said quickly, probably afraid that he'd be killed if he didn't.

"Good." John eased up on the pressure on his gun. Behind him, he heard more of Scanguards' men enter.

"The rooms are empty," Zane announced. "Tons of mattresses, bedding, and the like. I can still smell them."

"Thanks, Zane." John glared at the thug in front of him. "Where are the girls?"

"They're long gone."

"Explain. Where are they?"

"On a container ship. On their way to Russia."

"Fuck!" John cursed. "Who is behind this?"

"I don't know," the man claimed.

John whipped him across the face with his gun, making blood splash from his mouth, while he grunted in pain. "Who?"

"I've never met him."

John glanced over to the other man who was held at gunpoint by Grayson.

"I haven't met him either. He sends us text messages. Tells us where to snatch the girls, which ones to grab. He gives us all the details. Which ship to put them on."

John looked back at his captive. "Is that true?"

The man motioned to the cell phone on the desk. "You can check for yourself. But there's no number. We can't call him, he can only call us."

"How do you get paid?"

"Cash. He tells us where he leaves it, and we pick it up. Always a different place."

John looked over his shoulder to Benjamin. "Check the phone."

Benjamin did as he was told, while Oliver joined him and rummaged through the paperwork on the desk.

"He's telling the truth," Benjamin said after a few moments of silence.

John nodded. "And the girls, what happens to them once the ship arrives in Russia? Who takes them from there?"

Both thugs shook their heads.

"We only put them on the ship," Grayson's captive said. "Once they're loaded and the ship's gone, we're done."

John narrowed his eyes and growled.

"You have to believe me," the thug closest to him pleaded. "All we know is that the girls are special orders for some hot shots in Russia. They pick them specially. We just have to make sure they get on the ship. I don't know for sure, but I assume the boss has a crew on the other side to distribute them to whoever ordered them."

"Oh fuck," Oliver suddenly let out.

John whirled his head to him and saw him holding up a sheet of paper. "What?"

Oliver addressed the thugs, "Is this the manifest for the ship the girls are on?"

Both nodded.

Oliver cursed. "John, if I've figured out the time difference correctly, the ship with the girls will be arriving in Vladivostok in less than four hours."

"Shit!" John's heart sank into his knees.

"There's no way for us to get there before they dock," Oliver confirmed. "And once the ship docks, our chances of finding the girls are basically zero."

John squeezed his eyes shut. No, he couldn't give up. He could never face Savannah again if he couldn't bring her little girl home. It would break her heart. And he realized then that it would break his too. Over the last few days, Buffy had become part of his life, although he didn't know how it had happened. There had to be another way to getting to Buffy. A faster way.

"Then we just need to call in some help," Ryder said from behind him.

John turned to him and locked eyes with him, when he suddenly realized what Ryder was referring to. "You're right. Make the call." Then he holstered his gun. "Zane, lock these bastards up in our cells. We'll hand them over to Donnelly once the girls are safe and we've got their boss."

"Pleasure," Zane said, and from his facial expression John could tell that Zane was looking forward to inflicting a little pain on the bastards while transporting them back to HQ.

Fine by John.

29

John arrived back at Scanguards a little over half an hour later. Savannah was waiting for him in his office. When he reached the door, he stopped for a moment and took a deep breath. The news he had for her wasn't what they'd both hoped for. On top of it, he knew it was time to come clean, because the solution he and his colleagues had come up with in order to get to Vladivostok and save the girls before they were scattered all over Russia, was one that involved supernatural powers.

He felt his heart thundering in his chest. The moment of truth was here. And he had no idea how Savannah would react.

He knocked to announce himself, then opened the door and entered. Savannah spun around. She'd been looking out of the window where day was turning to night. Just like in his own home, the windows at Scanguards were coated with a special UV-impenetrable film that made it possible for a vampire to stand in front of it without being burned.

Still dressed in his Kevlar suit, he placed his helmet and gloves on the desk.

"You're back. Where is she?" Savannah looked past him. "Where is Buffy?"

He let the door snap shut behind him and walked toward her. "I'm sorry, Savannah, the girls weren't at the docks anymore. They've already been transported away."

Tears shot into Savannah's eyes and a sob tore from her throat. "Noooooo!"

He pulled her to him and wrapped his arms around her. "Shhhh! Don't cry. Not all is lost. We got the two guys who kidnapped them, and they talked. We know where they are. We know where Buffy is."

She lifted her head and looked at him with eyes filled with fear and just a smidgen of hope. "Where? Where's my baby?"

"On a ship headed for a Russian port."

"Oh God!"

He could see in her eyes what was going through her mind: the ordeal her daughter was going through, the despair she must be feeling, thinking that nobody was coming to rescue her. The loneliness, the hopelessness.

"We know which ship they're on, and we know when they're arriving, and where. We'll be waiting for them." He hesitated.

She studied his face now. "Something else is wrong, isn't it?"

He wasn't surprised anymore that she could read him so easily. Maybe it would help in the end. Help her understand that he wouldn't hurt her, help her understand that he wasn't a monster, despite what he had to tell her now.

"There's something you need to know."

"Oh God, they touched her, didn't they? They touched my baby!"

He quickly shook his head and gripped Savannah's shoulders. "No, they didn't. It's not that. But there is something." He paused, not knowing how to start.

"You're scaring me, John. Please, what is it?"

"The ship Buffy and the other girls are on will dock in Vladivostok in three hours."

"Three hours?" As the words left her lips, an expression of horror and despair darkened her face. "No, no, no!"

"Listen to me. There is a way for me and my team to get there in time."

She let out a shrill laugh. "How? It must take what, eight hours, ten hours to fly there? You'll be too late."

"No. We'll be waiting for the ship to dock. We'll be there before them. Because we have something they don't. We have allies who can take us there. They'll transport us."

"What?" She looked at him, confused.

"Savannah, our allies, the people who'll help us save Buffy and the other girls, they're not human." He swallowed hard. "And neither am I."

She pulled free of him and took a step back. He let it happen. "That's crazy."

"It might sound crazy. But it's real. I'm real. My friends are called

Stealth Guardians. They're an ancient race able to teleport to anywhere in the world via their portals. They can get us to Russia in a few minutes."

She stared at him as if he'd lost his mind. In her shoes, he would have thought the same, because mankind's age-old dream of teleportation was just that, a dream scientists hadn't yet been able to turn into reality.

"They are a benevolent race who's made it their mission to protect the innocent. Just like we have, my colleagues and I here at Scanguards. We're not just simple bodyguards and security guys. We're not human, though we once were." He watched her intently now. "We were human before we were turned." He waited. Saw her contemplating his words, noticed her shake her head, witnessed the glimmer of emerging knowledge in her eyes. "I'm a vampire, Savannah."

~ ~ ~

At first, she thought she'd heard wrong. Vampire. She associated the word with fiction, with movies, TV shows, with the female TV heroine she'd named Buffy after. It wasn't real, she knew that, had never once believed that there was any truth to the centuries-old lore about creatures of the night who lived on the blood of humans. But John wouldn't joke about something like that, wouldn't choose this moment of all moments, where she was losing hope of ever seeing Buffy again, to dish up a lie. Not after all they'd been through together. Not after the things they'd told each other, the promise they'd made to each other that they'd be there to support each other, to be there for one another.

She looked at him. John stood there in utter silence, motionless and rigid. As if waiting for the axe to fall. And in that silence, every moment they'd spent in each other's company came rushing back to her. Details suddenly emerged that she'd dismissed: the fact that he hadn't eaten when she had, the lack of a mirror in his home, the claim that he'd run out of coffee, the blood on his chin.

But there were other things that contradicted his claim that he was a vampire. She glanced at the window. The sun was setting now, but earlier, during daylight, John had been in this office, with the sun shining into the room. And he'd driven his car during daylight, moved around his house freely as if the sun didn't bother him.

Slowly, Savannah shook her head. "But the sun… it didn't burn you. We were outside together. You can't be what you say you are." She couldn't say the word, though she was surprised at herself that she was so calm. Maybe nothing could scare or upset her anymore. Because the worst thing that could happen had already happened to her: Buffy was gone, and her hope of getting her back was fading fast.

"Search your memory, and you'll remember that I was never outside. Always in a room, or the car, my house, this building. Never outside while the sun was up."

"But the sun comes through the windows."

"Special UV-coating. We use it everywhere in this building, in our homes, our cars. So we can move freely during daylight hours. Because the sun does burn us, kill us if we're exposed for too long."

She accepted the explanation, but did that mean he was telling the truth? Could she take his word at face value? "I want to believe you, John. I want to believe that everything you're saying is the truth, that the guardians you speak of are real and that teleportation is real. That there is a way to get Buffy back. I want to believe it, but I… I don't know how. I have no hope left. And I fear that what you're telling me is in my imagination, that this conversation isn't even taking place, it's just in my mind, because I so desperately want to save Buffy."

"You need proof."

Savannah nodded.

"I can show you who I really am. I just want you to be prepared for what you'll see. Most people are frightened when a vampire shows his true face. But I want you to remember that I would never hurt you. I may have piercing fangs and sharp claws, red eyes and the strength of a hundred men, but you have nothing to fear from me. I will always protect you. And Buffy. Will you believe me?"

"I will," she said, without hesitation. She knew with certainty that John didn't mean her any harm. She'd always felt that, felt it from the first moment she'd met him. That belief had grown stronger over the last few days.

"Then look at me," he demanded softly.

He lifted his arms and drew her gaze upon them. His beautiful strong hands suddenly changed, his fingers growing long sharp barbs where his fingernails were. Savannah drew in a quick breath and lifted her eyes to his face, while her heart started beating frantically.

"Don't be afraid," John begged. His lips parted and slowly two teeth started to lengthen, one to each side of his incisors, until they were fully formed piercing sharp fangs where his canines had been.

"Oh my God."

She pressed her hand to her chest, willing her heart to slow, when she noticed John's eyes change color. First, the chocolate brown irises turned golden, then red. She'd seen the golden color before, had noticed it when they'd made love and thought that it had been a play of light. Now she knew. She'd seen a part of his vampire side, a part that had slipped through in the throes of passion.

There was no doubt now. He was a vampire. A creature who fed on the blood of humans.

She reached her hand out to him, took a step or two toward him.

"Don't," he demanded. "Please, Savannah, don't touch me now."

Her breath hitched. "You said you wouldn't hurt me." Or had that been a lie?

"I won't." He swallowed. "But when I'm in my vampire form, I'm not as civilized as usual. I have a harder time controlling my desire for you. If you touch me in my current form, I'll try to kiss you, and you won't be able to stop me."

A sigh of relief worked its way up her throat and rolled over her lips. "What makes you think that I would stop you from kissing me? We made love last night."

"Before you knew what I was. I don't expect you to still want me, now that you know what I am. What I hid from you."

She slowly nodded. "I should be mad at you for not telling me."

"Yes. I took advantage of you. Of your vulnerability."

"You did what was best at the time. I wasn't ready to see the truth. Now I am. Because the truth is my only hope now. The truth about you and your allies, because only a miracle can save Buffy now. And you're that miracle. You and your friends. So I'm not gonna refuse to see what's right in front of me. I'm not gonna question what I can see with my own eyes." She took another step toward him and ran her index finger over his lips. "Or what I can feel beneath my touch."

She moved her finger, intent on touching his fang.

A firm hand wrapped around her wrist so fast she hadn't seen it coming.

She sucked in a breath, but she wasn't scared, only surprised. "Let me touch them."

A shaky breath burst from John's mouth. "Savannah, a vampire's fangs are very sensitive."

"I won't hurt you," she promised.

He chuckled unexpectedly. "That's not what I meant. If you touch my fangs, it'll feel like an orgasm to me."

"Oh!" She hadn't expected that, but now that she knew, the temptation to touch him was even greater. "Let go of my wrist, please."

He immediately released her hand, proving to her that he was still in control of himself, even in his vampire form. He was still the Southern gentleman he'd always been.

"I need to do this," she said, "so I know that I'm not dreaming."

"Savannah, darlin', I hope you know what you're doing." Despite his words, John didn't protest any further and let her proceed.

Slowly, she slid her finger onto his teeth and rubbed over his incisors backward to one of his fangs. When she touched the razor-sharp canine, a jolt went through John, and suddenly the color of his eyes changed again.

"Your eyes shimmer golden," she murmured.

"Because I'm aroused." Both his hands were on her shoulders now, but she didn't feel any barbs on his fingers any longer. She felt him draw her closer to his body, pressing her to him. "I need to kiss you. I need to feel you."

Under her finger, his fang suddenly receded back into its socket and turned into a normal tooth again. She met his eyes and slid her hand to his nape, pulling his head closer to hers.

"Yes," she murmured.

His lips were on her before the word was even out of her mouth, and he kissed her with a passion she understood now. The passion of a man who carried a powerful beast inside him. A beast she could embrace, because she knew that it was her daughter's salvation. And her own too. A beast she knew she could love without reservations.

30

John felt Savannah yield to him in a manner so trusting, he couldn't believe his luck. She wasn't afraid of him, wasn't running screaming from his office, wasn't staring at him in disgust. She had accepted him. Accepted the vampire in him. The vampire who craved her even more now.

A firm knock on the door made him release Savannah's lips and look over his shoulder. "Yes?"

The door opened, and Virginia entered. The redhead was not only a Stealth Guardian, and a member of her race's ruling body, but also Wesley's mate.

"We're ready, John," she announced.

"Thanks for coming so quickly, Virginia." He reluctantly let go of Savannah. "Savannah, this is Virginia. She's one of the Stealth Guardians I told you about."

Virginia raised an eyebrow. "I didn't realize she knew."

"I only just found out," Savannah said, and offered her hand to Virginia, who shook it. "I'm so grateful to you and everybody involved in trying to get my daughter back."

"For a woman who just found out that there are preternatural creatures roaming this world, you seem remarkably calm," Virginia said.

"I was hoping for a miracle. I'm not going to reject it, just because it arrived in the form of vampires and Stealth Guardians."

Virginia directed her gaze to John. "Smart woman." Then she motioned to the door behind her. "We've gotta go. We found a portal in Vladivostok. Logan and Enya are transporting directly there and will be expecting us."

John nodded his approval, then turned to Savannah. He cupped her cheek. "I'll bring her back to you. I promise."

"I know. I trust you."

"I'll call my protégée Deirdre to come and keep you company while I'm gone. Stay in my office, until she arrives. Okay?"

"Is she a vampire, too?"

"Yes. And she's a good woman. You can trust her."

"If you trust her, I trust her."

When she smiled at him, John pivoted, snatched his helmet and gloves from the desk, and left with Virginia. On the way downstairs he placed a quick call to Deirdre to give her instructions to take care of Savannah. In Scanguards' lobby, several people were waiting for them: the four hybrids and Zane. Zane was wearing the same kind of Kevlar suit as John, helmet in hand. As luck would have it, Luther was in San Francisco this week and had lent his own suit to Zane for this mission. They would need the protection: it would be afternoon local time when they arrived in Vladivostok.

"That won't be enough people," John said.

"I can only take so many with me in the portal, or we'd have to do several trips. And with Logan and Enya, we're more than enough to take care of the traffickers." She motioned to Zane. "Zane filled me in on everything. They're human, and from what you encountered at the port earlier, they don't exactly have an army. Trust me: four hybrids, two vampires, and three Stealth Guardians can defeat fifty humans."

John knew that, but there were kids involved, kids they had to protect, and when it came to kids, one could never be too cautious.

"I hope there are enough for all of us to take a bite out of," Zane threw in, his eyes glimmering with bloodlust. "I didn't get much to do in Oakland. And scaring the crap out of those two thugs was hardly any fun."

"Well, then let's go," John announced.

The only portal in San Francisco through which a Stealth Guardian could travel, was in a tunnel in the 16th Street BART station in the Mission district, only a few blocks away from Scanguards' headquarters. Virginia led them there on foot. Once inside the station, they walked down the stairs and around a corner where for a moment they would be shielded from the passengers waiting for the next train.

"Now, hold hands."

"What?" Zane asked in disgust.

"I need to make us all invisible, but because we're so many, I can't do it with my mind; takes too much energy. I need to do it by touch." She took Zane's hand. "Now hold hands with one of your colleagues. We need to create a chain."

"Do it!" John ordered and offered his hand.

There were no more protests, and moments later, they emerged from their temporary hiding place, now invisible, and walked into the tunnel. A couple of hundred yards into it, Virginia stopped and pressed her hand against the stone wall. Within seconds, a section of the wall disappeared, revealing a cave.

"Get inside," she ordered, and one by one, the hybrids, as well as Zane and John crowded into the space. Virginia joined them. "Two of you need to hold onto me. And everybody else has to hold onto them. Don't let go, or you'll be left behind." Suddenly the opening closed, and darkness descended upon them. "Oh, and it might be a little bumpy if this is your first ride."

Bumpy was an understatement.

John felt as if he was being hurled into the air and tossed around like a ragdoll in an oversized dryer. But he didn't let go of Virginia, nor of Benjamin, who was holding onto him for dear life. Luckily, the ride only took several seconds. Before he even realized it, he felt solid ground under his feet again, and the tumbling stopped.

"Bumpy, my ass," Zane growled. "You might as well have tossed us into hell."

Involuntarily, John had to grin. Zane was fearless and never displayed any discomfort about anything, but it appeared he wasn't keen on a repeat of this particular experience.

"That was cool!" Grayson proclaimed.

"Oh yeah!" Damian confirmed.

Ryder simply rolled his eyes, as if he didn't believe Damian's and Grayson's show of bravado.

When they exited the portal, Logan and Enya were waiting for them. John familiarized himself with his surroundings. They were in an abandoned factory. He slipped on his helmet and gloves, and noticed Zane doing the same.

"We procured a truck," Logan announced.

"What Logan means is, we stole one," Enya corrected him. The blond female looked rather petite, but according to Wesley, she was a formidable fighter and no less capable than her male brethren. "We figured out the route. It'll take about twenty minutes to reach the port."

When they exited the factory, John looked up at the sky. It was overcast, and in the distance, dark clouds were visible. He didn't mind the cloudy weather, because it would provide an extra shield against the sun, but the dark clouds worried him somewhat, because they could develop into thunderclouds pretty quickly.

They piled into the large truck, weapons at the ready, and drove off. Enya used her smartphone to guide Logan through the unfamiliar city and direct him toward the dock at the port where the cargo ship carrying the girls was scheduled to arrive.

They didn't seem out of place when they arrived at the docks in the old, beat up truck. Nobody gave them a second glance.

"That way," Enya ordered, pointing to a dock around a bend, away from the hustle and bustle of the main docks, where containers were being loaded and unloaded.

When they turned the corner in the truck, John was glad that the area was somewhat shielded from the other docks. It would make it easier to avoid being seen by innocent bystanders. It figured that the kidnappers wanted to unload the girls in an area where nobody would see them and ask any questions.

"Park over there," Enya said now, and Logan pulled behind a large shipping container and brought the truck to a stop.

"The ship's already docking, look!" Grayson said from behind him.

John turned his head and looked out the side window. The hybrid was right. The ship was already being tied up in its berth. Yet, it still took almost an hour until the unloading began. The wait was excruciating, but John knew that it would be easier to fight the kidnappers once they had started unloading their victims. If Scanguards acted before the kids were on solid ground, too much could go wrong.

"Grayson, Ryder, you're responsible for scanning the containers with your thermal cameras. We need to know which container the girls are in," John instructed. "I doubt they'll walk them off the ship and risk somebody seeing them."

Zane nodded in agreement. "That's what I would do."

John looked at Virginia. "Virginia, how many of us can each of you cloak with your mind so we can move freely and not have to hold hands?"

"We can each take two at least, so that's good." She exchanged a look with Enya and Logan. "I'll take you and Zane, Logan can take care of the twins, and Enya will take Grayson and Ryder."

Both Enya and Logan nodded.

"Okay, Enya, you, Grayson, and Ryder will secure the girls, once we have their location. The rest of you, we're taking out the kidnappers. I want no one to escape. Are we clear?"

"Now you're talking," Zane said.

"Are you saying to kill all of them?" Virginia asked. "Don't you want to interrogate them?"

"If it's safe to leave one alive, sure. But the girls' safety comes first. Seeing how the kingpin behind this operated with the hacker and the two thugs we picked up in Oakland, I doubt they know who he is. He's too careful. If it's safe, we'll ask them questions, but if they try to run, kill them."

"And if they don't try to run?" Zane asked. "You saying we'll have to let them live if they talk?" Displeasure spread on Zane's face.

"Don't worry. Once they've told us what they know, they'll die too." After all, here in Russia, they couldn't very well hand these criminals over to the authorities. And they needed to be punished, one way or another.

"Glad we cleared that up," Zane said dryly.

"Hey guys," Ryder suddenly said. "That container, the red one they're lowering down right now... I see a whole bunch of heat signatures in there. All huddled in a corner."

"Yeah, I see it too," Grayson confirmed. "Could be a good dozen kids. Must be them."

"Okay, get ready. Wait until the container has been lowered and disconnected from the crane. We don't want them to pick it up again if they notice something," John instructed.

With one eye John watched the container, with the other the gangplank, where three man appeared. Carrying small travel bags, they marched down and headed for the red container.

"They're packing heat," Damian said.

John had noticed the bulges under their jackets too. Guns.

"Let's go," John ordered. "Virginia, Enya, Logan. Cloak us."

"Done," all three said in unison.

All of them exited the truck, and while John could still see all members of his team, he trusted that they were now invisible to everybody else. John looked around, but he couldn't see anybody else approaching the container or leaving the ship. Could they be so lucky as to only have to deal with three men? This was going too well.

All of a sudden, lightning split the sky, accompanied by a thunderclap. John looked up into the sky. The dark clouds he'd seen in the distance were now right above the city and the docks.

"Shit!" John hissed and exchanged a look with Virginia.

"Rain," she said with concern, just as the first drops hit the ground. "If this lasts, we're not gonna be invisible for long."

"John," Grayson's voice came through the mic. "Customs truck approaching. To your left."

John spun his head in the indicated direction and saw the white van with Cyrillic script on its sides and front hood. "How do you know it's customs?"

"I took a few years of Russian. Trust me."

"Fuck!" John cursed. "Get out of the rain, all of you, take cover where you can. We're gonna have to wait until they leave."

He watched his colleagues scatter, taking cover where they could find it. John motioned to a stack of pallets covered with a tarp, and ran toward it, Virginia and Zane following him. They pressed themselves close to it, the overhanging tarp providing some protection from the rain.

The van stopped near the red container, and two men got out. They marched toward the three who'd just come down the gangplank. The three didn't appear to be surprised or scared. Instead, they walked straight toward them, exchanging handshakes. Then one of the three men from the ship pulled a thick envelope from his jacket pocket and handed it to the customs official.

"Payoff," John said, looking at Zane, who nodded.

"Customs knows what's in the container. They want their cut."

That changed things. John would never risk the lives of innocent government officials, but these guys were dirty. And if they allowed child trafficking, they had to be taken out, or this practice would continue.

"Change of plans," John said into his mic. "Treat the customs officials as hostiles. They're going down."

The two customs officers turned and walked back to their van.

"Move in, now! Don't let them get away. Damian, Benjamin, Logan, you take the customs guys. Enya, your team secures the girls. We'll take the three from the ship. Everybody, attack!"

John charged toward the three thugs from the ship, who were now making their way to the red container. Zane and Virginia were by his side. He felt the rain pelting down on him now, and though it didn't penetrate the Kevlar suit, the drops clung to the material, making his silhouette visible to anybody who was looking in his direction. Which one of the men suddenly did.

Startled, the man froze. Then his head whipped from left to right, then back again, and with a curse in Russian, he alerted his friends. All three drew their guns and aimed.

"Fuck!"

Still running, John took the safety off his semi-automatic, when a shot hit him. He felt the impact, and it jerked him back for a moment, but he caught himself quickly and kept running, aiming his own weapon now. However, the rain pounding down on him obscured his vision, the water clinging to his visor like rain to a windshield whose wipers weren't working.

Loud thunder exploded in the sky, just as more shots rang out, those from his own gun, and the weapons of his colleagues. One of the men from the ship dropped to the ground like a felled tree, while the other two ran for cover.

John didn't have time to see how the twins were faring with the two customs officials, while he dodged the kidnappers' bullets. They had taken cover behind a stack of pallets, while John was still out in the open, crossing the large empty space between the warehouse and the ship.

His idea of taking out the criminals silently and stealthily, or to question them before killing them, had gone up in smoke, or rather, in rain. This was getting messy.

"I'll get around the other side," Zane announced over the mic and ran between two containers toward the right.

"Shit, Zane!" Virginia hissed. "You'll be out of my range."

But Zane didn't reply. And it didn't matter much anyway. They were already partially visible.

Finally John reached the stack of pallets where the thugs were hiding. He tried to look through the gaps in the wood and saw movement, but couldn't get a clear view through his wet visor. Nevertheless, he aimed his gun through the gap and pulled the trigger.

A man cried out, then cursed in Russian. He'd hit the guy, but not killed him. Next to John, Virginia appeared, her gun ready as well. John focused again, trying to figure out which way the guy had run, when he suddenly saw a nozzle pointed in his general direction.

"Duck!" he screamed to Virginia and they both dove for the ground.

More lightning lit up the sky, and thunder rolled over them like a tank charging into a war zone. John looked over to Virginia, but she was unharmed. He motioned for her to stay down, then looked around for anything he could use to distract the two criminals. He ripped a two-foot-long plank from one of the outer pallets, and lifted it with his left hand, waving it in the air, while he gripped his gun tightly with his right.

As expected, there was a movement on the other side of the stack. The thug fired, aiming for the plank, which splintered. John dropped it, and aimed. This time the bullet found its mark. The man dropped like a sack of potatoes.

Then another shot sounded from behind the stack.

"Got 'em," Zane confirmed through the mic.

"The three men from the ship are dead," John announced through his mic. "What about the customs guys?"

"Both dead as a doornail," Benjamin confirmed.

"Pushing up daisies," Damian added.

"Greedy bastards," Logan said dryly through the mic. "They didn't leave me anything."

"Grayson? The girls?" John asked.

"Container is locked with a chain. Ryder is getting a bolt cutter."

"Ryder? Check in."

"On my way back."

"Hurry! I'm sure we'll have company soon. Somebody will have heard the shots." Though John hoped that the thunder and the pounding rain had obscured some of the sounds.

John marched toward the red container, past the customs van, where the twins loaded the bodies into the back.

"Good thinking," he praised them on passing. At least from afar people would only see the empty customs van, and not the dead bodies. It would buy his team precious time to get away.

He pressed his mic. "Zane, get rid of the bodies of the three guys."

"Already on it."

John looked over his shoulder and saw Zane dropping one of the guys into the water. Virginia was busy searching the pockets of the second guy. Satisfied that his team was doing what needed to be done, he approached the red container, just as Ryder came around the corner and joined Enya and Grayson who were waiting there, scanning the area for anybody who might see them.

"Are we all visible again?" John asked Enya.

She nodded. "Wasn't much point wasting energy once we all got drenched."

"Okay." He nodded to Ryder. "Open it up." Then he added, "Get ready, just in case they've got a guard in there with the kids."

Both Enya and Grayson aimed their weapons at the door. Ryder used the bolt cutter on the chain, snapping the metal, then tugged on the chain to free it from the door. He looked over his shoulder.

"Open it," John instructed, "and stand back. I'm going in first."

Ryder pulled the heavy door back. As soon as John could see inside, he focused his eyes. Then relaxed.

"Weapons down," he said quietly, so as not to alarm the precious cargo. "Enya, join me. Virginia, meet us inside. The rest of you stay outside, cover us."

John slowly walked into the dark space. With his vampire vision, he could already see what a human couldn't: in the back of the container, the captured girls had huddled together in fear, clinging to each other on their mattresses.

John lifted his visor. He sighed when he saw the girls' horrified faces. "Don't be afraid. We're taking you home to your parents now," he said softly. "I'm John, and this is Enya."

There were gasps and sobs, as if the children didn't believe him. And why should they?

Behind him the door opened wider, letting in a bit more light.

With Enya by his side, John approached the girls, then crouched down when he reached the mattresses. "Jennifer? Mary? Carol?" He'd memorized their names from their files and hoped by addressing them by their names, some of their fears would dissipate. "Sarah? Jane? Cindy? Are you all okay? Andrea? Heather?"

"I'm Jane," one of the girls replied.

"Are you taking us home now?" another one whimpered.

"Yes, honey, we're taking you home now."

A few girls started crying, but several inched closer. Finally, he could see them all. His eyes darted from one to the other. And with every second, his heart pounded more violently.

"Buffy?" His pulse beat into this throat. "Buffy? Where are you?"

But the only black girl he saw didn't look like Buffy at all. He counted the girls. Twelve.

"There should be thirteen." He exchanged a panicked look with Enya, then stared back at the girls. "Where's Buffy? Where is she?"

The girl who'd identified herself as Jane came closer. "Buffy?"

He nodded and pulled a photo from a pocket in his suit, turned it to her so she could see it. "This is Buffy. Have you seen her?"

She looked at the photo, concentrated on it, then looked up. "Yes."

"Where is she?"

"The man took her."

Horror filled him. "What man? Where? When?"

"Before they put us on the ship. The man came and picked her up."

"She was never on the ship with you?"

Jane shook her head.

Tears welled up in his eyes, and he didn't bother pushing them back. "Oh, God!"

To his surprise the girl suddenly asked, "Are you her daddy?"

He met Jane's gaze. And because he didn't know how else to describe his relationship to her, he said, "I promised her Mommy to bring her home."

31

In John's office, Deirdre put the receiver back on the phone. "They're back."

Savannah pressed her hand to her chest and sighed. "Where is Buffy?"

"All the girls are downstairs in the medical center, being checked out."

Before Deirdre could even finish the sentence, Savannah was already at the door and ripped it open. "Let's go. Show me where it is."

"We can't just go down there."

"If you don't show me where it is, I'll go by myself."

"Ah, shit!" Deirdre cursed, but jumped up and joined her. "You're a pain in the butt."

"So are you."

"Yeah, well, we can't all be as cuddly as John." Deirdre's voice practically dripped of sarcasm.

They hurried to the elevators. "You don't like him much, do you?"

Deirdre shrugged. "He should have let me go to Russia with him, but no, he made me babysit you." When Savannah raised her eyebrows, she added. "No offense, but I'd rather be helping take out the assholes who took those kids than sitting around twiddling my thumbs."

The elevator doors opened, and they rushed in. Deirdre looked at the buttons and hesitated.

"Well, are we going or not?"

"Hey, don't get pissy with me." Somebody passed by the elevator and Deirdre called out to him, "Hey, which level is the medical center?"

The guy stopped, gave her a strange look, then answered, "Lower level two."

Deirdre hit the button and the elevator doors closed.

Before Savannah could comment on the fact that Deirdre didn't know where the medical center was located, Deirdre cut her off with a glare. "I just started here, okay? And it's not like I'd ever need the medical center myself."

"I didn't say anything."

"You were going to."

Savannah refrained from answering back. Clearly, the woman had issues. When the elevator door finally opened, Savannah stepped into the hallway. It wasn't very hard to figure out which way the medical facility was located, since a myriad of voices drifted to her from a set of double doors. Kids' voices.

Savannah's heart leapt, and she started running. She pushed the double doors open and rushed into the large room. Several doors led from there to other, smaller rooms. Some of them were open, and she could see girls sitting on examination benches and on chairs. In the main room, there were partitioned off areas for various purposes. Here, too, she saw many kids, as well as several adults. Vampires, she assumed.

One person she recognized from behind. "John!"

He spun around. Their eyes locked. What she saw in them turned her blood to ice. "No!" She shook her head and let her gaze wander around the large room, let it fall on each child, examine each face. She walked farther into the room, turned this way and that. But there was no sign of Buffy.

She pivoted back to John, and he was already there, already gripping her shoulders, holding her so she wouldn't collapse.

"Where is she, John? Where is my baby?" Tears stung her eyes.

"She was never on the boat. She was picked up before the ship left for Russia. The children confirmed it. A man came just before the ship left and took her with him."

She slammed her hand over her mouth, but the sob tore from her chest nevertheless. "No, no, John, no!"

John wrapped her in his arms and pressed her to his chest. "Don't give up, Savannah, because I won't. She's still in the country. She's still here. And I'm gonna find her."

"But how?" she wailed. "She's gone, my baby's gone."

"The girls gave us a description of the man who took her, and we still have the two guys who held the girls at the port in Oakland."

She looked up at him. "What makes you think they'll tell you who he is?"

"They'll talk, because I'll make them fear me. I'll show them what I will do to them if they don't tell me all they know." He slowly released her.

"You'll torture them." She made no judgement, only an observation.

"Yes."

"I want to be there."

"No. I don't want you to see this."

"I need to see it," she insisted.

He hesitated for several seconds, then reached for her hand. "Come."

John led her outside and down the corridor, then opened the door to a staircase. They descended one level, then entered another corridor.

"What happened in Russia?" she finally asked.

John gave her sideways glance. "The men involved are dead. They had a couple of customs officials on their payroll so they could smuggle the girls into the country. We got rid of them too. We went through their papers, anything they had on them. My team is currently combing through everything to see if they had anything that'll identify their boss. The girls gave us a description of the man who took Buffy away. Detective Donnelly is on his way. He's bringing a sketch artist with him so we can get a picture."

She nodded. It was a long shot, but she appreciated that John wasn't giving up.

"What'll happen to the girls?"

"We'll make sure they're healthy, feed them, clothe them. But we can't turn them over to their parents until we know where the head of the operation is holed up."

"Why not?"

"Because if he finds out we rescued the girls, he might go underground forever, and then we lose our chance of finding Buffy."

"Oh, God."

"It won't come to that. We'll keep the girls comfortable until then."

Fear nearly choked her. "But what if he already knows that you rescued the girls?"

"He doesn't. The guys in Russia had no chance of contacting anybody before they died. From what we could piece together so far, there was a truck waiting for them, and the three men who transported the girls by ship were supposed to drive them cross-country. The trip would take several days. Nobody will realize for a few days that the girls aren't on their way to their destination. Only then will whoever ordered them contact the kingpin and complain. We have time until then."

"I hope you're right."

John pointed to a door. "They're in there. Are you sure you want to be present? It might get bloody."

Savannah tipped her chin up. "You can't stop me."

"I guess I already knew that."

Using his keycard, John opened the door and marched inside ahead of her. She followed. The room was as large as her own bedroom, but it was sparsely furnished. In fact, there was no real furniture. The two cots in the room were built in, and the small table was affixed to the wall, the two chairs mere stools fastened to the concrete floor. A metal toilet without toilet seat and a tiny sink were located in one corner. The walls were bare. Neon lights on the ceiling illuminated the room.

The two men in the cell shot up on their cots. They looked worn out, their gazes guarded as they looked at John. Then they fell onto her, and both guys jolted. They recognized her, though she didn't recognize them. After all, they'd worn masks.

"Stand up!" John demanded in an icy voice.

Both men immediately stood up.

"You withheld information from me!" John thundered. "And you know what happens to people who keep things from me? They get hurt." He swiped his hand across the chest of one of the men, slicing his shirt to shreds.

The man yelled out in pain. "No! No! Stop!"

Savannah noticed the blood that now drenched the shredded shirt. John had used his claws on the man. And though it should frighten her to see the man she'd made love to use violence without flinching, she remained calm and without fear. He was doing this for her, for Buffy.

Shoving the hurt man back onto his cot with his hands pressed to his bleeding wounds, John directed his gaze to the second criminal. "Unless you want me to do the same or worse to you, you'd better talk." John flashed his fangs at the man.

"Oh God! No! What are you?" He stumbled backwards, hitting the back of his knees on the edge of the cot.

But John didn't let him fall. He snatched him by his shirt and pulled him closer. "Do we understand each other?"

Shaking, the man nodded. "Anything you want. Please, don't hurt me."

Savannah recognized his voice now. He'd been the driver the night they'd tried to kidnap her.

"There was a thirteenth girl." He motioned to Savannah. "My friend's daughter. She wasn't on the ship. According to the girls we rescued, she was never on the ship. Who was the man who picked her up?"

"I don't know."

John dug his claws into the man's shoulder, making him cry out in pain.

"I really don't know," he said quickly. "The boss sent him. He sent us a text message. Said not to put the girl on the ship; that a client, the man who'd ordered her, would come pick her up in person. We were to hand her over without questions. That's what we did." He looked to his associate for confirmation.

The injured man nodded. "It's true. That man picked her up."

"Did he have a name?"

"He didn't give one. And we didn't ask."

"What did he look like?"

The man in John's grip tried to shrug, but John's painful claws stopped him. "Like a businessman, you know, suit, nice-looking, blond, maybe around fifty. That's all, I swear. I don't know who he was."

"What else?"

The man hesitated. Then he seemed to remember something. "Yeah, he had an accent. Not sure, but it sounded Eastern European, maybe Russian, or Slavic. I don't know, I'm not good with accents."

"Another thing: when you kidnapped the little girl, were you supposed to kidnap her mother too?"

The man chanced a look at Savannah, then lowered his lids in shame. "Yes. But she wasn't there. So we took only the girl."

"Your boss ordered you to try it again, didn't he?"

Again, the man nodded.

"God, you guys aren't just evil, you're stupid too, aren't you?" John let go of the man and tossed him back on his cot. "You can rot in here for all I care."

John turned and took Savannah's elbow. "We're done here." Again he used his keycard to open the cell door and ushered her outside.

In the corridor, he looked at her. "Are you okay?"

She nodded. "What did you mean by them being stupid?"

John sighed. "They're too stupid to see it, but it's evident: the man who picked up Buffy was their boss."

"What?" Her breath hitched. "How do you know?"

"The man behind this operation has been extremely careful that nobody working for him knows too much. But then he sends a client to pick up a child from the kidnappers he employs? Exposing the location where he keeps the girls captive until they can be put on a ship? A location he presumably wants to continue using? He's not that stupid. But he counted on his henchmen to be too stupid to put two and two together. He took Buffy for himself; she was never meant for a client in Russia. And he tried to have you kidnapped after the ship had already left for Russia. He wants you and Buffy for himself."

"Oh John, how are we gonna find him? From the description the kidnapper gave, it can't be Alexi. He's blond, and he has a heavy accent, yes, but he's too young by at least twenty years. And if it's not Alexi, who then?"

"We'll know what he looks like soon. And then we'll hunt him down."

32

On his way to his office, John's cell phone pinged with a text message from reception.

Detective Donnelly here to see you.

Coming, John texted back.

He put his hand on the small of Savannah's back and ushered her down the corridor. "Donnelly is here. Let's see what he's got."

"Do you think he'll be able to help? I mean, he sent me to you in the first place," she said doubtfully.

"There's something you need to know about our relationship with the police."

"Yes?"

"Donnelly knows that we're vampires, and whenever the police suspect that a case might involve preternatural creatures like vampires and the like, he sends the case to us. So when he couldn't find any leads in the real world, he asked me to evaluate the situation and see if I could find any connection to vampires. If we don't find anything, we send the case back to them."

"Are you saying that vampires are behind this?"

"No. The fact that many of the children were kidnapped during daytime hours led me to believe that no vampires were involved. I still believe that, now even more so. None of the thugs we've encountered so far were vampires."

"But if there are no vampires involved, why didn't you send this back to Donnelly to deal with?"

John met her inquisitive gaze. "I was supposed to. But I couldn't."

Understanding suddenly lit up her eyes. "That's what that argument between you and Samson was about. He didn't want you to help me, did he?"

John sighed. He didn't want her to get the wrong impression about Samson. "Samson only did what he had to do. We're short-staffed. We didn't have the capacity to take on this case."

"But you took it anyway."

He took her hand and squeezed it. "Because I couldn't bear to see you suffer."

"But how did you convince Samson?"

John let out a slow breath. "I told him I'd quit if he didn't let me work this case."

She stopped and turned to him. "You risked your job for me?"

He'd risk much more for her if it came to it. He'd risk his life. For her and for Buffy. But she didn't need to know that. "It's just a job."

"Oh John, I don't know what to say."

"You don't have to say anything. I just need you to stay strong. We'll get through this. Will you do that?"

"Yes, John."

He tugged at her hand. "Now let's talk to Donnelly." He pushed the door at the end of the corridor open and entered the reception area.

Donnelly shot up from the seating area, and the woman sitting with him did the same. He waved. "John."

John walked to him and shook his hand. "Mike, good to see you."

Donnelly turned to Savannah. "Evening, Ms. Rice."

"Hello, Detective Donnelly."

"Grayson got me caught up on everything. I brought a sketch artist to work with the children. This is Emily Bolton."

They exchanged greetings, then John said, "Ms. Bolton, I'll have somebody escort you down to the medical facility. I believe the children are still down there being checked out."

It took only a minute for John to arrange an escort to take the sketch artist to the children, before the three of them went to John's office. Once the door was closed behind them, Donnelly sighed.

"I have some news for you too," Donnelly announced.

"I hope it's good news. We could use it," John said.

"Well, you tell me. Remember the ransom note you had analyzed? Well, there was indeed a chemical substance on it. It's actually a compound used in dry cleaning facilities. Which gives us reason to believe that the paper was stored at a dry cleaners."

"Can we narrow it down any further?"

"Afraid not."

"There must be hundreds of dry cleaners in the Bay Area," John mused.

"That's all I have. It'll take us weeks to check them all out to see if any of them might have a connection to the trafficking ring."

"We don't have time," Savannah said, her voice shaky. "We need to find Buffy now."

"I know, Ms. Rice. I understand. But I've got nothing other than a hunch on where the paper is from. There were no fingerprints, no DNA, nothing." He looked at John. "Were you able to trace the phone number used to contact the kidnappers?"

John shook his head. "No. I put Thomas on it. But we got nothing, no location, no IP address."

"IP address, that's it!" Savannah suddenly said excitedly. "The hacker."

"What about the hacker?" John asked.

"Remember how he told you that he traced his boss by the email address he used and told you that each time it came from a different location? He was able to trace the IP addresses from wherever this man sent his email communications via the malware he'd sent in his link." She snatched a quick breath. "Is the hacker still in one of your cells?"

"Yes. What do you need to know?"

"I need to find out if he kept a record of the IP addresses. And if the malware is still active and still sending data back to him."

John reached for the phone and dialed a number. The call connected immediately. "Thomas? Can you talk to Otto Watson, the hacker we've got locked up downstairs, and ask him whether he kept a record of the IP addresses he tracked his boss's email address to? Apparently, he tricked his boss into installing malware on his computer that tracks his IP."

"Clever guy. When do you need it by?"

"Five minutes ago."

"I'm on it."

"Oh, and Thomas, when you have those IP addresses, send them to my computer. And can you somehow check whether the malware is still sending back any data we can use to pinpoint him in real time?"

"Sure."

John hung up and looked at Savannah. "It won't be long." He moved behind his desk and sat down, then quickly logged into his computer. He turned up the volume on his notifications, then drummed his fingers on the desk.

Savannah started pacing. Donnelly rounded the desk and leaned against it, looking down at John.

"So, uh, Grayson said, the kidnappers were just, uh, regular guys, right? Any chance their boss is different?" he asked cautiously.

"Mike, you can stop being cryptic. Savannah knows about us. She knows what I am." He slanted Savannah a look and she met it. "And she's not afraid of us." She'd touched his fangs, kissed him, trusted him. He couldn't ask for more.

Donnelly said, "Oh, well, then we're on the same page. So, you don't think the kingpin is a vampire?"

"I can't be sure, but at this point I see nothing that makes me suspect that he is. The kids didn't know what time of day it was when he came to take Buffy."

Just then, the computer pinged, and John looked at the screen. Thomas had sent him a file. He opened it. "The IP addresses. And a note. Thomas thinks the guy might have ditched his computer. Nothing has pinged back from it in the last couple of days." He looked at Savannah. "What do you need me to do now?"

Savannah was already walking around the desk. "Let me sit. I'll do it."

He made way for her and let her take his seat.

He watched her as her fingers flew over the keyboard and her right hand clicked the mouse, copying and pasting items, plotting them on a map, and doing so over and over again. She was confident in what she was doing, and driven. Ten minutes later, she turned her head. "I've got all the locations. Detective, we just need to overlay this map with one containing all dry cleaners in the area and see if any match."

Donnelly nodded. "No problem. Let me do that." He motioned to the keyboard. "May I?"

Savannah got up and Donnelly took her seat. "I'll just need to log into our database," he explained. "Give me a sec."

John put his hand on Savannah's shoulder, squeezing it gently, and she smiled at him for the first time since he'd returned from Russia with bad news. Finally, he could see hope blossoming in her eyes again.

"Here we go," Donnelly said after a few moments and pointed to the screen showing a large map of the city. "Bingo." He pointed to several of the locations that Savannah had marked. "All these are dry cleaners, or dry cleaning facilities. This is good. I'll make a few calls, see what the department has on these locations and the owners and their employees. It might take an hour or two. Can I stay here and use your office?"

"Of course," John said. "We'll help you with anything you need."

Donnelly waved him off. "Nothing for you to do right now. Why don't you take a few moments to relax and let me work on this?"

"I get the feeling you're throwing me out of my own office," John said with a raised eyebrow.

"Glad you got the hint. I'll ping you when I've got something."

John nodded. "Come, Savannah."

"I can't just do nothing."

"You've done enough," he assured her.

"But there must be something I can do."

Donnelly looked up from the computer. "Why don't you see how the kids are? I'm sure they'd love to see a friendly face."

Grateful for Donnelly's suggestion, John took Savannah's hand. "I think that's a brilliant idea."

33

When Savannah and John reached the medical center in the basement, it was empty except for the doctor, whom John introduced as Maya, and one child, who suffered from dehydration and lay in a hospital bed, a drip attached to her arm.

"Where is everybody?" John asked.

"We checked all the kids out; they're fine. And hungry. They're all up in the H lounge," Maya said. "I ordered some food for this little one here." She smiled at the child in the bed and ran her hand over her head. "Chocolate ice cream and cookies, right?"

The little girl, who was a little shorter than Buffy and probably only nine years old, smiled weakly.

"Why don't you guys go up to the H lounge and see what's taking them so long?" Maya suggested.

"Sure thing," John agreed.

On their way up, Savannah asked, "H lounge, that was the lounge where you brought me, right? What does H stand for?"

"Human," John said without hesitation. "It's meant for our human employees and guests. There's also a V lounge." He cast her a quick look, as if to check whether he should continue. "Only vampires are allowed there, because we serve blood there."

"What do you mean by serve? Do you keep humans there to drink from?"

John chuckled unexpectedly. "No. Of course not. There's a bar with blood on tap. The company purchases it from a blood bank."

"Does that mean you don't drink from humans? You don't bite them?" If that was the case, it would mean they were rather civilized.

"Yes and no."

When she raised an eyebrow, he continued. "Some of us live entirely on bottled blood, others drink from their human mates, few of us go out to hunt these days. We prefer to have permission to drink from a human. It's more gratifying."

"Gratifying?" She wasn't sure what he meant by that.

He sighed. "A vampire's bite is very sensual. Many of us like to combine the act of feeding with the act of sex, because it heightens the pleasure."

"For the vampire?"

"For both partners, the human, too. That's why we prefer to drink from those we are drawn to sexually and emotionally. It's a way for us to share ourselves with our human partners."

"But doesn't that mean you're turning them into vampires too, I mean, by biting them?"

"That's not how it works. Only in death can a human be turned."

"I guess television got a lot of things wrong then."

"They also got a lot of things right. But we're not the bloodthirsty monsters they make us out to be on *Buffy the Vampire Slayer*. We're more like *Angel* than *Nosferatu*. Sometimes troubled by our wish to hold onto our humanity, but also driven by our need for blood. It's a delicate balance."

She contemplated his words. "I can see that. But you seem to be in control of that need."

They stopped in front of the H lounge, and John gave her a long look. "Savannah, I wish I could say you're right. But I'm not in control, not when I'm around you. There were many times, when I wanted nothing more than to sink my fangs into your lovely neck and drink from you. And it took every ounce of my strength not to do it. I don't know how long I can still hold back that need."

She gasped, and her chest lifted. With parted lips, she stared at him. But it wasn't fear that paralyzed her. It was something he'd said earlier, that the bite would heighten her pleasure.

"I don't want you to be afraid of me. I know this is not the time to ask your permission, not with everything you're going through, and I would never act without your consent, but when this is over… when this is behind us… I will ask for permission."

She shivered involuntarily.

John opened the door to the lounge for her, clearly not expecting an answer, and ushered her inside. The kids were running around, filling plates with food, marveling at the many choices, and looking happy and relaxed. A large number of adults, mostly women, mingled with them. Each woman seemed to have taken charge of one girl, focusing all her attention on the child, and catering to her every need.

"Who are all these women? Are they vampires?" Savannah whispered to John.

"Some of them are, but some of them are human. Most are the wives and daughters of the vampires who run Scanguards. Samson's wife is here, Delilah." He pointed to a beautiful woman with long dark hair and a warm smile who was handing a napkin to a little girl whose mouth was covered with chocolate. "And you met their daughter already, Isabelle. She's a hybrid."

"A hybrid? What is that?"

"She's part human, part vampire."

"Does that mean her mother is human?"

"Yes."

Savannah ran her eyes over Delilah. She wore a casual dress with a plunging neckline, revealing her flawless neck. There were no blemishes on her skin. "You said a vampire bites his partner. But I see no marks on her neck."

"And you won't, though he likely drinks from her every night." She felt John's hand on the small of her back, gently touching her. "When we bite our partners, we seal the puncture wounds with our saliva to heal them instantly. It prevents the skin from scarring."

Savannah felt heat radiate through her. "Oh."

"And we don't always drink from the neck." She felt him move closer, so she could feel his hot breath at her ear. "There are many inviting spots." Her nipples pebbled. "Like those."

Suddenly he stepped away, dropping his lids as if ashamed. "I'm sorry, Savannah. I got carried away. I shouldn't talk to you like that. It's not the right time. Not the right place."

She reached for his hand and squeezed it. "I owe you so much. For everything you're doing."

He shook his head. "Please promise me something. If and when you say yes, don't do it because you think you owe me something. You don't. I'm doing this as much for me as for you. I lost a child. I know what it feels like. And I don't want you to go through it. I'm doing this because I couldn't save my own child. You don't owe me anything. All you owe me is a truthful answer. Whenever you're ready for it."

"You're an honorable man, John. You're more than any woman could ever hope for."

He smiled. "Come, why don't I introduce you to Delilah?"

As if she'd heard them, Delilah looked in their direction and waved for John and Savannah to join her.

"Delilah, this is Savannah," John introduced them. "Savannah, this is Delilah, Samson's wife."

When Savannah shook Delilah's hand, John added, "I've filled Savannah in on everything. She knows about us."

Delilah smiled. "I'm glad. I hate hiding things, but sometimes it's necessary."

Then John looked past her and said, "I see Samson. Excuse me for a moment." He marched away to the far end of the lounge, where Samson stood talking to Amaury. They were the only other men in the room, and were keeping to themselves, maybe so as not to frighten the young girls who seemed to feel comfortable in the company of the other women.

In another corner, the sketch artist Detective Donnelly had brought to Scanguards was sitting at a table with two girls, who were talking animatedly and making gestures to describe the man they'd seen.

"I'm sorry to hear that your daughter is still missing," Delilah said.

Savannah sighed. "I think we have a lead. Detective Donnelly is working on it right now. But the waiting is driving me crazy."

Delilah smiled at the little girl who sat next to her on the large sectional. "More ice cream?" she asked.

"May I?" the girl asked excitedly.

When Delilah nodded, the girl jumped up and ran to a cart that seemed to have been brought in specially and looked at the display of different ice cream flavors.

"It's so nice of you all to do this for the kids," Savannah said.

"We figured they'd be hungry, and we wanted to take their minds off what they've been through. So, when Samson told me that the kids had arrived, I called all the other wives and asked them to come." She pointed around the room. "The blonde with the pixie haircut is Nina, Amaury's wife. And you've met her boys, the twins, Benjamin and Damian."

"She's their mother?" Savannah's mouth gaped open. "But she can't be older than twenty-five herself!"

"Actually, she must be forty-eight or forty-nine now. I lose track."

"That's impossible. And you don't look like you could have a son Grayson's age either."

"Well, thank you. But I assure you, he's my son. But we don't age, you know, Nina, myself, and the other wives."

Savannah leaned closer and dropped her voice so none of the nearby children could overhear them. "But John said you're human."

"I am. But we're blood-bonded to our vampire husbands. And as long as they're alive, we remain the age we were when we first bonded."

"So you're immortal?"

"Not exactly. We can die."

"Like John's wife?"

A sad smile flashed over Delilah's face. "He told you about that?"

Savannah nodded.

"It was tragic. But, yes, we can die from accidents just like any human, but we remain young and healthy, and our husbands' blood can heal injuries and illnesses we might contract."

"Your husband's blood. Are you saying…" She couldn't finish the sentence or the thought.

"Yes, I drink his blood on occasion. That's what keeps our bond strong, and my body young."

Stunned, Savannah stared at Delilah. A human who drank a vampire's blood? She'd never imagined that. There were a lot of things she'd never imagined. She'd never imagined this world she'd been thrown into. But it was real.

Delilah chuckled, when a young Chinese woman holding a little Asian girl by the hand walked past their seating area. "Ursula, let me introduce you."

She approached with the child.

"This is Savannah Rice; Savannah this is Ursula. She's Oliver's wife. You probably haven't met him yet, but you will."

"Pleased to meet you, Ursula," Savannah said and shook hands with her.

"We're all keeping Buffy in our thoughts," she said. "She'll make it through this. I can feel it." Then she motioned to the girl tugging at her hand. "I think somebody wants more cookies." She allowed the girl to pull her toward the food area.

Delilah laughed. "Their parents are gonna be annoyed with us for spoiling them like this."

"Their parents won't mind, as long as they've got their little ones back." Tears suddenly stung in Savannah's eyes.

The girl Delilah had been taking care of came back with a large bowl of ice cream. "Are you crying?"

Savannah sniffled. "No, honey, I've just got something in my eyes."

"Oh, okay. But it looks like you're crying." She offered Savannah her bowl. "Do you want some of my ice cream?"

At that, tears started running down her cheeks. A girl who only hours ago had been locked up in a dark and dirty shipping container was offering to console her. There was still so much good in this world, despite all the evil.

And now Savannah had the support of all of Scanguards, a company of vampires and preternatural creatures more powerful than she could have ever imagined.

"We'll find Buffy," Delilah said softly. "We'll find her."

34

John was watching Savannah from a corner of the H lounge where the assembled men had withdrawn in order to not disturb the children, when the door opened and Donnelly entered. John waved to the detective to join him, Samson, and Amaury. He'd been relieved to see that Samson was in the room. It had given him an excuse to leave Savannah. Just in time, because ever since they'd started talking about blood, his need to bite her had grown by leaps and bounds. And he knew it was wrong in so many ways. She was a mother in fear for her child, and not in the right frame of mind to make any kind of decision, let alone the decision to allow a vampire to bite her. He was a bastard for even having these thoughts at a time like this.

Donnelly greeted them all and immediately reported his news. "I've got something. SFPD's organized crime unit has been looking at an individual who's suspected of money laundering. They haven't been able to prove anything so far, and that's why this case has been under the radar, and I hadn't heard anything about it. But listen to this: the guy owns a string of dry cleaners under various business names. Incidentally, the IP addresses our hacker, Otto Watson, was able to trace from the emails he received, lead back to several of these dry cleaning shops."

"Finally, something!" John let out.

"Not so fast, John. We have a name, but not much else. The organized crime unit doesn't have a location for him. He moves around too much, and they don't have the resources to surveil every single one of his business locations."

"Who is he?" John asked.

"Name's Sergei Viktorov, Russian national. Immigration has no information on him ever even entering the country. We assume that he's here under a false name, but we've not been able to find anything further on that."

"A Russian, that fits," John said. "What else?"

"They sent over a photo, but as I said, since immigration has no record of him, and the DMV hasn't got anything for a Sergei Viktorov either, we can't even be sure it's him." He reached into the pocket and pulled out a photo. "I printed it out on your printer. But the colors are a bit off."

"Let me see it," John demanded and took the picture from Donnelly.

John perused the picture. Just like the children and the two kidnappers had said, the man was in his fifties and blond.

"My colleagues told me something else, too."

John lifted his gaze back to Donnelly. "What's that?"

"Rumor is that Viktorov has a preference for young meat, sisters, twins, mothers and daughters. According to Vice, some prostitutes in the Tenderloin reported that a man matching his description has offered to pay for women who would bring their virgin daughters with them so one would watch while he fucked the other."

"Disgusting asshole!" Samson cursed.

"Fucking bastard," John grunted. "It sounds like him." And he'd set his sight on Savannah and Buffy. John's blood started to boil at the thought of what Viktorov was planning.

"Are you okay if I show this picture to the girls?" Donnelly asked.

"Let's compare it to what your sketch artist has come up with first," John suggested.

Donnelly was already turning in the direction of the sketch artist, when John saw Savannah approaching them. Quickly he said to Donnelly, "Mike, not a word about Viktorov's reputation to Savannah. It'll only upset her, and it won't serve any purpose."

"Understood."

Savannah made a beeline for Donnelly. "Do you have news?"

Donnelly cast a quick glance at John, then nodded. "We think we know who it is. A Russian named Sergei Viktorov. I was just about to compare the photo we got to what the sketch artist has drawn."

"Let me see." She took the photo from Donnelly's hand and looked at it. Her mouth dropped open. "Oh, no! Oh God no!"

With one step, John was by her side and gripped her arm. "What's wrong?"

She looked at him, eyes wide, while she lifted the photo higher. "This man, I know him. He came to my office. He shook my hand." Her face distorted in disgust.

"Who is he?" John asked.

"Viktor Stricklund. He claimed to be from Sweden. Wanted a business meeting about cyber security for his company." She choked out the words. "Oh, God, John, that's how he knew about you. He said my assistant arranged the meeting, but I couldn't check with Rachel, because she was out sick. He probably never had an appointment. He must have somehow found out that Rachel was out sick and then pretended that she set up the meeting, knowing I couldn't verify it. And when Alexi told him that I had a family emergency, I told him that my daughter had disappeared." She swallowed. "He pretended to be concerned. He offered his help, said he knew people who could search for her. To get rid of him, I told him that I'd already hired a private investigator." Tears now ran down her cheeks. "He played me. And I didn't see it."

John nodded. "He's brazen. He wanted to make sure he knew what steps you'd taken. I assume he showed up in your office before you received the ransom note?"

She nodded.

John exchanged a look with Donnelly. "Show the picture to the kids. Confirm that he's the same guy who took Buffy."

Donnelly nodded, took the picture back and walked to the sketch artist and the two kids she was working with. John pulled Savannah into his arms. "We'll get him, darlin', we'll get him now."

John caught Samson's look, as the Scanguards CEO said, "I'll have Thomas run his photo through our database, just in case."

John knew he was referring to the database of known vampires across the country that Scanguards had put together. "Thanks."

"And I'm sure Thomas or Eddie can get into the servers of

Homeland Security to see if anything comes up under a Swedish national named Viktor Stricklund. Maybe that's the passport he travels under," Amaury added.

Savannah turned in John's arms, wiped her tears away and addressed Samson and Amaury, "I'm sorry. I shouldn't fall apart like this. Thank you for all your help. I'm so grateful. But I'm sure the name he gave me is just as fake as everything else about him. We won't find him like that." She sniffled. "There's only one way he'll show himself."

John gripped her shoulders and made her look at him.

She met his gaze. "And we all know what will draw him out."

John shook his head. Without her saying it, he knew what she meant. "No! I won't allow it."

"It's not your choice, John. It's mine."

He saw red right there and then. With a quick nod at his bosses, he bit out an "Excuse us" and snatched Savannah by her arm, dragging her toward the nearest door.

"John, let go of me!" she protested, but he ignored her and flung the door open that led into the kitchen and supply rooms adjacent to the lounge.

"We're gonna have a word," he bit out and dragged her along the corridor and around the corner, glancing at the signs on the doors, until he found one saying *Break Room*. He pushed the door open and entered with Savannah in tow.

A female employee sat at a table, reading a magazine and drinking a coffee. She whipped her head in their direction.

"Out!" John commanded, and the woman scrambled to her feet and rushed out of the room. When the door shut behind her, John let go of Savannah and flipped the lock shut so nobody could barge in and interrupt them.

When he turned back to Savannah, she glared at him, her hands braced on her hips. "What the fuck, John?"

"That was gonna be my line!" he replied just as furious. "Are you fucking crazy proposing what I think you are? Offering yourself as bait to this madman?"

She narrowed her eyes. "Not as bait! I'm offering myself in exchange for Buffy. So she doesn't have to live through this nightmare any longer."

"That's fucking nuts! He'll never let her go if you offer yourself. He'll take you both! That was his plan all along. And now you want to deliver yourself to him on a silver platter? Over my fucking charred body!"

"It's not your decision! She's my daughter! And I'll fucking do what I think is best."

"The fuck you will!"

"You can't stop me!"

"Can't I? Watch me!"

"You have no right to tell me what to do!"

"I don't care whether I have the right or not! I'm not gonna stand here and watch you put yourself in danger." Because it would break him. It would shatter what was left of his heart.

"You have to."

"No! I'm not gonna lose you. I've been through this once. I'm not gonna do it again. I'm not gonna let the woman I love walk into certain doom. I won't do it. Damn it!"

Savannah's eyes widened, and she sucked in a shaky breath.

Had he suddenly scared her into submission? "What? Damn it, Savannah!"

She shook her head. "You love me?"

Only then did he realize what he'd said. For a second, he froze. But he knew it was true. "I love you more than I thought I could ever love again. And not just you. I love Buffy. I love her like the child I lost. I love her because she's part of you. And I'll do anything to get her back for you. But I can't let you do this. I can't lose you both."

Tears started welling up in her eyes, and she sniffled. "Oh, John. I didn't know… After what you told me about Nicolette… I didn't think you could feel anything…"

He sucked in a much-needed breath of air, and with it, some of his rage dissipated. "I didn't either. But, you, Savannah, you made me feel again. And I can't throw that away. I can't let this bastard steal that from me. From us."

She took a step toward him and put her hand on his chest. When she lifted her gaze to look at him, there was calm determination shining from her eyes. "If you truly love me, then you have to let me go. Buffy is part of me. If I don't do this for her, I'll never be able to forgive myself. And I'll never be happy again. It would kill the love I have for you. Because I do love you. I don't know how it happened or why."

John put his hand over hers. Knowing that she loved him, that she felt for him what he felt for her, would have been the most joyous revelation he could have ever imagined, had it not been for her request to let her go.

"But what if he takes you both?"

"You'll make sure that he won't. I trust you. I trust you to save Buffy. And once she's safe, then you'll come for me too. I'll trust in that too. And then we'll be together. All three of us."

He knew her mind was made up. No matter how long he argued with her, Savannah wouldn't change her decision. Resigned, he said, "We'll do as you say. Under one condition."

"What condition?"

"You let me drink your blood now."

35

John's request stunned her into silence. Ever since he'd told her about the effect a vampire's bite had on a human, Savannah hadn't been able to get the thought out of her head.

"I'm not asking because I crave your blood, though I do, but because it will help me track you if anything goes wrong during the exchange."

She tilted her head to the side, looking at him quizzically. "Track me? How?"

"If I have your blood in me, I'll be able to follow your trail in case he takes you away. Vampires have a strong sense of smell, like bloodhounds. With your blood in me I'll be able to track you over long distances. It'll ensure that I won't lose you."

"But why not use an electronic tracker?"

"We have to assume that he'll take every precaution and search you. If he suspects you're wearing a tracker, he might have you strip."

At that thought, Savannah felt a shudder of disgust run down her spine. "You're right. It's best."

"I'm sorry," he said. "This is not how I imagined it. I hadn't planned on forcing this on you. I wanted you to choose freely. To decide for yourself if, and when, I would bite you." He dropped his lids and looked away. "I know you're not ready for this. It's not the right place, or the right time. I'll make it quick."

Savannah put her hand under his chin and lifted it, so he had to meet her gaze. "And shortchange me?" She shook her head, smiling. "Oh, John. Please don't make it quick. Do it the way you wanted our first time to be. I want to experience what it's like to feel your fangs piercing my skin. You told me it was a pleasurable act. Let me feel that pleasure." Because if something went wrong, then this would be their first and last time. If Viktorov managed to snatch her away, or if he killed her when he realized that he'd lost, this would be their only time.

But she couldn't say that. She couldn't give those thoughts voice.

"Are you sure, darlin'?"

"I've never been so sure of anything. Show me what it's like to love a vampire and to be loved by him. Show me what my future will be like." If she indeed had a future. If she was so lucky.

John pulled her to him, sliding one arm around her waist. His chocolate-colored eyes turned molten, a golden shimmer framing his irises. "I will always cherish this moment, though if I had a choice I would do this differently. But I can promise you that what you feel will be my true self."

He slanted his lips over her mouth and kissed her gently, nibbling softly on her lips, his tongue sliding over the seam of it to ask for entry. On a breath, she parted her lips and received him. Her tongue met his for a dance as old as time. Immediately arousal swept through her cells. He could do that to her in an instant, fill her body with the kind of need only he could satisfy.

Already, she felt his hands on her clothes, felt him undressing her, shoving her top over her head to lay her torso bare. She felt his hands on her breasts then, kneading them, teasing her nipples. But they didn't stay there. Instead they got to work on her pants.

"John, I thought you wanted to drink my blood," she said, panting.

"I do," he said, his voice thick with lust, "but I have to be inside you. For our first time, I need to make love to you when I bite you."

"Oh God!" She glanced around the room. A kitchenette in one corner, a row of lockers along another wall, a small table and several chairs. "How? Where?"

"Don't worry about that, darlin'," he assured her and stripped her of her pants. Then he opened his cargo pants and shoved them and his boxer briefs down to mid-thigh.

His cock sprang free, hard and heavy, ready to impale her. She reached for his erection, wrapped her hand around it, and felt it twitch in her palm.

But then he lifted her up and moved them both a few steps, until her back connected with the wall. He held her there, suspended, as if she were as light as a feather. He pressed his body to hers, spreading her legs, and she wrapped them around him.

His hard-on nudged at her center.

"My God, you're wet," he groaned and plunged into her without preamble. As if nailing her to the wall.

A shudder charged through her body, and her interior muscles spasmed around him.

"Just like that, darlin', that's exactly what I need." He drew back his hips and thrust back into her. His eyes were fully golden now, and his lips had parted, showing the tips of his fangs.

She reached for his face, and he didn't draw back. With her index finger, she touched one fang and caressed it. His cock spasmed inside her, thrusting wildly.

"Fuck!" he cursed.

Breathing heavily, he severed the contact to her finger and dipped his head to the crook of her neck. Savannah obliged him and tilted her head to the side to give him better access, to offer herself to him.

"Take me, John, I'm yours."

She felt his tongue lick over her skin and shivered. Her entire body began to tingle pleasantly. Then she felt them, the sharp tips of his fangs touching her skin, exerting pressure, and then, suddenly, a sharp pain that lasted only a millisecond. Finally, she felt his fangs drive deeper, lodge in her neck, settle there, and draw blood from her vein.

Even though John had prepared her for this feeling, had told her how pleasurable it was, she wasn't prepared. Everything around her began to disappear. Her vision swam, nothing seemed to be in focus, because all she could see and feel and hear and smell was John. He was all around her, inside her, with her. With every draw on her vein, every drop of blood he took from her, he gave her something else: utter bliss. Not just physical pleasure, but emotional satisfaction too. Her body hummed with energy, with hope and love.

While John drank from her, his hips worked frantically and his strong arms held her suspended against the wall. He was pounding into her now, his cock stiffer and thicker than she'd ever felt before. As if her blood was filling his cock so he could take her even harder. His pelvic bone slammed against her clit with every thrust, igniting her over and over again. Waves of pleasure traveled through her, and there seemed to be no end in sight.

She felt dizzy with pleasure now, while orgasm after orgasm claimed her body. Yet she didn't want him to stop. "More, oh John, take more."

She heard him moan and thought she could hear his heart beat like a drum against her every time their bodies slammed together. She clung to him, her fingernails digging into his shoulders to urge him on, her ankles crossed behind his back to drive his cock deeper into her. She was wild now, wilder than she'd ever been before. If only she'd known that something like this was possible, that a man like John existed. No, not a man. A vampire. Her vampire.

Suddenly, she felt him spasm inside her. Warmth filled her channel, and cool air wafted against her neck. John had withdrawn his fangs. Now he licked over the incisions, then kissed the spot gently.

When he lifted his head to look at her, his eyes were as red as a traffic light. But within seconds, they turned back to their golden color. His erection was still inside her, still moving, though much slower now.

He moved his head from side to side as if shaking it, as if he was unable to understand what had happened between them.

"This is more than I ever expected. It's a miracle to find love once, but to find it a second time is more than that."

She caressed his cheek lovingly. "It's fate."

And if fate allowed it, they would have a future. Together.

36

Savannah had used the hacker's email to send a message to Sergei Viktorov.

I'll offer myself in exchange for Buffy's release. Choose the time and place. Bring Buffy. I will surrender when I see her. Savannah Rice, she'd written. After discussing with John and several others at Scanguards that Viktorov would wonder whether the police and her private investigator were on his tail, she'd added a postscript. *Did you really think I wouldn't figure out that you used a second-rate hacker to get access to my daughter's photos? Unfortunately, he was too stupid to figure out how to find you. I wish you'd worked with somebody smarter. I guess you won.*

The message was meant to reassure Viktorov that Savannah had no idea who he really was and how to find him. It had its desired effect. Within two hours, Viktorov replied. He'd specified a meeting place and threatened that he would kill Buffy if he so much as got a whiff of Savannah's private investigator or the police, or if she was even a minute late. The little time he allowed for Savannah to get to the meeting place ensured that Scanguards had no time to prepare a counter-offensive.

The exchange was on.

"Do everything he says," John instructed her now, his hands framing her face, his voice soft. "Trust me. You might not see me, you might not hear me, but I will be there. Wherever you go, I'll be close-by. Don't look for me. Don't try to communicate with me. I don't want him to become suspicious."

Savannah nodded. "I trust you."

John pressed a kiss to her lips, then leaned his forehead to hers. "This ends tonight. I promise you. Now go."

He released her, and she turned on her heel and left Scanguards' headquarters through the front door. She shivered, both from fear and the cool night air, but she didn't look back. John had kept all his promises until now, and she knew he would keep this one too.

At a brisk pace, she walked several blocks, then turned west on 18th Street and continued walking as fast as she could. She checked her watch to make sure she would make it and increased her speed. Her heart beat faster, not just because of the increased cardio activity, but also because she was afraid. Afraid that something would go wrong, afraid that Viktorov wouldn't be bringing Buffy and was leading her into a trap. But she had to accept that risk.

At Guerrero Street, a major thoroughfare, the pedestrian light turned red just as she reached the intersection. She looked at her wristwatch again, then at the traffic. It was coming up on midnight, and the normally busy traffic in the area was easing up. Without waiting for the light to turn green, she dashed across the lanes. A car driving way too fast honked at her, but she continued running and reached the other side in time. She didn't break her stride and continued running to the end of the next block. Across the other side of Dolores Street, she saw the popular park that stretched up the hill. The pedestrian light to cross to the park was green, and she hurried along, racing alongside the park until she reached the next corner: Church Street. This was the spot Viktorov had chosen for the exchange.

She stopped at the corner, her chest heaving, her heart pounding. Her eyes darted around the area. A homeless man hung around the entrance of an apartment building on the opposite side of the street, and two youngsters were smoking and drinking nearby. From farther up on Church Street, she heard a streetcar approaching.

She glanced around the parked cars, but they all appeared empty. Nobody's engine was running. Where the hell was Viktorov? Was he playing with her?

A ringing cell phone startled her. She whirled around, trying to see who had approached her without her noticing. There was nobody. Yet the ringing continued. Looking left and right, she saw nobody. The same ringtone continued. She zeroed in on it. It seemed to be coming from a trashcan. Carefully, she approached and saw a faint light. There, in the area above the trash receptacle that was reserved for recycling, lay a cell phone. She reached for it and pressed the accept button.

"About time, Savannah," a male voice said.

She recognized it immediately: Viktor Stricklund, the man who'd had the audacity to come to her office and offer his help. But she couldn't give away that she knew who he was. "Yes?" she said instead, allowing her fear to color her voice.

There was a movement next to her, and from the corner of her eye she saw the streetcar slowing for its stop. Two people got off, one was a man in a business suit, a scarf around his neck and a hat pulled deep into his face.

"I'm glad we're finally connecting," Viktorov said on the phone.

She stared at the man who was now coming toward her, but he wasn't holding a phone in his hand.

"But before we can meet in person," Viktorov continued, "I need to make sure you're alone."

"I'm alone," she insisted.

"Whatever you say. See the MUNI train? Get on it. Now."

The stranger walked past her without stopping. There was a beeping sound, indicating that the doors of the train were about to close. Savannah ran to the nearest door and jumped onto the steps. Seconds later, the doors closed and the train was in motion.

"Hello?" she said into the phone, but Viktorov had disconnected the call.

She dropped onto the nearest seat and glanced around without trying to be too obvious. Maybe a dozen people were in this carriage, and though she couldn't see everybody's face, nobody looked like Viktorov in terms of size and stature.

For several minutes, the train continued on its route, stopping once and letting off passengers. Nobody got on the train. What was Viktorov trying to do? Where the hell was he?

The cell phone in her hand rang again. She picked it up immediately. "Yes?"

"At the next stop get off the train. Then walk one block to Duboce Avenue and get onto the N-Judah train heading outbound."

Before she could say anything, he'd disconnected the call. Savannah jumped up from her seat and walked to the door. Moments later the train stopped and she touched the handlebar to open the door. On the sidewalk she turned left and hurried to the next intersection. The N-train was already coming out of the tunnel, and she had to run to get to the stop on the other side of the street to catch it.

Breathing heavily, Savannah reached the last door of the train and got on. She let herself fall into the nearest seat and looked around. There were more people on this train than the previous one, but she knew that was normal. The N-train was always busy.

Clutching the cell phone with both hands, she stared down at it, willing it to ring. It didn't. After another stop, the train entered a tunnel, and for the minute and a half that it made its way through it, the cell phone lost the signal. When the train finally emerged on the other side, and stopped right after the tunnel, the signal finally came back. She kept staring at the display, wondering if she'd missed a call, but nothing happened. The train continued on its route, another stop, and more people got off, then another one. And still no word from Viktorov.

Cold sweat was now running down Savannah's back. If Viktorov was doing this to make her even more nervous than she already was, it was working.

The ringing of the cell phone in her hand nearly stopped her heart.

"Yes?"

"Get off at the next stop. Walk up Hillway Avenue. On Parnassus, turn left, then take Medical Center Way."

Again, he disconnected the call immediately after his short instructions.

She did as he said, and alighted at the next stop. She crossed the street and looked up. Hillway Avenue was one of the steepest streets in San Francisco. Already exhausted, she started climbing it. By the time she reached the top, she needed to take a deep breath of air and a few seconds to calm her thundering heart. This was Parnassus, the location of the UCSF Medical Center. She'd been here many times with Buffy. She'd given birth to her here.

It was foggy and windy up here, and she shivered. There was little traffic now. Savannah crossed the street and headed for Medical Center Way, a dimly lit winding way that led behind the hospital and its research facilities up on the hill. A deep forest of Eucalyptus trees and other trees and shrubs provided a greenspace next to the concrete buildings.

She hurried along the narrow, deserted street, and the cell phone rang again. She pressed the button to answer it, but didn't even get a chance to reply.

"Take the stairs on the left. All the way up."

She stopped and looked up to her left. There, in the dark, was indeed a set of stairs, leading up the steep hill. She could have easily missed them. Breathing hard, she set her foot on the first step. She heard a sound behind her and spun around. But there was nothing. Only darkness.

Her nerves were frayed, she knew it. And her body was exhausted. It was what Viktorov intended. He wanted to make sure that she wouldn't have any energy left to fight. And she had no choice but to comply.

It took several minutes for her to make it up to the top. When she set her foot on the pavement of the parking lot she'd reached, she looked down at the display of the cell phone. Where would he send her next?

"Welcome!"

Savannah snapped her head up and stared at the middle of the parking lot. Every drop of blood in her body froze in her veins.

"Oh, no! Oh God no!" she cried out.

37

Still invisible, like John and Logan had been during the entire pursuit through the city, John froze the moment he and his Stealth Guardian companion cleared the stairs and reached the parking lot a few steps behind Savannah. What he saw was worse than he'd expected.

Viktorov was indeed waiting for Savannah, and he had, as promised, brought Buffy with him. John had expected Viktorov to have a gun to Buffy's head or maybe a knife, something to ensure that Savannah made no false move, and that anybody approaching, trying to save Buffy, would think twice about it for fear Viktorov would kill the child before a rescuer could reach her.

In fact, John had been counting on it. Hence he'd devised his plan to approach invisibly with Logan's help. Logan was cloaking him with his mind, eliminating the need to touch. What John hadn't counted on was that Viktorov would go far beyond a gun or a knife: he had blindfolded Buffy and put her in a suicide vest. This changed everything.

Buffy stood about twenty yards away from Viktorov, who was leaning casually against the back of a dark SUV. She was slouched against the thick post of a street lamp that illuminated the otherwise empty parking lot high above UCSF Medical Center, her hands tied behind her back so she couldn't run away. Nor could she see what was going on around her, which probably added to her fear.

"Well," Viktorov said in a casual voice, "we're finally all together. Remember me?"

"I remember you. Now let her go, let Buffy go. You've got me like you wanted," Savannah replied.

"Mommy? Mommy?" Buffy cried out.

"Yes, baby, I'm here now."

Buffy started crying. John exchanged a look with Logan, indicating with signs what to do next. Logan understood and nodded. Making sure he made no sound, John walked across the parking lot to Buffy until he was behind the pole she was tied to.

"Everything will be fine, baby," Savannah reassured her daughter.

"Yeah, about that," Viktorov said and chuckled. "Slight change of plans. You're both coming with me."

"You bastard!" Savannah yelled at him.

"Buffy," John whispered into the girl's ear. Her head jerked up in response and she began to struggle against her ties. "Don't say anything now. Just listen. I'm your Mommy's friend. I'm going to untie you."

Buffy stopped struggling, while John blocked out the conversation that was now unfolding between Viktorov and Savannah.

"Good. I'll cut the rope around your wrists, but you have to pretend you're still tied up. Can you do that? We don't want the bad man to see that I'm freeing you. Okay?"

She nodded, but didn't speak.

"You're a brave girl," he praised her and willed his fingers to turn into sharp claws. With them, he sliced through the rope, caught it, and quietly laid it on the ground.

"Let her go!" Savannah demanded again.

"You see, I can't do that," Viktorov said. "The moment I saw the picture of you and her together, I knew what I'd been missing. A mother and daughter, both beautiful in their own right, but together, stunning!"

"Don't!" Savannah snapped.

"Oh please, as if you don't have your own fantasies. We all have them. I'm just more liberated and willing to act on them. You'll see. You'll enjoy it in the end."

John wanted to curse. Sick bastard! He rose again behind the pole and put one hand on Buffy's shoulder.

"Now we need to get this vest off you. Bend your upper body forward a little. Slowly so he doesn't notice what you're doing." Luckily, Viktorov was currently concentrating on Savannah.

Guided by John's hand, Buffy moved away from the pole a few inches.

"That's good, Buffy. Now stay still. You'll feel my hands at your back. I need to make sure there are no wires criss-crossing your back, before I can cut through the fasteners."

While he touched her back to feel if Viktorov had run any wires underneath or across the ties that held the vest in place, he looked back to where Savannah and Viktorov were standing. Viktorov now held a gun in one hand, aiming it at Savannah, while he pressed his thumb onto a device in his other hand.

Logan had approached them and was close enough to examine the device. When he turned his head toward John, he mouthed, *dead man's switch.*

John understood immediately. If Viktorov let go of the device and removed his thumb from the spring-operated switch, the vest would explode.

"You promised to let her go if I came to you," Savannah said, her voice desperate.

"I don't always keep my promises," Viktorov replied. "Now get in the fucking car!" He lifted his hand holding the dead man's switch as a threat. "Or I'm gonna blow your precious little girl to bits."

Slowly, Savannah approached Viktorov.

John made a sign to Logan. It was now or never. John got to work on Buffy's vest, carefully cutting through the three fasteners that tied the vest in the back. They were no obstacle for his claws. But Buffy's arms were in armholes. It would take too much movement to free her from the vest, and Viktorov would notice from the corner of his eye and know that something was afoot. John had to go about things a different way.

"Buffy," he whispered in her ear, "I'm going to cut the vest along your sides, underneath your arms now, so lean back against the pole again and keep your head up. When I've cut through it and give you the command, you'll drop down on the ground, and I'll pull the vest up. Make yourself into a ball, okay?"

She nodded.

"Good girl."

He cut through the thick material on one side, holding on to the vest with the other hand, so it wouldn't drop to the floor. Then he did the same on the other side. Buffy was now essentially free of the vest.

Logan stared at him and Buffy from his spot near Viktorov. Their gazes connected, and John nodded, giving him the sign. Logan took a step toward Viktorov, reached his hand out, nodded at John, then clasped his hand over Viktorov's fist holding the dead man's switch.

Viktorov cried out in panic. "What the fuck?"

"Now, Buffy."

Buffy dropped to the ground, while John pulled the vest off her and flung it to the other end of the parking lot. The vest was still in the air, when John dropped down and covered Buffy with his body, shielding her from danger.

A gunshot echoed through the night.

John spun his head around. There, near the car, Logan was fighting with Viktorov, one hand still on his fist holding the detonation device. Blood was seeping from Logan's shoulder, and judging by Viktorov's reaction, Logan was now visible. And a few feet from him, Savannah held her hand to her side. Blood was seeping through her fingers.

"Fuck!" The bullet had gone through Logan and struck her too.

And with Logan's left arm incapacitated, and his right still holding onto the dead man's switch, he couldn't fight Viktorov. John tossed a look in the direction he'd flung the vest. It had landed at the edge of the parking lot, near an embankment covered in bushes and trees. Far enough away.

"Logan!" John screamed. "Let go of the switch."

Still covering Buffy with his body, he watched as Logan followed his command, then slammed his now available fist into Viktorov's face, before gripping the gun.

John stayed down on the ground for another few seconds, but nothing happened. There was no explosion. He turned his head to look at the vest. It still lay there intact.

He lifted himself off Buffy and ripped her blindfold off, before lifting her into his arms.

Logan was now pinning Viktorov to the ground and Savannah had picked up the gun and was pointing it at her assailant, though it was clear she was hurting.

With Buffy in his arms, he ran to her.

"I've got her," he said and dropped Buffy to her feet.

Buffy immediately wrapped her arms around her mother, and John took the gun from Savannah's hand. She cast him a weak, but happy smile. Then he pried her hand away from the wound at her side and looked at it.

"He only grazed you," John said with relief. "I'll heal you once we're done with him." Then he stroked over Buffy's hair. "Take care of your Mommy for me, okay, Buffy?"

"Yes."

He turned to Logan and stared down at Viktorov. "You can let go of him now, Logan. I've got him. Thanks." He lent Logan a hand to help him up while he pointed the gun at Viktorov. "The bullet went right through you. I'll give you blood to heal the wound if you want." He knew Stealth Guardians healed fast, but vampire blood would speed up the healing process even more.

Logan nodded gratefully. "Appreciate it, man."

Then John leaned closer to Logan and dropped his voice, "Make sure Savannah and Buffy don't see what I'm about to do."

"Sure thing."

Logan walked past him to take care of the two most important people in John's life. Soon, he would be able to take care of them himself, but first, he had to deliver justice to a man who was pure evil.

John glared down at the man and extended his fangs. Shocked, Viktorov stared at him and tried to crawl backwards, hoping for escape. There would be none. John's gaze fell on the dead man's switch that lay nearby. He focused on it. It had broken apart when Logan had dropped it. It was a fake. Viktorov had never planned on killing Buffy. He'd only used the suicide vest as a threat so Savannah would comply.

John glared at Viktorov. "Only place you're going is to hell." He put the safety on the gun and dropped it behind him, then jumped onto

Viktorov. The predator had just become the prey.

Viktorov screamed. "What are you?" He lifted his hands, trying to shield himself.

John growled. "I'm your worst nightmare." He swiped his claws across his victim's torso, leaving four long bloody cuts that laid bare muscle and sinew.

"Ahhhhh!" Viktorov screamed in pain.

"Since I've got your attention now, let's talk! Where are the names and addresses of the people who were to take delivery of the kidnapped girls?"

"I don't know what you're talking about," he claimed.

Another swipe with his claws, this time in the other direction, and Viktorov yelled out in pain again.

"Your torso will look like a checkered tablecloth when I'm done with you," John warned. "Now talk! The names! The addresses! Give them to me, and I'll let you go."

Viktorov whimpered. "On my phone. There's a list." He motioned to his jacket pocket.

John reached inside it and pulled it out. The screen was locked. He reached for Viktorov's right hand and pressed his thumb on the button, unlocking the cell phone. "Where?"

"In the notes."

John navigated to it, and scrolled through the notes. Dozens of names and addresses, all in Russia, were listed there together with the names of the girls and a dollar amount.

"You sick fuck!" John hissed.

"It's all there. Now let me go."

"You're right, it's all there." He shoved the phone into his pocket, then pressed Viktorov's right hand flat onto the ground, palm up and sliced off his thumb with his claws.

Among Viktorov's screams of pain, John explained calmly, "So I can unlock your phone again later. You know, when you're dead."

"No! You promised!"

"Oh, yeah, forgot to mention: I don't keep all my promises either." He leaned closer, holding the struggling asshole to the ground. "I should let you suffer longer, but you're lucky: there's a woman here and her child, and I don't want them to have to listen to your screams for much longer. But then, you wouldn't understand that, would you? Because you love to see women and children suffer."

John sliced through Viktorov's torso with both hands now, the sharp barbs at the ends of his fingers leaving deep cuts until he hit bone. Viktorov's screams were blood-curdling, but John couldn't stop. He had to make him pay for the pain he'd caused those children and their families, for the pain he was still causing some of them.

When he felt Viktorov's ribcage, he ripped it open, bones cracking. Then he plunged his claws into the cavity and grabbed the bastard's still beating heart. He squeezed it, then ripped it out. Looked at it, then dropped it.

It was done.

John sat back on his heels, his heart pounding, adrenaline flowing, his chest heaving, when he suddenly felt a soft hand on his shoulder. He whipped his head to the side. Savannah looked past him at the mutilated corpse.

"Thank you," she murmured. "Thank you for saving Buffy. And for killing him."

He turned his body fully and wrapped his arms around her legs, pressing his face into her thighs, while he took several steadying breaths. Her hand was gentle, when she stroked his hair. After a moment, he lifted his face to look at her.

"You shouldn't have had to see this."

"No, I had to. Now I feel safe again."

He rose and pulled her into his arms, then looked to where Buffy stood, holding Logan's hand, looking at them.

"We'll have to tell her what you are," Savannah said. "But I think she'll be fine."

"She's a brave little girl." He smiled at Buffy, then turned his head back to Savannah. "We know where the kidnapped girls were supposed to be delivered to. We'll go after them. Take them out."

Savannah clung to him now. "Please stay with me and Buffy. Let somebody else do it. You've done enough." She pressed her lips to his, and he kissed her back for a brief moment, then severed his lips from hers and looked deep into her eyes. Despite everything she'd seen him do, the violence she knew he was capable of, she had no reservations about him. She still wanted him. Still loved him.

Slowly John nodded. "I'll stay with you. And with Buffy. You're my family now."

Savannah was right, he didn't have to take out the Russian pedophiles on Viktorov's list himself. Besides, he already had somebody in mind who would be more than willing to go after them. And eliminate them one by one.

38

Ten days later, John entered the V lounge of Scanguards' headquarters. There were few people around, but in the far corner, in front of the fireplace, he saw Samson, who'd requested his presence. Next to him sat Amaury and Gabriel. However, John was surprised to also find Deirdre among them. He hadn't heard that she was back, although he'd seen news reports from Russia, confirming that her mission was a success.

"Take a seat, John," Samson invited him and pointed toward the bar in the middle of the lounge. "Drink?"

John declined with a wave of his hand. He wasn't drinking bottled blood these days. Just like Amaury and Samson, who only drank from their mates. Gabriel, whose mate was a vampire, had a half-empty glass of blood in front of him; same as Deirdre, who drank from hers through a straw.

"Evening, all. Deirdre, good to know you made it back."

To his surprise, she smiled at him. She looked content and relaxed, and perfectly at ease. "Why wouldn't I? Logan has always been a great driver. Though I must admit, now that I'm not a Stealth Guardian anymore, I understand that it can be a little disorienting for other creatures to travel in the portals."

"It was the easiest way to get you into Russia," Amaury said. "Particularly with all the weapons you insisted on taking with you."

"I like to be prepared."

"Give us a full report. I've seen your field reports, but I'd like a summary. Is it done? All of it?" Samson said.

Confidently, Deirdre nodded. "Logan and I found every single man on the list we found on Viktorov's phone. And not just the ones who were supposed to receive the last shipment; we were able to find the clients for previous shipments too."

"How did you take them out?" John asked. "The news reports out of

Russia were kind of sketchy."

"Let's just say they all died a violent death. I made sure they knew why they had to die. Wouldn't be much point in killing them silently, would it now?"

Gabriel and Samson raised their eyebrows, but Amaury simply grunted. John could only agree with Deirdre's actions. They'd all deserved it for kidnapping and then abusing innocent children.

"It was very satisfying to see them beg for their lives," Deirdre continued. "I let them suffer a little, you know, pretend that they could buy their way out of it. They really thought that their money could save them."

As it had turned out, most of the men were Russian oligarchs, many of them connected to the Kremlin and its corrupt government.

"Looks like you enjoyed this a little too much, Deirdre," Samson said.

She gave a one-shouldered shrug. "Nobody said I wasn't allowed to enjoy my job. And it is my job now, isn't it?" She cast John a quick look. "A real job this time, not a pretend one like the one you gave me."

Samson looked at John. "Yeah, about that, John. You could have told me that you wanted to offer Deirdre a job here."

"You thought she wasn't ready. And I knew she was."

"Well, next time you want to hire somebody, make a better case for it." Then he looked back to Deirdre. "As for you, Deirdre, yes, you've got a job here."

"Chief assassin?" she suggested.

The three Scanguards bosses exchanged eyerolls.

"This was a one-off," Gabriel said. "We don't employ assassins. This is a security company. We protect people."

"Same thing," Deirdre claimed. "I protected innocents by killing their tormentors."

John suppressed a smile. Deirdre was right. She'd done the right thing.

Samson sighed and exchanged a look with Gabriel, then gave him a sign to continue.

"You'll undergo our bodyguard training, learn the rules we live by," Gabriel said. "That will have to be enough."

Deirdre nodded. "It's good enough for now." Then she sighed. "How are the girls Logan and I brought back from Russia?"

Deirdre and Logan had transported almost a dozen other girls back from Russia, in addition to the ones John and his team had rescued from the ship in Vladivostok.

Samson gave her a bittersweet smile. "Physically, they're mending. Maya is doing her best to make sure they heal. But emotionally, there will be scars. Particularly the ones who were in Russia for a few months, are in bad shape. They endured weeks of sexual abuse. We haven't been able to return them to their parents yet. Some of them are so distraught that we are worried they'll harm themselves, given the chance."

John's heart broke for the girls. "Have you thought about erasing their memories?" It was a gift vampires possessed, but used only in dire circumstances.

"We've discussed it with Maya and Dr. Drake. Both are of the opinion that it's the best way, rather than having these girls undergo years of therapy. We're taking care of it later tonight."

"I'm glad," John agreed. "And with what explanation will you send them back to their parents?"

"We're working on that with Detective Donnelly. They'll need to know the truth, or at least part of the truth. But we can't tell them everything."

John knew that Donnelly would come up with something that worked for everybody and threw no suspicion on Scanguards or revealed what had really happened.

"And Viktorov's money?" John asked.

"Thomas hacked into his accounts and transferred all of it out. He wired Savannah's ransom money back to her. The remaining money is going to a fund to benefit victims of sex trafficking."

"Good." Then John looked at Deirdre. "You probably don't know yet, but we've dealt with all the people who were involved in the trafficking stateside."

"You didn't kill the kidnappers?" she asked.

"Only Viktorov himself. We handed Otto Watson, the hacker, over to Donnelly. He'll receive a reduced sentence in exchange for his cooperation. The two kidnappers, the ones who kept the girls at the port in Oakland, will do hard time. Donnelly will keep Scanguards out of it, and the police chief and the mayor are backing us up."

"You should have killed those two," Deirdre said.

"I would have, had they touched the girls," John confessed, "but I don't kill indiscriminately. Don't worry, they're paying for their crimes. And they'll have nightmares for the rest of their lives."

Before handing them over to Donnelly, John had made sure that they knew what he was, and that he would rip their throats out if they ever breathed a word about vampires. He could have erased their memories, but he wanted them to know that vampires existed, and that the two kidnappers were on his personal shit list.

"So it's over, then?" Deirdre asked.

"Yeah, it's finally over."

Though for John, life was only just beginning. He'd gotten a second chance, and he was grabbing it with both hands and holding on with all his might.

39

Eight months later

Dressed only in a pair of jogging pants, which he'd slipped into after showering upon returning home just before sunrise, John stood in the kitchen of his house and opened the pantry. Then he looked over his shoulder and stared at Buffy. She was dressed, her hair neatly combed, and ready for school.

"Are you sure you want peanut butter and *banana*? That can't taste good."

Buffy let out a long-suffering sigh, like a teenager annoyed at her parent. She even rolled her eyes as if she'd practiced it a thousand times. "I don't criticize your taste in blood. Believe me: peanut butter and banana is awesome. Way better than jelly."

He smirked. "I'm gonna have to take your word for it, my little slayer."

A smile flashed across Buffy's face, just like it always did, when he called her by her nickname. Since the night he'd saved her and her mother, Buffy knew all about vampires, and the nickname was a joke between them. She'd accepted him without question and trusted him one hundred percent.

He grabbed a banana and turned back to the counter to prepare Buffy's sandwich.

"John, can I ask you something?" she asked.

"Sure, fire away."

"Ahm..."

When she hesitated, he turned to look at her. "Something wrong? Is somebody giving you trouble at school?"

"No, no, school is fine. You don't have to beat anybody up for me."

He shook his head and laughed. "Good, 'cause I'm not going to beat up a bully; I'd rather teach you how to take care of him yourself." When she didn't say anything, he asked, "So what did you want to ask?"

She shrugged. "I forgot."

But her expression said otherwise. And Buffy wasn't a shy kid. When she wanted to know something, she asked a question, no matter how direct or embarrassing it might be.

He was ready to sit her down and ask what was wrong, when he heard the bedroom door open and close. The sound of bare feet on the wooden floor reached his ears and made his heart leap.

"Mommy's awake," he said and winked at Buffy.

He wrapped the sandwich and turned to the door. Savannah, dressed in a long white silky bathrobe entered the kitchen. He let his eyes roam over her, and his cock jerked at the lovely sight. She was getting more beautiful every day, her belly ripe with his child, her skin healthy and glowing.

"Morning, Mommy," Buffy said cheerfully.

"Morning, baby," she replied and embraced Buffy, stroking her hand over her head and squeezing her, while her eyes locked with John's. "Morning, my love."

"Morning, darlin'," he murmured.

You look sexy as hell, he added with his mind, sending those words to her via their telepathic bond, so Buffy wouldn't have to witness how totally smitten he was with her mother. Not that they could hide their love for each other, or wanted to, but kids could be funny when it came to their parents displaying too much physical affection for each other.

And you're blind. I'm not sexy, I'm fat.

Smiling, Savannah looked at her daughter. "Ready for school, Buffy?"

She nodded. Then she went on tip-toes to whisper to her mother, even though she should know by now that his vampiric hearing would pick up the words nevertheless. "Mommy, I wanted to ask him, but…"

"…you're afraid he'll say no?" Savannah finished the sentence.

Buffy nodded.

"But you want it. Just ask him. I know he wants it too."

"Are you sure?"

Savannah nodded and chuckled. Finally, Buffy turned around and looked up at him. "John?"

"Yes, my little slayer?"

She took a step closer and clasped her hands in front of her stomach. "You know, now that I'm gonna have a little brother soon, and you're gonna be his daddy... I was wondering, you know, wouldn't it be weird if I still call you John when my brother gets to call you Daddy?"

John felt a smile split his face. He knew what she was getting at, and he couldn't be happier about it. "Yes, Buffy?"

She took a deep breath. "Do you think it would be okay if I called you Daddy, too?"

He opened his arms. "I've been hoping for a long time that you'd want that." Buffy ran into his arms and he lifted her up and squeezed her.

She wrapped her arms around his neck and hugged him tightly. "Thank you, Daddy!"

Past Buffy's shoulder he looked at Savannah, who looked at them with tears in her eyes. "You'll always be my firstborn, my little slayer." He kissed her on the cheek.

The doorbell rang at that moment.

"That'll be Ryder. Time for school," John said and dropped Buffy back on her feet.

"I'll get the door," Savannah offered. The moment she left the kitchen, Buffy winked at him. "You know that my teachers are all crazy about him?"

"About Ryder?"

Buffy chuckled. "Yes, Miss Peabody always stares at him like she wants to undress him when he drops me off at school."

John raised an eyebrow. At eleven, Buffy shouldn't really be aware of those things yet. Or was he old-fashioned? "How do you know what that look is like?"

Buffy shrugged casually. "It's the same way Mommy looks at you."

He was saved from responding by Ryder breezing into the kitchen. "Morning, John. Hey, kiddo, you ready?"

"Morning, Ryder," John greeted him, while Buffy snatched her bag from the chair.

"I'm ready."

John grabbed the sandwich from the counter and handed it to Buffy. "Don't forget that."

"Thanks, Daddy!" she replied and slipped the sandwich into her bag.

Ryder shot him a surprised look and mouthed: *Daddy?*

John smiled proudly.

"Well, let's go then, or we'll be late," Ryder said and took Buffy by the hand.

After more goodbyes, it was suddenly silent in the house again. Savannah leaned against the doorframe to the kitchen and smiled at him.

John walked to her. "I have it on good authority that you look at me as if you want to undress me."

She chuckled, her gaze sweeping over his bare chest and down to his jogging pants. "If that's true, then I don't think I'd have a lot to do."

"Good, 'cause I don't really want you to exert yourself in your condition." He slid a hand over her belly and caressed her. "Mmm, I love the feel of this." He reached for the belt and loosened it, until her robe fell open in the front, revealing her nakedness. But then, he already knew that she wore nothing underneath. In the eight months they'd lived together, she'd never worn anything beneath that robe.

He reached inside her robe with both hands, sliding his hands over her pregnant belly, then to her hips, and finally to her ass. Savannah tipped her head up in invitation. He captured her lips and kissed her, while he palmed her ass and pressed his chest against her heavy breasts. He loved the feel of her like this, lush, ripe, all woman. Making love to her had become better with every day, more intimate, more sensual. And even now, with Savannah seven months pregnant with his son, he couldn't keep his hands off her. To his delight, she'd yet to refuse him.

When he took his lips off hers, he leaned his forehead to hers. "How you feeling this morning?"

She slid her hands over his naked chest, making him shiver with pleasure. "I missed you last night," she said, instead of answering his question. Or maybe it was an answer. Or an invitation.

"You did?" he murmured and kissed a path down her tempting neck. Hunger suddenly surged. He needed to feed, and ever since they'd blood-bonded, she'd become his sole source of nourishment. "I missed you too."

"Are you hungry?"

"Famished."

She brought her hands to her breasts and cupped them. "They feel so heavy lately."

The hint was clear. He put his hands over hers, squeezing the heavy fruit. "They're gorgeous." He dipped his head, slid her hand aside and pulled one nipple into his mouth. He licked over it gently, and felt her shudder in response. Then he let the nipple plop from his mouth and looked up at Savannah watching him. "You want me to bite your tits today?"

"Yes."

"Does that turn you on?"

Even after all this time, she still dropped her lids as if embarrassed about her desires.

"Well, it's easy to find out, isn't it?" he asked and dropped one hand between her legs. He found her pussy warm and wet. Unable to resist, he bathed his fingers in her heat. "Oh, darlin', I love the way you welcome me home in the mornings." He drove his finger into her channel and noticed her eyelids flutter and a moan tumble over her lips. "So ready for me." Just as he was ready for her. His cock was as hard as granite.

He pulled her away from the doorframe and pressed her against the wall next to it. Savannah leaned her head back, thrusting her breasts out. As much as he needed to be inside her, he needed that bite first. He dipped his head to her gorgeous tits and licked first over one then over the other nipple. "Delicious," he murmured.

"Are you trying to torture me?"

He grinned. "My wife seems a little impatient this morning." He dropped his hand to her pussy again and began to caress her.

"Hmm," she moaned.

He found her clit engorged and eager for his touch. "I want you to come when I drink from you. Can you do that for me?"

"John," she said on a strangled breath, "hurry, I'm almost there."

"Good!" He wrapped his lips around her nipple and extended his fangs. Then he drove the sharp tips into her flesh. A shudder charged through her, and rich blood filled his mouth. He swallowed it and felt a bolt of energy shoot through him. God, this feeling alone could make him come. But he held himself in check. This wasn't just about his nourishment or pleasure. This was just as much about hers. So while he drank her blood, he stroked her clit tenderly, his movements becoming increasingly faster and more intense. He could read her reaction so easily now, knew when she was close, and knew what she needed.

He sent her over the edge with his next stroke and felt her pant out her release. Reluctantly, he pulled his fangs from her breast and licked over the tiny incisions, closing them instantly. He'd taken enough from her for today; now he wanted something else.

He turned her to face the wall to get her in a position that they were taking more frequently ever since Savannah's stomach had grown so big that taking her in missionary had become uncomfortable for her. Luckily, his wicked wife enjoyed being taken from behind, in a position that allowed her little movement and put him in charge. And her at his mercy.

He gripped her shoulders and slipped the silk robe from her body, revealing her smooth back and sexy-as-hell ass. Savannah braced her hands against the wall and took a step back so she could bend over.

"I love the way you offer yourself to me," he murmured and stripped himself of his jogging pants.

"Then you should take what's offered." Her voice was pure seduction. In the time they'd been together, the sexy woman he'd taken without finesse at their first encounter had turned into a seductress who knew all his weaknesses and exploited them with shocking regularity.

She knew how much he loved it when she talked dirty to him and submitted to his insatiable desires for sex and blood. And that she let him fuck her wherever it pleased him: against a wall, in the kitchen, the bathroom, the garage, even outside in the garden at night when nobody could see them. No place was safe.

"I'm looking forward to our new house being finished so we can christen all the rooms," he said behind her as he gripped her hips. He adjusted his cock and drove into her drenched pussy.

Savannah's moan was confirmation that she welcomed his invading cock. Her sheath was still quivering from her orgasm, and he knew it wouldn't take much to make her come again.

"John," she said on a breath, "I need you to fuck me hard today. I've been aching for you all night."

He withdrew and plunged into her again. "What a horny wife I have. So hot, so fucking sexy," he murmured, as he slid back and forth inside her, loving the feel of her clenching muscles squeezing his cock. Gripping her hips even tighter, he increased his tempo and gave her what she needed, what they both needed.

"Yes, John, yes, that's good," she cried out.

He lifted his hands from her hips and reached forward, cupping her heavy breasts, while his hips kept moving, his cock thrusting hard and deep. "I love your tits, darlin'. When I'm done here, when I've shot my seed into you, I'm going to suck on your tits once more, drink more of your blood. You want that?"

She moaned in agreement.

"Good. 'Cause you make me hungry."

"I'm hungry, too, John. I need your blood today. I need you."

She didn't need to ask him twice. He brought one wrist to his lips, extended his fangs and pricked his skin, so blood dropped from the small incisions. Then he extended his arm and offered her his wrist. "Drink from me, darlin', so you'll be strong."

And so his son would grow strong in her belly.

When she drank from his wrist, a jolt went through his body, and his cock took on a mind of its own. He started pounding into her, taking her hard, plunging deep and fast. Whenever she drank from him, it was like that, because the blood made her strong and as insatiable as him.

Her muscles suddenly spasmed around him, pulling him over the edge with her. He came in long, hot spurts, filling her channel, while their bodies quaked and shook from the power of their orgasms.

"Oh, John," she murmured, letting out a deep breath. "So good."

He brushed her hair away from her neck and pressed a kiss to it. "Give me a minute or two, and we'll make it even better."

How come you always know what I want? she asked via their telepathic bond.

Because it's what I want, too.

~ ~ ~

ABOUT THE AUTHOR

Tina Folsom was born in Germany and has been living in English speaking countries for over 25 years, since 2001 in San Francisco, where she's married to an American.

Tina has always been a bit of a globe trotter: after living in Lausanne, Switzerland, she briefly worked on a cruise ship in the Mediterranean, then lived a year in Munich, before moving to London. There, she became an accountant. But after 8 years she decided to move overseas.

In New York she studied drama at the American Academy of Dramatic Arts, then moved to Los Angeles a year later to pursue studies in screenwriting. This is also where she met her husband, who she followed to San Francisco three months after first meeting him.

In San Francisco, Tina worked as a tax accountant and even opened her own firm, then went into real estate, however, she missed writing. In 2008 she wrote her first romance and never looked back.

She's always loved vampires and decided that vampire and paranormal romance was her calling. She now has over 36 novels in English and dozens in other languages (Spanish, German, and French) and continues to write, as well as have her existing novels translated.

For more about Tina Folsom:

www.tinawritesromance.com
http://www.facebook.com/TinaFolsomFans
Twitter: @Tina_Folsom
Email: tina@tinawritesromance.com

Printed in Great Britain
by Amazon